Kore's Field

Kore's Field

A myth retold

N.C. Sellars

This is a work of fiction. Names, characters, places, and incidents are products of the author's imagination. Any resemblance to actual events, or persons, living or dead, is entirely coincidental.

Text Copyright ©2018 N.C. Sellars

Cover design by www.ebooklaunch.com

ISBN: 978-0-9998240-0-9

For Brad

I

My story is a quiet one. The greatest myth-makers will not remember it; few poets will ever reference it, and then only in passing. Even now, the rumors are rife with inconsistencies. Some present me as the very model of a devoted wife while others call me a weak victim. Or else they praise my act of sacrifice, yet condemn my motives. My husband receives no respite from criticism, either. According to various accounts he is a selfish fool, a wise king, or some combination of the two.

The gossips can't even agree on my fate. One says a hero rescued me before I could taste death, while another swears I saw Kore face-to-face and stirred her pity with my harrowing tale. I leave it only to you, Reader, to decide what is true.

My story is a quiet one. You must listen carefully, for it begins and ends in the most curious of places:

A wheat field.

That morning many years ago, when it all began, I heard the army before I saw it.

The great crash of the battering ram against the castle gates didn't come as a surprise; for days we had waited for the cascade of soldiers to come pouring down the mountain. It was the early hour that alarmed me. I crept to the window and peered out, exposing as little of my face as possible. Dark shapes moved from the vineyards and into the orchards, lit only by the moon. I could only guess they had descended without torches. A bold, yet dangerous, ploy. A second crash sounded in the distance and I lunged for my trunk, breaking the latches and throwing off the lid in one fluid movement. The gates were old and ill-tended; it wouldn't take long for invaders to crush them.

I dug through the trunk, pulling out the clothes gathered for me and specially set aside for that day. They didn't fit quite right; the shoes were too big and the bodice slipped even though I laced the stays as tight as they could bear. One by one I pulled on each layer; autumn was approaching early and the balmy days of high summer were a distant memory. I took a deep breath and crossed the chamber. As I reached for the door latch I caught a glimpse of myself in the tiny glass hanging on the wall and saw a stranger staring back. With a trembling hand, I opened the door.

The stairs were deserted. Again: not surprising. Most of the guards had been called to supplement the army. The nobles had abandoned the kingdom weeks before, as soon as the first whispers of the Itomian invasion reached their ears. Several servants had followed suit. Despite the king's orders to remain in the castle they had fled in droves, slipping through hidden doors and vanishing over garden walls in the dead of night. I stood in the doorway for a moment, waiting for a guard to come charging toward me and order me back into the tower, but none ever came. I picked my way slowly down the swirling steps, pausing again when I reached the door at the base. I pressed my ear to the wood, hardly daring to breathe as I listened for sounds of battle on the other side. When I heard nothing, I turned the handle, slipped through the heavy door, and ran.

The corridor stretched before me like an endless stone tunnel with smaller hallways splitting off left and right. I counted them carefully as I sprinted past, praying I hadn't made a mistake and missed one. Half the torches were unlit, leaving large pockets of shadow that left me second-guessing my instructions. I had never seen this corridor before; I could only rely on the information provided to me by others. I turned left, finding myself in a darkened hallway. I slowed my pace for fear of colliding with a wall and knocking myself senseless. My breath came in short gasps and for the briefest moment I squeezed my eyes shut, pleading with the gods to guide me to safety.

"Here!" a man's voice shouted. "Down here! More men to the gates!"

A handful of guards thundered past. I flattened myself against the wall and listened for their footsteps to fade. Another crash sent the castle trembling and for the first time, I heard screams. They were shrill and somehow deep, as though bursting from a place of inhuman agony. The sound ripped through my ears and made me wish I could do something, anything, to help the poor man in such pain, even if it meant bringing his final moments to an end.

I hesitated only a few seconds longer, to be certain the footsteps were gone. I kept one hand on the cool stone as I walked, feeling for the kitchen door. I knew it was short and narrow, positioned just below the great hall to give the servants quick access while burdened with heavy trays for feasts. Not that Myrilla had enjoyed much feasting in recent years. It's difficult to bake bread when your fields are barren of grain.

The surface beneath my fingers changed from stone to wood. I felt for the latch and lifted it slowly, muffling the click with the fabric from my skirt. It swung open easily and I stepped into the kitchen. It was a disaster: overturned bowls and limp vegetables scattered across every surface. Shrunken carrots and wilted lettuce and diseased potatoes. A pitiful harvest if there ever was one. The coals in the stove burned on, unaware of the violent tide creeping closer. I darted past the work tables and tore open the door to the gardens, exhaling with relief.

For the first time all night, I felt safe. The royal gardens were a maze of paved walkways and stone walls. Laid out behind the castle and inaccessible to anyone but the royal court and a few hand-chosen servants, they carried an air of mystique and secrecy. Logic told me the Itomians cared nothing about the gardens and would have no reservations about swarming and destroying them in pursuit of victory, but I still felt secure as I recited the maids' instructions under my breath.

"Three right turns," I whispered. "Three right turns and then you'll come to the fountain. Just after the fountain—"

"Lord Blackwall!"

I froze. Heavy footfalls carried toward me, but I couldn't tell which direction they were coming from. I looked for a shrub or low tree to hide beneath, to no avail. They were all too small or else had already dropped their leaves. I couldn't afford to make the slightest sound. Panic descended as I ran along the closest garden wall, searching for the door. I finally found it, covered in peeling dark paint with a key jutting from the hole. I turned the key and stepped inside, then let it swing gently closed, not daring to bolt it.

The voices stopped just on the other side of the wall. I strained to hear the speakers' accent, though neither Myrillan nor Itomian would be much help to me.

"One of the volunteers saw someone leave through the kitchens." He spoke in the thick, heavy brogue of the Itomians. I couldn't help shuddering in disgust.

"Man or woman?"

"Woman."

The second speaker was unimpressed. "A woman's no threat to us."

"But she can't have gotten far—"

"Let her run. The prince needs all hands to help take the throne room."

Still bickering, their voices grew fainter and soon vanished altogether. I stayed crouched in the garden, unable to stop myself smiling. I couldn't believe my luck. I rose to my feet and prepared to resume my search for the south castle gate once more when a tangle of overgrown vines on the back garden wall caught my eye. Early dawn light spilled through the cracks between the vines and I realized they weren't covering the wall at all, but an ancient iron gate. My relief swelled as I wove my hands into the brambles and pushed hard. It opened with a metallic creak and I saw neither battle nor carnage nor even a single soldier, but an open field bordered by trees on three sides. I could barely make out the temple in the distance, perched on the eastern hill and hovering just above the pointed silhouettes of the treetops. The sky had turned pink since I'd entered the garden and any moment now the sun would rise and give me away.

I picked up my heavy skirts and, wasting no time, darted toward the trees. If I could just reach their cover I'd vanish forever. The Itomian prince could dethrone Myrilla's king, but his triumph would be short-lived. After all, Itomius had plenty of enemies; it wouldn't be difficult to convince one of Myrilla's neighbors to take action on my behalf.

My feet pounded the hard earth and I had nearly reached the tree line when I tripped and fell forward. At first I thought I'd caught my toe on a stone or fumbled in the too-large shoes, but a sharp pain erupted from my ankle. I scrambled to my feet, only vaguely aware of the blood dripping into my shoe. I made for the trees once more, but I hadn't taken two steps when a strong hand caught my arm.

"Kern, we've got a runner!"

It wasn't the same voice I'd heard in the gardens; this man's was rougher, to the point where I could barely understand him. But I understood enough to know he wasn't planning to let go of my arm any time soon. I threw my whole weight against him, hoping to startle him into releasing me, but he just held tighter.

"You're a fierce one, no question," he said, laughing. "The prince'll be glad we didn't let you get away. He'll want a good look at you, I'm sure."

Fear coursed through my body and I drove my elbow back as hard as I could. I must have caught the man in the throat because he choked and sputtered and loosened his grip slightly. Before I could run, however, he spun me around and raised his hand so fast I didn't even see it fly. My neck snapped back and I stumbled and sank to my knees, cradling my cheek. Water gushed from my eye and I tasted rust. When I pulled my hand away my fingers were bloody.

A second man—Kern, I assumed—appeared. He was older and looked weary from fighting. No blood stained his clothes, though a bow dangled from his hand. The dawn light etched deep lines around his eyes and he looked at me with something like pity. He pulled me up and studied my face. "For the love of the gods, Sir Hartford," he swore, "you didn't have to bludgeon her."

"She attacked me!" Sir Hartford shouted. "She nearly crushed my throat!"

"You're wearing mail, it can't have been too terrible. Prince Admetus wants all survivors brought back to the castle in the best health as possible. Those were our orders. That's why I clipped her foot with the arrow, instead of aiming for her heart."

"Sounds like the perfect excuse for a missed shot," sneered Sir Hartford. "Some marksman you make, old man—"

"Please." I interrupted their quarrel. "Please let me go. I'll be no trouble, I swear it. I'm nothing, nobody, I won't be missed. You'll never see or hear from me again. Just let me go and I'll be eternally in your debt."

Kern gave me that pitying look again. "I'm sorry, sweetheart, truly. But we're under orders. We have to bring you back to the castle. The prince won't tolerate disobedience in the field."

"Don't! Don't, I beg you—" I dragged my feet but my resistance was fruitless. They ignored my pleas and cruelly led me back the way I'd come. Shock numbed me and eventually I walked with them, as complicit as a child. I simply could not believe my change in fortune. I'd planned this escape for months, learning and studying, waiting for the perfect opportunity. Now it lay in shambles around me, destroyed by a hateful, pagan prince.

Kern and Sir Hartford escorted me past the twisted, broken front gates and through the castle doors. The sun had risen fully and cast its pure, lemony light over the destruction left by the battle. Scarlet rivers ran in the street and bodies littered the walk. Most were grown, but others disturbingly small. I tried very hard not to look too closely at anything. I took in my surroundings in small gasps of color, avoiding any lingering sights. We passed through the entry hall and the great banquet hall; both were swarmed with Itomian soldiers filling their bellies with wine from the castle cellars and celebrating merrily.

By the time we reached the throne room Kern and Sir Hartford had all but forgotten about me. A large cluster of prisoners huddled near the wall, and it was there they took me. I sat on the cold stone floor, surrounded by disinterested Itomian soldiers trading war stories in their barbaric accents. I glanced at my companions; most were young families or elderly folk. I felt eyes on me and turned to see a little boy with a rag wrapped tightly around his forearm. He stared at me, his eyes wide, and I wiped my cheek with my apron, smearing it with blood. Behind me, an old man coughed and wheezed in a way that made the hair on my arms stand up. It didn't stop, and when a lady sitting nearby asked one of the soldiers to have mercy and bring the old man something to drink, the soldier just jabbed the butt of his spear into the woman's shoulder. The cluster became much quieter after that.

In spite of the many bodies surrounding me, the throne room felt cool. I ignored the shuffling soldiers and kept my eyes on the door behind the dais. I knew it led to the king's private chamber, and I felt sure he was waiting within. He'd never ride out to battle; he probably hadn't even seen the enemy's army. I could picture him and his frigid wife on the other side of the door, probably toasting Myrilla's fall with crystal goblets and royal wine. From what I heard in rumors, that was how they handled most of the kingdom's problems. They'd known for weeks that the Itomian prince was planning an invasion, and all they'd done to stop it was take a few servants from the kitchens and order them to keep watch at the castle walls.

The old man stopped coughing, and at the same time I felt a gnarled hand close around my wrist. I pulled my gaze from the chamber door and turned to find the old man staring into nothingness with milky eyes.

"Tell me what's happening, please," he said, his voice thick with phlegm.

I didn't want to speak, certain my voice would give me away to an elderly Myrillan, but the plum-colored splotches on his scalp, visible through tufts of white hair, stirred my sympathy. I shifted closer to him and tilted my head toward his. "We're in the throne room with probably two hundred other Myrillans," I said quietly, so no one else could hear. "The Itomian soldiers are double our number, at least, with more pouring in every minute."

"What standards do you see?"

"There's a gold lion on a rust red field. And"—I craned my neck, trying to catch a glimpse of the limp flags—"what looks like a…silver pig…on a white field striped with crimson."

The old man nodded. "It's a boar. The wild boar of Itomius. The lion belongs to Warkenland; Prince Admetus must have promised their king tribute in return for alliance. It's the way of young princes to make pledges before holding currency in their hands."

I looked at him with new respect. "Are you a soldier, sir?"

His weathered face cracked with a grin. "I was, many years ago. When the grain still grew and Kore smiled down on us."

It was difficult not to scoff. "That must have been well in the past, sir, for Kore has never smiled down on me."

He looked like he was about to say something else, but before he could speak a great shout went up from the soldiers. With the rest of the Myrillans I turned to see the chamber door open and the king emerge, trailed by the queen. We rose upon his entry, a chorus of scraping feet and muffled groans. I gripped the old man's elbow and held him steady, afraid he would crumple without support. Just as I suspected, the king held a crystal goblet in one hand and a staff in the other. Both he and the queen were richly dressed in the Myrillan style: sweeping robes for him and draped silks for her. A finely wrought gold crown sat on the king's head, and he looked out at the crowd of defeated Myrillans crammed into the throne room as though it were all a masque that had caught him off guard.

"Have no fear, my people," he called, almost jovially, and raised his cup. "I've not been deaf to your cries. Our enemy is breaching the gates, but we shall triumph in the end."

Silence filled the room. In a strange way, the king's command was obeyed: the people feared no more. The terror that had gripped the Myrillan hearts around me dissolved into contempt. Even the Itomian soldiers took pause in their celebration to turn their disdainful faces toward the king, studying him as if he were mad.

The king took no notice of the palpable hostility, he only drained his cup and called for more wine. A trembling servant obliged; his hands shook so violently that the wine sloshed from the cup and splattered the hem of the king's robes. Before the servant could stammer an apology the king hurled the goblet to the floor, where it shattered into a thousand crystal fragments.

"Fool!" the king screamed. "Count yourself lucky I have been stripped of my arms, else you'd taste my steel in your gut. As it is, I'll have to satisfy myself watching you lick these shards from the floor."

He brought his crushing hand down on the servant's shoulder, forcing the man to his knees. The servant begged for mercy, but before the king shoved the poor man's face into the stone, he glanced up, as though to make sure we were all watching.

It was then, at that very moment, that I made my fatal mistake. I didn't understand it at the time, but many years later I overheard a conversation between two courtiers that shone light on my error. They were talking about the challenges of deer hunting, and one of them remarked, "What deer don't realize is that they have the advantage. They think that just because they don't have fangs or claws, their only defense is to run. But they're wrong. The deer that lives the longest isn't the fastest one—it's the deer who knows *when* to run and, more importantly, knows when to keep still."

To this day, I wonder what would have happened if I had kept still. Perhaps I would have blended seamlessly with the broken Myrillans surrounding me, indistinguishable from the young mother beside me clutching her baby. Indeed, every person's attention was fixed on the horrific spectacle up on the dais, and I was no exception. But when the king's eyes passed over mine, I turned my face away ever so slightly, afraid he would recognize me.

In an instant his rage had vanished, replaced with glee. I heard the servant whimper as the king released him, and the air relaxed considerably. Up on the dais, towering over every Myrillan subject, the king took a step forward and held out his hand.

"I see my long-lost niece has finally arrived," he said, beaming at me. "How good of you to join us at last, Princess Alyce."

II

Silence rippled through the throne room, immediately followed by an outbreak of whispers. The sound of my name being hissed over and over—"Princess Alyce, Princess Alyce"—breezed through the Myrillan crowd, while the enemy soldiers only glanced at each other in confusion. Amidst the whispers I heard a woman remark, as clear as a chime, "By the gods, all these years I thought she was dead."

I considered staying put; surrounded by my countrymen I felt a camaraderie I'd never known before. But when the king was in one of his rages I knew it was better to quietly comply. Keeping my eyes down, I smoothed the front of my dress with shaking hands and walked to the dais. The soldiers parted without a word, momentarily forgetting their spears and arrows. I stopped before the king, who took my chin in his meaty hand and lifted it, forcing my eyes to meet his. He smiled to himself, as though savoring a private joke.

"You'll want to get cleaned up before our honored guest arrives. Take her to the chamber and find something decent for her to wear," he said to the handful of servants cowering behind him. "The queen will go with you to ensure our dear princess looks her very best."

The servants bowed and my aunt took my arm. Her fingers dug into my skin; I could feel their chilliness even through my sleeve. Cold and silent, she had terrified me more than the king on the few occasions our paths crossed. With iron-like strength she pulled me toward the chamber door. I had no choice but to follow her, though her wooden feet halted when a trumpet blast sounded from outside the throne room. All heads turned toward the doors, which swung open with a bright bang. A man with yellow hair and beard swaggered into the hall, not bothering to conceal his delight.

"Kneel for Prince Admetus, conqueror and savior."

Most of the Myrillans did as he ordered, and those who didn't were forced to their knees by the soldiers. The servants around us dropped down obediently and only those left of the royal court— the king, the queen, and I—remained standing on the dais. I watched the influx of soldiers, fascinated and horrified. I had heard of Prince Admetus, son of the Itomian king, only through rumor. Vicious and cunning, he craved a kingdom of his own. A privilege that, as a second son, he would likely never enjoy except by taking it with force.

You may have heard the rumor that the prince blazed into the throne room riding a chariot pulled by a lion and a wild boar. As fantastic as this sounds, it is not correct. The prince entered the throne room on foot, flanked by standard-bearers and leading a sea of soldiers. My skin prickled at their sheer number. For the first time in my life I understood the true meaning of terror. With their blood-stained armor and swords and spears clutched in their hands they looked capable of any measure of violence. They might kill us in our own castle, or parade us naked through the streets like slaves. Whatever the prince desired. We were utterly powerless against one man's whims.

The prince approached the throne without invitation, grinning like a boy who's just won a very clever game. The sweat of battle glittered on his golden forehead and his eyes crinkled with amusement. He was handsome, but in a bland way. Most princes are. The only fault in his perfect face lay in his nose. It swung slightly to the left, as though it had once been broken and not healed properly.

My uncle held out his hands in a gesture of welcome. He looked more the gracious host than ever. "Welcome to Myrilla, Prince Admetus," he said. "I hope you find my fair kingdom to your liking."

"I like it very much," the prince replied, in his strange dialect. Soldiers continued to pour into the throne room behind him, filling every crevice. My eyes darted over the colorful standards, each marking a different noble in service to Itomius. Among the lions and boars I saw goats and sheep stitched into colorful flags.

My uncle clapped his hands for more wine. The same servant who'd barely escaped with his life presented a flagon and two new crystal cups, which he filled.

"Here are my terms, Prince," said the king, gesturing for the prince to take a cup. "I am not the fool you think I am. I know how valuable my kingdom is, and I know your father won't supply you with enough soldiers to secure it. When my people hear of their new sovereign, a rebellion will rise faster than your armies can fly. Keep me here as king and I will pay Itomius such tribute that even your slaves will eat like royalty. Our finest harvests will be reserved for you. Our loyalty will be challenged by none. Kore will bestow you with such blessings that you could never imagine, if only you leave me as regent."

I kept my face carefully blank lest any scorn show. Only my uncle would be so foolhardy as to make such an offer. The outrageous generosity underscored his fear at being turned out of his own castle. Myrilla's fields were so poorly tended they could scarcely feed their own people, much less pay tribute to a larger kingdom. And to speak of Kore in such a presumptuous manner was enough to earn a curse from the gods upon our entire house. I had seen many suffer after uttering far less inflammatory statements concerning the gods. Kore will not be used for any man's personal gain. Not even a king's.

I was fuming silently over the king's plan when his thunderous voice filled the throne room again: "And you may have my niece, the Princess Alyce, as your wife."

Every face—including mine—turned to my uncle. I took an involuntary step backwards, hoping somehow I could vanish from his proposal. But my aunt, mistaking my alarm for an attempt at flight, tightened her grip on my arm and stood me before the prince.

The yellow-bearded man joined the prince at the front of the dais and ran his eyes over me. Apparently very unimpressed, his mouth twisted into a smirk. "This is a servant," he spat. "Do you truly expect us to believe she's royalty? I've seen cattle-hands' daughters who look more like a princess than this girl."

A few of the soldiers snickered appreciatively and my cheeks colored with shame. I felt the prince watching me with the same scrutiny, taking in my muddy dress and tangled hair. For a split second I saw myself as he must have: a powerless nobody with dirt and blood splattered on her face, hardly worth calling a princess.

Then, from the corner of my eye, I caught sight of the blind old man kneeling on the hard floor and my self-pity evaporated into rage. This was my kingdom and these were my people. I'd failed to escape, but I'd fought for my freedom that morning and had nearly won it. I was mere steps away from starting my journey as Myrilla's rightful queen when this idiotic prince's soldiers had quenched my hope, and now he dared to let his comrade mock me. If my mouth weren't so dry I'd have spat in his face.

"Look at her eyes," said my uncle, reveling in his new role of matchmaker. "As grey as the Great Sea. Hair darker and softer than freshly turned soil. Her royal blood can be traced all the way back to the gods themselves. Let Myrilla's princess be the vessel for a new generation of Itomian princes."

Humiliation made me blush once more. No uncle should speak so crudely of his niece. I waited for the prince to protest, to say he had some heathen wife or lover waiting for him at home, or that his gods forbade marriage to any foreign princess. Instead, he fixed his eyes on my uncle and spoke with the confidence that only comes from uncontested triumph. "Your boasting is in vain, Falwyn. You may bluster all you like of your people's loyalty, but your gods delivered Myrilla into my hands. Half your soldiers laid down their arms and joined our ranks. Your Kore has already blessed me beyond measure; she started when she turned her face from you."

My uncle said nothing to this. My aunt gripped my arm tighter and pushed me slightly closer to the prince, using me as a shield against the prince's harsh words. Harsh, and true. A chill ran down my spine when I thought about Kore's temple on the hill, cold and empty. The last priest knew this would happen; he had tried to warn the king, but because of my uncle's stubbornness we all now paid the price. If the prince and the priest were right, if Kore had truly removed her favor from my uncle, then I was his final lot to play. He lost no time in assuring the prince of my greatest asset as a princess.

"She's clean," my uncle said desperately. "A virgin. I swear it on her life. Have your physicians examine her—"

"Enough." The prince held up his hand. "My men are weary from battle and I have no interest in your petty arguments. Here are my terms: I will be crowned King of Myrilla. All soldiers and citizens who swear loyalty to me will be permitted to stay. Those who refuse may peaceably leave and settle elsewhere. Each departing family will receive a gift of grain and wine to sustain them during their travel, provided from the royal storehouses."

"And what of my fate, Prince?"

The prince narrowed his eyes in disgust. "You'll have your life. For the moment, you and your family may stay in the castle. Once I am crowned other arrangements will be made."

My uncle smiled tightly. "I am sure the gods will bless you for your generosity," he said, in a voice that meant just the opposite.

The prince smiled back. "Just as I am sure they won't spare you for hiding behind your niece." His soldiers smirked and he studied me with what I took to be a mixture of contempt and pity. I met his gaze with tremulous resolve. He had defeated my uncle, but I would not be conquered so easily.

"One of your terms, however, I will accept," he said, his eyes locked on mine. "I will have your niece. Princess Alyce will be my wife."

III

Looking back on it now, the moment those words left the prince's mouth was the moment my aunt and uncle lost their power over me. Of course, I didn't realize it at the time. Living in such fear and isolation is not easily undone, even under the most ideal circumstances. For me, being handed over to a foreign prince I'd never met while my kingdom lay in shambles from war...I felt as though I'd passed from one imprisonment to another.

The prince's first act was to take possession of the king's bedchamber. My aunt and uncle were bustled out of sight while the prince ordered all their things to be carried into one of the lesser bedrooms and deposited there. I could easily picture my uncle fuming and growing increasingly red in the face as their fine golden sculptures and other trinkets were piled haphazardly and shunted into corners. Not that very much finery remained—of the little treasure owned by Myrilla, most had been sold to finance my uncle's feckless military campaigns.

While the prince settled into his new quarters, I took my place in the chamber next to his. It was the second best in the whole castle, and I suppose I should have been flattered, but I felt so sick with worry I couldn't enjoy its luxurious furnishings or the view of the grounds from the large, open windows. My anxiety was only inflamed by the woman the prince had placed in charge of housekeeping. She had a wide, cheerful face and seemed perfectly at home ordering around the foreign servants, though she herself was Myrillan. With her hands on her hips, she surveyed the chamber and

21

said, "I know it's not the loveliest of rooms, but don't worry, Princess. You won't be staying here long."

She gave me a meaningful wink and returned to her task of bossing and sniping. I knew she meant well, but my stomach filled with sour bile at the reminder of the impending wedding. In a matter of days—three, to be precise—I would be the prince's wife.

Suddenly the thought of remaining in the castle for one more second became unbearable. I gripped the bedpost, unsure where to go, or where I would be permitted to wander, when one of my new maids came in. I didn't know her name; I thought of my former maids with a pang of sadness. Faithful to the last, they had remained with me in the tower until the battle drew so close I insisted they depart. I could not protect them from harm should Myrilla fall to its enemies. They had kissed my hem in farewell and assured me the gods would bless me for such kindness.

The new maid eyed me nervously. "Are you unwell, Princess?"

I shook my head. "Not at all, only in need of some fresh air. I'd be very grateful if you fetched me a pen and a scrap of parchment, please"

She curtseyed and withdrew, dodging two servants carrying a small trunk. They set it on the floor and furrowed their brows in bewilderment. "The prince ordered us to move your belongings in here, Princess," said one, "but this is all we found. There was nothing else in the tower."

"Very well, thank you," I said absently. Did they expect to find glittering jewels and chests of gold in a prison? I tried not to look at the broken latches, remembering how hastily I'd dressed only a few hours before. The aftertaste of hope and longing turned my tongue bitter.

The maid returned with the pen and parchment and I scrawled a hasty note to the prince, asking permission to journey to Kore's temple to ask the gods' blessing for our marriage. I expected him to deny my request, or at the very least force me to travel under military escort, but he did neither. He replied quickly, wishing me safe travels and assuring me in his note that the road to the temple would be kept clear for me and my companions. I snickered quietly and tried to imagine what it would be like to have companions I trusted enough to invite on such an intimate journey. I shook my head and threw the prince's note into the fire. As I reached for my cloak, I noticed the maid fidgeting.

"What is it?" I said, my fatigue making me sound more annoyed than I really was.

She flushed. "I only wanted to ask, Princess, if you would like me to draw you a bath before you set out. You've had such a difficult morning, I thought you might find it soothing."

I looked down at my hands, still dirty from my fall in the field so many hours ago. I hadn't changed out of my servant's garb, and the blood on my cheek had dried into a dark, cracked scab. A difficult morning, indeed.

I managed to smile at the maid. "When I return," I said gently, "a bath would be lovely."

My walk was silent, apart from the wind in the fruit trees and my pounding heart. The prince had kept his word: the road was empty apart from me, though I did not doubt for a moment that his soldiers lay hidden along the way, ready to drag me back to the castle if I attempted escape. The temple stood at the top of a hill, a half mile or so from the castle. On the other side of the temple lay the village, though it was more of a marketplace than anything else. Farmers and craftsmen filled the stalls with their goods to sell and trade each day, then packed everything up and returned to their farms in the evening. At night the village lay completely empty, apart from a few stay dogs and cats, and before dawn the whole routine began once more. For the longest time I thought all kingdoms functioned this way. The first time I visited the sprawling city centers of Warkenland and Itomius it came as quite a shock when I realized that not only did their cities stay lit well into the night, but people *lived* there as well.

Halfway to the temple I had to stop and sit down for a moment. The walk had drained my energy and I hadn't eaten a proper meal all day. As I rested I closed my eyes and tipped my head back, letting the sun warm my face. The smell of the fading leaves and fresh soil filled my mind with memories of festivals from my childhood long ago, before my parents had departed to the gods, leaving my uncle to neglect the practice of honoring Kore with celebrations during each planting and harvest.

I continued on my way, finally arriving at the temple. Its pale pink columns, crafted of marble hewn from Myrilla's farthest mountain border, spiraled high overhead, supporting the great roof. I climbed the steps and approached the threshold, which of course was empty. No priest had resided in Myrilla since my uncle banished the last one. I craned my neck, taking in the great altar. Intricate pictures of the wheat harvest, blossoming flowers, and spring plantings were carved into various panels. The images next to the high, narrow windows had worn down slightly, their sharp edges softened from wind and rain and time. The carvings closest to the center, however, remained pristine and unharmed by the elements.

The temple's interior glowed with beautiful rosy light, though it was very cold. At the far wall I saw an elderly woman pacing back and forth before the altar, murmuring her prayers and chanting praises to Kore. As I waited quietly, wondering when she would finish, I studied the floor; the red and brown lines shone like veins in the marble. The distant smell of charred grain, offered in the centuries before me, clouded my mind. Shaking myself, I rubbed my arms and looked at the center picture behind the altar. Carved into the pink stone was the God of Souls' great hand reaching down toward a wheat field tended by Kore. Perhaps it was my imagination, but the heavy-headed stalks seemed to cower from the powerfully muscled hand, fearing that it would rip them from the nourishing earth and crush them in his fist.

The woman finished her prayers and turned to leave. Though the temple was empty apart from us two, I moved closer to the wall as if to give her more room to pass by. I watched her make her way slowly toward the bright threshold, struck by her countenance. Her carriage was stooped under the weight of her many years, but her face was as alert and sharp as a curious young girl's. She didn't shrink from the pictures above the altar, neither did the heavy silence disturb her in the least. She seemed perfectly at ease in the temple, so long abandoned. I was seized with the sudden urge to follow her and ask her blessing. Or better yet, ask her to plead to the gods on my behalf, since clearly they had forgotten me. But I stayed rooted to the cold, smooth floor, paralyzed by my own cowardice.

The woman reached the pool of light at the threshold, then looked over her shoulder at me. She didn't speak a word, but her dark eyes pierced me so deeply I felt sure she had guessed my thoughts.

Upon my return from the temple the seamstresses were waiting to take my measurements for my bridal gown; they had such little time to work on it that they whipped their twine around my waist, hips, and chest with lightning speed. They happily assured me—beneath perspiring brows—that I would look stunning in spite of the time constraints. I managed to thank them and even smiled, mostly to keep from vomiting.

The rest of the afternoon and evening passed with bizarre normalcy. I bathed and whiled away the time in my room, grudgingly sketching out my plans for the bridal chamber and listing which plants I required. Once the sun had set I found myself anxiously glancing at the door every few moments. I feared the prince would send for me and insist we share dinner in the great hall. Mercifully, one of the maids arrived with a tray for my dinner and news that the prince was otherwise occupied.

I woke the next morning in my unfamiliar bed and experienced a brief shock from the sunlight flooding the room. When I sufficiently recovered I dressed in one of the few gowns remaining in my aunt's wardrobe, restored to my new chamber the previous day. Unfortunately, it was ill-fitting and smelled musty. The housekeeping woman, arriving to update me on the bridal gown progress, wrinkled her nose when she saw it.

"It isn't the loveliest frock in the world, is it, Princess?" she said, as kindly as she could. "Not to worry, the prince brought bolts upon bolts of silk and wool from Itomius. You'll have your pick of colors. As soon as the seamstresses finish your gown for tomorrow they'll start on a whole new wardrobe for you. You'll have a trunk full of clothes before you know it."

There was a knock at the door and one of the maids answered it. A servant entered with my breakfast on a tray. An egg cooked in its shell alongside a buttered artichoke, with blackberry tea to drink. She placed it on the table and, with a little bow, departed. I had not yet adjusted to the comings and goings of my room; in the tower my door almost never opened, and any visit was clandestine and hurried. I sat at the table and peeled off one of the artichoke leaves. The housekeeper watched me eat for a moment, then ventured quietly,

25

"Are you planning to prepare the chamber today, Princess? I know it's a very private matter..."

I sipped the cold, tart tea before answering. Tiny bits of fruit floated in the dark purple liquid. Choosing the plants for the wedding chamber was traditionally an experience shared between mothers and daughters. Even poor young women whose choice was limited to wildflowers in the cornfields always performed the task with their mothers. Or at least an aunt, cousin, or close female friend. For a princess to do such a thing alone was almost tragic, though solitude was preferable to the company of my one living female relative. I shuddered at the thought of strolling through the royal gardens with my aunt, her swift and critical gaze condemning my every move.

"I shall go alone," I told her, determined to sound resolved. "It shouldn't take very long, anyway. I have a good idea of what I need." I gestured to my sketch, which had been scribbled over and crossed out so many times it was hardly recognizable.

But the housekeeper must have noticed the slight slump to my shoulders as I studied my ragged piece of paper. Too wise to comment on my poorly disguised misery, she sank into a curtsey. "Of course, Princess Alyce. But if you are willing, may I suggest you bring a couple of maids with you? Trina loves the fresh air and Bethine has been terribly idle today. A morning spent in the gardens carrying your bridal plants might remind her how to properly sweep out a fireplace."

I nodded. "That's a fine idea. Call for them at once."

It may sound strange to you, Reader, for a princess to spend hours walking the castle gardens and filling baskets with plants, but I assure you there was nothing strange about it. You must understand: to place plants and flowers indoors means more to royal Myrillans than simply stuffing a fistful of stems into an empty pot. That is the peasant way. I was descended from Kore herself. Her divine skill flowed in my veins—diluted by generations upon generations of time, but present nevertheless. When she wed the God of Souls she was said to have plaited honeysuckle vines around their nuptial bed and whispered scores of roses out of the walls. Trumpet flowers sprouted from the mortar and sang out with the first light of dawn. When her husband rose in the morning they say his bare feet touched not cold stone, but fresh grass. Her great-great-great-granddaughter, Queen Roselyne, known as the First Rose of Myrilla, purportedly sewed a veil of white rose petals for her wedding, and hung curtains of blue lilies and sage around her marriage bed.

My own wedding chamber was sure to be a scene of disappointment. The few flowers I managed to find in the gardens were dull and nearly wilted. The seamstresses had already scourged the royal grounds for any decent looking blooms they might sew onto my wedding gown, and hadn't left much in their wake. Every garden gate revealed more evidence of neglect. Weeds, rot, slugs, and plants destroyed by insects assaulted me from every side. I seethed with each stem I cut with my little gardening knife, tossing ashen roses and faded morning flower vines into the baskets. The fire flowers had long died and the pale pink Lady's Lips would not bloom for weeks. Every lily had already been cut, though their haunting, sweet fragrance remained. I filled the baskets as well as I could—ignoring Bethine's steady stream of murmured complaints—and led the maids back toward the castle.

We had just passed the autumn garden when I noticed a familiar door covered in peeling black paint. The door I was so certain would lead me to my freedom. I hadn't noticed it earlier; it looked so different in the daylight. I stopped suddenly, much to the maids' surprise, and stared at it a long moment.

I felt the maids' growing discomfort behind me. "Princess Alyce?" said Trina, shifting the basket in her arms. "What's wrong?"

I didn't answer her question. With a trembling hand I touched the key—still in the keyhole—and pushed open the door. It squeaked on its hinges, startling me. It had opened silently the previous morning. I stepped inside and when I heard the maids following I raised my hand for them to stop.

"Wait here," I said. "I'll be back shortly."

I let the door close behind me and surveyed the garden. It was as wild and unkempt as I remembered. Overgrown vines covered the walls and invaded the stone walkway. Rotten fruit littered the spotty grass, filling the air with a sickly-sweet scent, and the few flowers that had survived were being choked by weeds before my eyes. I didn't dare pick any of them; I hated this garden with every part of me. I spotted the little hidden gate in the back wall and my rage grew. When I last walked this path I had been so sure of my escape. But it had betrayed me. It hadn't led me to freedom at all, only despair and a lifetime of loneliness, bound to a monster.

I slipped through the little gate and found myself at the edge of the field once more. Grief charged at me with such force that I sank to my knees. Dry dirt stained my gown but I didn't care. I rested my forehead in my hand and wept for the first time since the foreign prince had invaded. Hot tears swelled in my eyes, running down my cheeks and dripping from my chin. A parade of images flashed through my mind: my uncle's delightful smile as he discovered me in the throne room, the old man and his milky eyes, the awful prince studying me with that smirk, and the hand of the God of Souls reaching down to tear the wheat from the earth.

You can imagine my surprise, then, as I opened my eyes and noticed a small clump of wheat swaying in the breeze. It wasn't the plump, brilliant golden wheat of a healthy harvest; it was pale and scrawny and looked like it might blow away at any moment. But it was the only wheat growing in sight. I watched it struggle against the wind, then grasped it in my fist and cut it free. Wheat was Kore's crop, the most holy in Myrilla. We hadn't enjoyed a proper harvest in years; many people believed the fields were barren, including myself. But perhaps if I placed wheat in my wedding chamber—even wheat as feeble and pitiful as this—then Kore might bless the land once more.

I wasn't so foolish to think she might bless me as well.

It was late in the evening when I finished arranging the plants in the prince's chamber. It was hardly a beautiful spectacle, but I couldn't help my limited resources. I folded my arms and scanned the room, looking for any remaining bits to be trimmed. Finding none, I started to tuck my knife into my pocket, then stopped. I looked over my shoulder at the great marriage bed, with its heavy bedclothes folded neatly, awaiting our arrival the next night. Gripped by foreboding, my heart leapt to my throat and before I could stop myself I rushed to the bed and lifted the corner of the blanket on the left side. The knife sweated in my hand as I shoved it beneath the mattress, where it was swallowed by the thick, downy layers.

My blood was still pounding when I returned to my room and readied myself for bed. The maids were gone for the evening; I had dismissed them when they brought the last of the baskets into the prince's chamber, much to their relief. I had just cleaned my teeth and pulled on my dressing gown when I heard a knock at the door. I opened it, expecting to see the housekeeper or another servant, but it was the prince.

I stared at him, mute with surprise. I hadn't laid eyes on him since the throne room, when he stood sneering at me in his bloodstained armor. For a wild moment I thought he might have found the knife, but he merely peered into the room.

"May I come in?"

I stood aside and let him pass. He studied the furnishings, the fire, the view, all in that curious way he looked at everything, as though waiting for it to displease him. He rested his hands on the windowsill, looking down into the courtyard, then turned to me. "I heard you were in our chamber earlier, arranging flowers."

"I was, yes," I said, narrowing my eyes at his ignorance.

"Apparently I'm not allowed to sleep there tonight. It's one of your peculiar Myrillan traditions, or so I'm told."

"What a terrible inconvenience," I said, unable to stop the bitterness creeping into my voice.

He gave me a sharp look. We glared at each other for a moment, two strangers connected by nothing more than hostility and a dethroned king's foolishness. The tense silence stretched, and then the prince poked at the fire with his boot. "I'll leave you now," he said wearily. "I only came by to tell you that I've chosen your new name."

"New name?" I said, scowling.

"Tomorrow when we wed you'll become queen. You must have a new name." For a moment he looked almost apologetic. "It's a mere formality. I chose one that's quite close to Alyce, so the scribes won't be confused."

New anger surged through me. What an absurd tradition, formality or not. Rooted in Itomius, of course. No Myrillan-born man would ever force his wife to change her name. "Well, what is it?" I demanded tartly. "What name did you choose that's more suitable than my own?"

He looked into the fire, his face glowing orange and gold in its light. "You'll be called Alcestis. Queen Alcestis."

IV

The next morning the prince was crowned King of Myrilla. The speed of the arrangements shocked me. One moment Trina was rousing me from sleep and in the next I was standing in the throne room watching the prince take my uncle's crown and place it on his own head. Hardly anyone attended—or was even invited to attend. The great room looked sparse and bare as the prince took his seat on the throne. His friends and chosen courtiers stood in the places of honor while my maids and I huddled a short distance away, awkward and out of place. The prince looked so noble and grave as he promised to honor Kore and seek the gods' favor for the people of Myrilla that I wondered for a moment if I had gotten it wrong. Perhaps we were the barbarians, and not he.

No sooner had the coronation ended than the final preparations for the wedding feast began. We were ushered from the throne room and paraded past scores of onlooking Myrillans toward the temple, where the prince had erected a great bower for the occasion. It stood at the top of the hill, with all the kingdom's fields and orchards spread out before it like a richly patterned carpet. The bower's roof was constructed of branches from the birch tree with garlands of rosemary and laurel entwined among the silvery twigs. Rosemary's perfume is sacred to Kore while laurel is the royal symbol of Itomius. It was supposed to represent the unity of our two kingdoms, and I heard many comment afterwards on the bower's great beauty. I thought it looked hideous.

A short distance away at the opposite ends of the bower stood two pavilions: one white and the other red. The white pavilion contained my household and a few servants hurrying about fetching whatever I needed for the ceremony. My aunt and uncle—invited to the wedding, but not the coronation—added new heights of tension to my already tight nerves. We were to wait there until the wedding began, and then process to the temple. I tried very hard not to think of the red pavilion. Waiting inside its walls of crimson linen was the bloodthirsty warlord who killed my people, the thief who stole my kingdom, and the master who would make me his slave.

My maids implored me to eat as they dressed me, or at least partake of some wine. But I shook my head to all their offers and reached for my flowers. They were terribly heavy, a waterfall of roses and lilies that tumbled over my arms and toward the ground. Like all brides in my kingdom, I dressed in green. The pale, fresh green of new shoots growing out of the earth, the green of leaves uncurling toward the sunlight. My train dragged over the grass, weighted with hundreds of white and yellow flowers sewn into the silk. The only crown I wore was a band of wheat, tightly plaited and interwoven with tiny pink roses and ivy. I was not a proper queen, after all. My queenship was merely a symptom of my marriage.

When the maids plucked the last stray petal from my hem I stepped around the screen. The servants froze in their tracks and bowed to me as if I were already queen. My aunt searched me with her eyes, seeking out any flaw while my uncle, furiously pacing the length of the pavilion, scarcely glanced at me.

"He's planning something," he muttered. "That little upstart is plotting something terrible for my kingdom and I won't have it. He'll probably burn all the fields and convert them into grazing land for his horrid beasts."

I knew better than to comment. I simply shifted the flowers in my arms and listened to the muffled voices on the other side of the pavilion's walls. A servant dressed in Itomian garb poked his head into the pavilion and beckoned to my uncle.

"His Majesty would like to begin the ceremony now," said the servant, his face reddening in embarrassment as he addressed Myrilla's former sovereign. "As the princess's closest relatives you and your wife are to enter the temple just before the bride."

31

He held the curtain aside to let them pass. My uncle stormed out first, still muttering about the injustice of it all and what a cheeky tyrant the prince was turning out to be. My aunt followed him like a silent shadow, never once looking back at me. I think that even then she had already erased me from her mind. I was a traitor now, though she seemed to have forgotten what little choice I had in the matter.

The servants trickled through the curtain after my aunt and uncle, while I remained in the pavilion. My attendants—chosen by the prince—were already in the temple, in accordance with the Myrillan custom. I had to wait on my own just as Kore had wandered the fields on her own when the God of Souls came and stole her away as his wife. It was a tradition shared by all Myrillan brides, but I wonder if any felt the parallel as acutely as I did on my wedding day. My eyes traveled over the pavilion's silk walls, searching wildly for a gap that I could slip through and make my escape.

At that moment, the musicians began plucking their lyres, signaling me to emerge from the pavilion and join the prince. I clutched my flowers and gripped the front flap with white fingers. It took every measure of strength I possessed to pull the silk curtain aside and step into the sunlight. Once I did, however, I nearly dropped the bouquet in surprise.

Thousands of people spread out before me, lining the path to the temple like an ocean split in two. Every living Myrillan must have been present, and all their eyes were fastened on me. My heart pounded in my ears and I attempted to swallow my terror. The temple looked so far away; the thought of walking toward a miserable future bound to a pagan prince rooted my feet firmly to the ground. Cold sweat broke out on my forehead; I lifted my free hand to wipe it away, but it didn't feel like it belonged to me anymore. The people continued to watch me, waiting with blurry faces. Tears gathered in my eyes and I blinked them back, determined not to look weak in front of the entire kingdom, especially the prince. I felt like I was trapped in some terrible dream, but it was all too real. I could not do it. I could not willfully marry the man who'd stolen my throne—

"Alyce?"

I gave a start, alarmed to see the prince standing to my right with his hand outstretched. Bulky Itomian armor covered his body and a dark crimson cape poured from his shoulders. My uncle's crown sat on his golden head, I noticed with chagrin, as natural as if it had always been there. "You're quite pale," he murmured in his thick accent, so only I could hear. "Is something the matter?"

Oh, the barrage of nasty retorts I could have given him! But to snap and snarl would make me look bitter, and only a defeated princess would surrender to bitterness. Renewed by the strength of my anger, I drew myself up and, instead of responding to his question, placed my hand on his arm. I touched him just enough to feel the cool steel beneath my fingertips, then pointed my feet at the temple.

I felt him looking at me, his face carefully blank as he took in my crown of plaited wheat and the flowers sewn into my green gown. He studied my profile and then he, too, faced the temple without another word.

Our walk to the temple was accompanied by music, which only ceased when we climbed the great pink marble steps. Since Myrilla had no priest, our ceremony was conducted by a military officer, in the Itomian tradition. I was startled to see the official was none other than Kern, the man who had clipped my foot with his arrow, dressed in formal armor and looking very out of place in the temple. If the whole business hadn't been so dreadful I would have burst out laughing.

Kern must have noticed my anxiety, for he gave me an encouraging little nod before taking on his role of distant stoicism. With his droning voice, he gave the same speech that was made at every Myrillan wedding, about Kore and the God of Souls. It was scrawled on a scrap of parchment, no doubt rescued from some forgotten room in the temple.

"The gods call us to them," he said, "just as the God of Souls called to Kore that fateful harvest day. We are to be imitators of the gods, that we may one day become gods ourselves. To wed the God of Souls, Kore had to die to her own wants and desires. She reminds us of this every year with the wheat, fruit, and flowers. Only a seed that has died and been buried can grow and bloom into something more beautiful than before. It is a painful process, but the reward is worth the cost. So it is with marriage. Both husband and wife must sacrifice their desires on the altar of love, each to benefit the other. Only then will these two truly know the love of the gods."

He read from the scroll, but his heavy dialect sounded so foreign to me I could scarcely understand a word he said. At the proper moment one of the Myrillan helpers held up the cask of grain, and I scooped up a handful to toss into the fire as a sacrifice to Kore. The prince did the same thing, asking for the God of Souls' blessing. There was more music and then the hideously awkward moment where the prince and I had to join hands and kiss.

The prince offered me his arm, leading me from the temple and down the steps. The entire ceremony had lasted half an hour at the most; it was difficult to believe anything had changed. I expected some monumental shift, some presentiment to settle within me, saying, "Your husband is the king and you are now queen," but it never came. I felt like the same Alyce as before. Alcestis was just a stranger with a queer name. As I walked with the prince I felt the same odd sensation as I had when I first stepped out of the pavilion; I looked down at my hand resting on the prince's armor and hardly recognized it as my own. Grief squeezed my chest; I knew the crowd was shouting greetings and praises but I heard none of it.

We proceeded to the wedding banquet waiting for us at the castle. Only the prince's close friends were invited, though in his calculated generosity he made sure the people outside the gates received helpings of meat and wine as well. A feast of ridiculous proportions was spread across the tables of the great hall, no doubt provided from the prince's wagons. Lamb and suckling pigs and roasted peacock, squash stuffed with sausage and a rainbow of vegetables and fruit. Wine was poured from generous hands and by the time puddings arrived (plum, cherry, lemon, rainberry, all sweeter than I've ever tasted) the newly installed court was rosy-cheeked and merry. As queen I sat at my husband's right hand and carefully sampled every dish that was placed before me, hoping the food would settle my churning stomach. My one relief was that as soon as the ceremony had ended, the prince ordered my aunt and uncle into their new lodgings: a house of exile on the edge of the kingdom.

I'm sure our wedding banquet included fine music and entertainment lasting well into the evening, but I remember little of it. I was sick with fear of the night to come. The knife that I'd hidden provided some consolation; it was the circumstances leading up to its possible use that I couldn't bear to imagine. I was young and naïve, but I'd heard enough whispers from my maids to know that men could cause terrible pain in the name of marriage, and a wise woman was one who took steps to protect herself.

Still, when the bell rang at midnight, announcing our imminent departure, my insides twisted into a tight coil. I tried to look as though I didn't mind the court's callous jests and bawdy jokes, but my face remained stony. When the prince stood and offered me his arm I had no choice but to accept it, though I wanted nothing more than to shove it away.

"We must bid you farewell, I'm afraid," announced the prince to the court, smiling broadly. "My bride and I have important business at hand."

"I hope it's more than that!" shouted one of the lords, to much laughter. I shuddered inwardly, cursing the prince for saddling us with such a wretched court. If they were always this silly and foolish I'd almost rather return to my prison tower.

For once I was thankful for Itomian traditions. We were allowed privacy our first night together whereas under Myrilla's laws royal wedding beds were presided over by the entire court. The prince had put a stop to that at once. He'd ordered the heavy curtains around the great bed to be torn down, saying the bolted door would provide enough seclusion for a man and his wife on their wedding night.

"Make yourself comfortable," said the prince, removing his armor and piling it carefully on a table near the windows. The curtains were loose to keep out the cool night air, and to prevent any breezes from disturbing my flowers. The prince folded his crimson cape and touched a creamy yellow rosebud I'd tucked into a crack in the mortar. "Pretty," he said, looking around the room with approval.

I said nothing, though I made sure to position myself close to the left side of the bed, where my knife lay hidden beneath the mattress. My head itched from the scratchy wheat of my crown; I pulled it gently from my hair and set it on the windowsill. I knew what was supposed to come next; I had to undress and slip into the fresh sheets like a willing bride. My hands started to loosen the stays in the back of my gown, but froze in refusal.

Thankfully, the prince chose that moment to visit the adjoining bathing chamber, so I was able to coerce my shaking fingers into unwrapping the gown and draping it over the chair by the fire. My bare feet skipped over the cold stone floor and I pulled back the heavy bedclothes, still dressed in my shift. Goosebumps rose on my arms, though from apprehension or the chilly air I couldn't be sure.

A few minutes later the prince emerged from the bathing chamber without a stitch of clothing. I looked away at once, my cheeks flushed with shame. I heard him smirk as he said, "Does my nakedness offend you?"

I did not answer, choosing instead to stubbornly adjust my shift before lying back on the pillows. I pulled the sheet up to my chin, loath that this idiotic prince should see any fleck of my skin.

He ignored my silence and I lay as still as stone as he climbed into the great bed. The mattress shifted and the frame creaked beneath his added weight, but I kept my eyes glued to the ceiling. I was keenly aware of every whiff of air entering and leaving my lungs. The fingers of my right hand trembled slightly, ready to dart into action. I silently begged the gods for courage and swiftness. I knew I would die for killing Myrilla's new ruler, but I would rather face an instant of death than a lifetime enslaved to a pagan.

The prince let out a long breath and tugged at the sheets until they covered him to his liking. I turned on my side, moving yet further away from him, so he could see only my back and not my face. My muscles were so tense I could have been mistaken for a statue in the bed. The prince finally ceased his beastly grunting and thrashing, and the room fell silent. I slipped my right hand beneath the mattress, under the pretense of adjusting the sheet. My fingers found the knife's handle and closed around it. The bone felt smooth and cold. With tiny, undetectable movements, I ran my thumb over the edge of the blade and noted how well I had sharpened it. It would do its work well, I realized with grim determination.

The prince grunted again and the mattress creaked as he rolled onto his side. Part of me knew that if he were intent on playing the part of a sinister husband, he would have done so already, but all my sensibility was quenched by panic. I knew nothing of decent kings— or decent men, for that matter—so when his arm brushed against my back I assumed the torrent against my body was about to begin. Squeezing my eyes shut, I ripped the knife from its hiding place and rounded on him with my arm outstretched, expecting to hear him scream in agony.

Instead, he caught my wrist, the blade inches from his chest. I cried out and opened my eyes, startled by his speed and his grip.

"Drop the knife," he said, as calmly as if remarking on the weather.

I grit my teeth in pain. His hand was crushing my bones, I was sure of it. I tried to pull away but he just held tighter. "You're hurting me," I gasped.

"Not as much as you were planning to hurt me. Drop the knife," he repeated firmly.

Once again, I squirmed, but it did no good. Candlelight danced along the blade as it trembled in my weakening grasp. Tears welled in my eyes and I let the knife fall from my hand. It dropped onto the soft bedclothes with a muffled thump, and the prince instantly released me. He snatched away the knife and set it beside the candle.

"Have you got any other blades hidden in here?" the prince asked in a flat voice. "It'll be better for you to tell me now; I won't be so merciful if I wake in the middle of the night to find you poking at me again."

I glared at him, all my fear replaced with reckless anger. "You're a monster."

"You are hardly the first to say so. Answer my question, wife."

My voice shook with rage. "I will never be your wife. There are no other blades in this room but if you try to touch me again I'll tear off your arm. I swear it."

"You have the same charm as your uncle," he muttered.

"I'm not joking. Come one inch closer to me and I'll scream."

"And who will save you? Every person in this castle is under strict orders not to enter this room tonight."

I said nothing. I knew he was right. He was King of Myrilla and I was his wife. I had duties to fulfill. He could do anything he liked to me and I'd have no choice but to bear it. Hot tears rushed to my eyes and I swallowed a hard lump in my throat, steeling myself for the pain and humiliation sure to come.

The prince watched me for a moment, then sighed in annoyance. "You needn't fear for your precious virtue. I've got it right here."

With one fluid motion, he grabbed the knife from the table and threw back the sheet. Before I could scream or back away or respond at all, he reached down and, with a careful flick of the blade, nicked the back of his knee. Bright blood dribbled from the cut and onto

37

the clean mattress. I blinked at the growing stain, confused, until he wiped the knife clean and returned it to the table. He drew the sheet over his body again, covering the red blot, and turned away from me.

"There. It's done. Now no one will know we're not truly wed," he said. "Marrying you was the price I had to pay for Myrilla. Nothing more." He pulled the sheets up to his shoulders. "Trust me, Alyce, I'd tear off my own arm before I'd ever bring myself to touch you."

V

I woke the next morning to pink skies and sunlight shining in my face. With the scent of rosemary and sweet flowers and the lemony light filtering softly through the window, I felt a rush of joy. The beauty of the room seemed to reach out and touch me. The delicate petals and leaves brushed my skin and lips; the mere proximity to their loveliness almost made me feel beautiful. Then the prince shifted on his side of the bed and the joy vanished. For a brief, wonderful moment I had forgotten the previous day's events; at the reminder I felt ashamed, different, tainted somehow. The flowers withdrew their perfume and the sheaf of wheat grew faded and dull. I had betrayed my people by marrying a barbaric prince; I could never enjoy even the simplest pleasures again.

I lay cold and still as the prince stirred beside me. I kept perfectly silent, listening to the unfamiliar movements of a bedmate rising from sleep. I heard him shuffle across the stone floor and slip into the adjoining chamber to empty his bladder. While he was gone I surveyed the room with a critical eye. The flowers looked pretty, but the arrangements were not particularly special. The wheat slumped listlessly, the delicate vines I had so carefully wrapped around the bed posts were coming loose, while the rosebuds I had inserted into the cracks in the stone wall had indeed opened, though half the petals had fallen onto the floor. It couldn't have looked more pitiful for a bridal chamber.

"Good morning," the prince mumbled as he emerged. I shut my eyes once more, not wanting to see his naked form again.

"Alyce?"

Still I said nothing. His servants would arrive soon to dress him, I silently reasoned, and he'd be out of my sight in the next room. Once he departed I would sweep up the scattered petals and fallen wheat berries, lest anyone else witness my embarrassment.

"I know you're awake," he said, interrupting my plans. "Do you want to know how I can tell?"

He could mock and cajole all he liked, but I wouldn't let him bait me. I let out a long, slow breath through my nose, resolutely ignoring him.

He moved throughout the room, his thick accent slowing his voice as it carried across the stone. "You're much too still," he observed. "When a person is truly asleep, their muscles alternate between relaxation and tension. You should shift and move every now and then, and vary your breathing. Let out a little whistle or snore through your nose. You're concentrating so hard on trying to look like you're sleeping that any fool can tell you're not."

Furious, I opened one eye to see him standing at the foot of the bed with a huge grin stamped on his witless, foreign face. I ran my eyes over him, unimpressed. Instead of calling for the servants to dress him like a true prince would, he had clutched at the first clothes to meet his hand and thrown them onto his body.

His tunic mussed his golden hair when he pulled it over his head. "Aren't you going to wish me a good morning, too?"

I kept my face neutral. I could smile and perform and convince the entire kingdom I was a happily married queen when needed, but in the privacy of our own room I owed this fool nothing. He was dying for me to speak, to ask him why he was dressed and on his way out the door at such an early hour, but I wouldn't give him the satisfaction. I just closed my eyes and let my head fall back on the pillow.

"I'm going to visit my chief herdsman," I heard him say. "He's keeping the flocks on the southern face of the mountain. I'll return in an hour or so."

I thought I heard him snicker one more time as he left the room, shutting the door behind him, but it could have just been the wind rustling the wheat piled on the sill.

My first several days married to the prince continued this way. Each morning I woke with the sun and waited for the prince to dress himself and leave for the mountain before getting out of bed. I kept very much to myself. Occasionally I ate with my maids, but other than that I barely saw anyone. I felt so embarrassed, so defeated, that I could hardly bring myself to walk the castle corridors. The prince was never unkind to me, nor was he benevolent; he merely treated me like a shadow. Something always present, but only noticeable on certain occasions. I couldn't bring myself to call him "king" as it reminded me too much of my uncle. Instead I referred to him in my mind as "the prince." Be assured, I was never so disrespectful to call him a mere prince to his face. On the rare occasions when we had to speak I simply called him "sir."

I avoided him whenever possible; I suspect he was doing the same to me. The most time we spent together was in the throne room, where we devoted each afternoon to receiving supplicants. Mostly farmers, all trying to take advantage of the prince's unfamiliarity and settle disputes in their favor. The prince patiently heard them all; he sat in my uncle's great carved throne, with me in a little chair to his left, and administered his justice. I say *his* justice, because that's precisely what it was. My opinion was neither welcome nor solicited. When we shared our evening meals in the great hall I ate little and said even less. At night we'd return to our chamber together, but almost never spoke. He'd take down his bow from where it hung over the fire and polish it carefully and eventually we would make our way to the bed like strangers.

During this time, I developed two habits I never expected. Like all other habits, I suppose, they began out of a need followed quickly by a desire to fill that need however possible. Sometimes the filling is healthy, sometimes it is not. A man needs to feel calm and emboldened for an unpleasant task, so he drinks wine until he forgets his troubles and can relax once more. A woman needs to feel important, so she makes herself look beautiful and snares whichever man first crosses her path, no matter how unsuitable he is. I needed to feel I still had a voice, an identity. Like a foolish girl I had thought Myrilla's fall in battle would lead to an opportunity for a position of power. Instead I had passed from one imprisonment to another, and was nearly going mad from it. Something had to be done.

41

So the first habit, which may sound strange to you, Reader, was that I started visiting the temple nearly every day. I don't even know what planted the idea in my mind—my aunt and uncle had not visited on a regular basis—but when I woke on the third morning of my marriage to the prince I felt so suffocated and desperate that I took a leaf from the prince's book and dressed myself, setting out for the temple just after sunrise. The guards paid me no notice; no one stopped or questioned me as I passed through the castle gates. On my walk to the temple I felt like a ghost of old Myrilla, surveying the wheat fields and orchards that had survived the invasion.

When I reached the temple, the sun shone through the windows, falling toward the veined floor in thick, pearly beams. Of course the temple was deserted, apart from the lone woman I'd seen the day before my wedding. She walked to and fro before the long altar, muttering her prayers. Above her, the carvings of the God of Souls' hand reaching toward the wheat stood out sharply against the smooth wall. I shivered at the sight, though it wasn't remotely chilly that morning.

The woman took no notice of me; if I had cleared my throat she might have acknowledged my presence with a welcoming glance or kind word, but I can't be certain. I don't know how your temples and places of worship function where you live, but in Myrilla you didn't always go to the temple to pray aloud. Not in those days, anyway. I later learned it wasn't unusual at all for a citizen to sit perfectly silent in the temple, just listening for the gods to speak.

I returned each day, content in my solitude until one morning the woman turned from the altar and fixed her dark eyes on me. "You've come again, Lady Queen," she said, proffering the sacred cloth filled with grain. "Do you wish to pray?"

I swallowed. "I have nothing to pray for."

"Then the gods will tell you what to say."

"Forgive me, but I must disagree. They've delivered me into the hands of a pagan husband. To ask for their favor would be a waste of time. And I doubt they wish to hear the hateful words filling my heart."

She lowered the sacred cloth and placed it back on the altar. "The gods know your words whether you say them aloud or not," she said quietly. "And while they would prefer your love, they will accept your hate. To the gods, even a rotten offering is better than no offering at all. Though you are young yet, you will learn this in time."

At that, I turned on my heel and marched straight out of the temple, in no mood to be patronized by a cloistered old woman who knew nothing of the outside world and its ways. I had come in hopes of receiving peace, but had gotten only lectures and humiliation in return. Nobody had to remind me of my naiveté; it greeted me every night when I lay in bed beside the perfect stranger who was supposed to be my husband.

Nevertheless, I continued my visits. I kept my eyes down and stayed well away from the intrusive woman, though as far as I knew we were the only two Myrillans who bothered to spend any time there. I should have found her presence comforting; instead her devoutness pestered me beyond reason.

My second habit sprang from more sinister roots. One morning I was passing through the throne room when I heard voices coming from the presence chamber behind the dais. This may not sound remarkable to you, but I assure you it was. The presence chamber was the site of the Myrillan king's royal council, where decisions affecting the kingdom's future were made. Heavy rugs covered the walls to protect the enclosed voices from any eavesdroppers. The design made the room so quiet that while the door was locked, no soldiers were needed to stand guard. Anyone speaking within could be confident of absolute privacy.

But I had grown up with my ears pressed against doors, always listening for the slightest sound. I never knew what might constitute a signal, or a message of some type. My hearing was as finely tuned as a doe's. So when I heard the prince utter the words "invasion" and "new Myrillan army" from the safety of his carpeted walls, I stopped. My heart in my throat, I climbed the steps of the dais and stood behind the throne, my back facing the door. To anyone it would look as though I was merely surveying the throne room with a thoughtful look on my face, when in fact my ears were racing to keep up with the prince's talk.

"I see no reason to wait for the campaign against one of the Southern kingdoms," he was saying. "They're too busy preparing for the rains to be on guard against a foreign army."

"It's a perfect plan," said a second voice. I recognized it as belonging to Turius, the yellow-bearded man who had announced to the entire throne room that I couldn't possibly be a princess. If anything his hatred of me had only intensified, and such was my reciprocal dislike that I rarely spoke to him when our paths crossed, lest I say something unbecoming to the prince's closest friend. My flesh crawled when I heard his voice. "These people are so grateful to you for liberating them that they'll gladly volunteer to fight for you. Though if you're not wholly settled on campaigning in the south, King Admetus, let me remind you of Grenlake. Their king is said to be unwell, and we both know what staunch enemies his children are."

"Grenlake borders Warkenland," said the prince, his voice accompanied by the sound of shuffling papers. "I wouldn't want King Torbold to mistake our aggression against his neighbors as aggression against him."

Turius goaded him. "Then bring him along as our ally. I'm sure he wouldn't mind more land to put his bulls out to pasture."

Much murmuring broke out following this, some in agreement while others made sounds of protest. I looked down at my knuckles, white from gripping the throne in anger. I had heard enough. I left the throne room, my thoughts whirling in my head. If the prince thought he could muster a new army so soon after his conquest then he must be completely mad. Myrilla was a small kingdom, so dwarfed by its powerful neighbors that, for the most part, nobody took notice of us. And that's how the Myrillans liked it. They were farmers, not soldiers. They were more interested in feeding their families than expanding their boundaries.

My anger led me back outside into the sunlight. I stood at the edge of the castle gardens and looked out at the endless maze of paths and walls. The temple rose on its hill, far beyond the tree line. But I had no desire to go back there, not with that woman with her prying eyes and ears lurking in the shadows of the altar. I paced back and forth for a moment, then found myself walking in the direction of the worn black door. I opened it and pocketed the key, greeted once more by the overrun wildness within. When the door closed behind me I felt utterly alone, in the best possible way. Here there were no war-thirsty princes or vengeful gods waiting for me to make a mistake. I truly felt that as long as I stayed within these walls, no one could touch me. I know how foolish it probably sounds to you, but my desperation had reached new heights. And if I could find solace there, so be it.

I chose a flowerbed near the far wall and knelt in the dirt. Savagely, I pulled at every weed I could spot, piling them on the path behind me. With each little space I cleared, I cleared away some of the prince's plans from my mind. I imagined the weeds as his maps and battle plans drawn up by those foolish friends and advisors of his and I tore them out of the earth to be burned. I ripped up his ignorance of the people he had sworn to lead with wisdom, and tossed away every bitter sneer and poorly disguised cross word from Turius.

Thus my second peculiar habit began. Some queens might think it beneath their dignity to paw through the dirt like a dog, but I had no such qualms. In fact, my anger against the prince, which had served as my motive in the beginning, soon gave way to genuine pleasure. The moment I left the temple each morning I made straight for the garden and only returned to the castle in time to change clothes before joining the prince in the throne room to receive citizens. I kept the key tucked beneath my side of the mattress where I was sure no one would find it. I even hid an apron in the garden, along with a handful of tools my maids had gathered for me after a few careful questions. I found great satisfaction in my work, as fumbling and slow as it were. Few days remained before true autumn set in, and I intended to draw as much as I could from them. I sang as I pulled weeds and pruned the mature plants, hoping that the sound of my voice would encourage new growth. I don't pretend to be an accomplished singer by any means, but I do believe the garden responded. Bright splashes of flowers soon sprang up in the neglected beds with each weed I cleared. At the end of every afternoon I sat on the grass and surveyed the progress, planning out where I would work next. The garden was not a small one, and would require many months of work. Still, I brushed the dirt from my hands and smiled, knowing that while it was hardly paradise, it was mine.

VI

Weeks passed, and the garden continued to take shape. Whenever I was in the castle I ignored the maps the prince insisted on leaving out on the table in our chamber, thinking only of the temple and my work in the garden. I never asked him about the council or his plans, and he never broached the subject with me. I preferred to think neither he nor any of his advisors existed. But then the day finally arrived when I could ignore him no longer.

It was a cool morning; one of those autumn days when the sky is such a clear, flat blue that you feel you can reach out and touch it like it's no more than an inverted porcelain bowl. So cheerful was my mood that I was singing to myself before I even reached the garden. I reached the ancient door, which creaked on its hinges as I turned the key and pushed it open. I closed my eyes and drew a deep breath, smiling with pure joy as the fresh scent filled my nose. The green stems and leaves, the black earth, the rainbow of petals and buds. It all held such promise. When I opened my eyes, however, I saw I was not alone. There stood the prince, examining a flowering shrub with great concentration. His back was to me; he slowly straightened and took in the vast spread of plants. I remained in the doorway, frozen with anger. He must have caught a whiff of the poisonous rage flowing from my body because he turned around and drew himself up when he saw me.

"I'm sorry," he said, though he certainly didn't look it. "I see I've intruded—"

"What are you doing here?" I demanded.

He gestured to the garden. "Forgive me, but my curiosity got the better of my senses. I've seen you disappear through that door nearly every day since I first came here." He had the audacity to grin at me. "It's beautiful, Alyce. Did you do all this yourself?"

I ignored his flattery. "You had no right to come here. This is my garden and no one is allowed inside without my permission. No one else even has a key. The door was locked. Curiosity aside, that should have been enough of a clue that what lay on the other side was not for your eyes. How did you get in here, anyway?"

He raised his eyebrows. "You can lock doors, but you can't lock walls."

It took me a moment to understand what he meant. Then, when the answer dawned on me I raced to the wall that faced the castle, scanning the carefully pruned vines for any damage. Any crushed leaves, any broken buds would have been enough to make me completely lose control. I grabbed an empty clay pot and turned it over, standing on the base as I inspected the highest climbers. The pot's lip was warped, and it rocked on the uneven stone. The prince put his hand on my waist to steady me and I nearly slapped it away.

"Everything's fine, I promise," he said. "As I climbed over I touched nothing but stone."

I glared down at him. "You think this is a joke, don't you? You think the whole world is just a big game, played for the purpose of amusing you. Nothing is serious, nothing is sacred."

Infuriatingly, he continued to smile. "You know that isn't true."

"Don't I?" All my hidden frustration spilled forth as I stepped down from the pot. "I remember that day in the throne room. You were beaming, radiant with joy, like a child who's just won at swordplay for the first time. It didn't matter to you in the slightest that you had destroyed half my kingdom, all in pursuit of a crown."

"I do remember that day," he countered, no longer smiling. "I remember your face, full of grief and despair and rage, and your cold pain as your uncle pushed you toward me again and again. I remember thinking of all the rumors I had heard about your grace and intelligence and sweetness. And I remember your utter silence, which, up until this moment, has been all that's existed between us."

I shook my head, flinging his kind words from my ears. "Don't use that as an excuse. You violated a sacred place today. I don't care how desperately you wanted to speak with me, it was a wretched thing to do."

"Almost as wretched as listening in on a private council."

My mouth snapped shut. I swallowed, perfectly aware of my flaming cheeks. So he knew. He probably had spies scattered all around the castle; I wagered he'd filled half the servants' pockets with coins in exchange for keeping their eyes on me.

"Only a foolish queen leaves matters of state to men," I said haughtily, clasping my shaking hands behind my back.

"I agree," he said, to my surprise. "But a wise queen wouldn't press her ear to the door like a kitchen girl."

My temper flared at the jibe. "That sounds very clever now, but don't expect me to believe for one moment that you'd actually allow me on your council. I've seen enough kings at war to know that. You'd patronize and ignore anything I said, until some lackey spat out the same advice, only he'd receive a knighthood for it."

"Well, you've never seen this king at war."

At that, I laughed bitterly. "Yes, I have."

"Not from my side. My style is a bit different from your uncle's. I prefer to strike while the proverbial iron is hot, rather than wait for it to crumble." He folded his arms and surveyed me. "But if you're so keen to give counsel, I'm ready to hear it. What do you have to say about the plans for invasion?"

I sensed a trap. I felt as though I were in the throne room with my uncle again, knowing he expected a particular answer, but not knowing what to say. I twisted my fingers together; anxiety formed a heavy ball in my stomach. "I-I'm not sure—"

"You must have some opinions. I'd like to hear them."

He might've liked to hear them, but he certainly wouldn't like the words I'd choose. The breeze picked up, scented with the blooming rosemary beside me. I traced the paving stone with my toe; the crushed herbs in the cracks released their sweet perfume. I looked up and met the prince's eyes. "I don't think you should do it."

He gave me an amused look. "What do you mean? Which campaign?"

"None of them. You've already taken one country, why do you wish to take another? What good could it possibly serve the people of Myrilla?" I glared at him, annoyed by his mirth. "There's no need to laugh. I haven't said anything funny."

"You're right, it isn't funny. It's very sweet, though. You're a precious girl, Alyce. Invasions are part of kings' business. Don't look at me like that; truly, I'm not patronizing you. Your gentleness will serve you well. I find your innocence charming."

"Let me tell you what isn't charming, sir," I snapped, unleashing every bit of anger that had built up inside me since we married. "How many people in this kingdom died of starvation during my uncle's reign. How many times the crops failed because he didn't observe the rites or keep the festivals. This is supposed to be a time of rebuilding, of restoration, not another time of war. The people want Kore's favor again, and that will only come with planting and harvest. That's all that matters here. The wheat was sown only four weeks ago. There is still much work to be done while we wait for the summer, rites to be observed, rituals to prepare. And while the harvest is nearly a year away people are already planning for the festival. I promise you, if you tell them that their fathers and sons and farmhands are to be called up to war at such a critical time, it will not endear you to them. They'll despise you for it."

His face was carefully blank. "Then what is your alternative suggestion, wife? I've yet to hear one."

"Myrilla was once the greatest producer of wheat and corn and nearly every crop known to man," I said. "It traded with all the kingdoms that touched its borders, and beyond. You can restore us to that, but the only way is by putting down your sword. If you want to make war, I can't stop you, but I beg you to at least wait until the storehouses are full once more."

He shook his head and touched a flower blooming on the shrub. One of the white petals fell off in his hand. "You Myrillans are all mad," he muttered. "Nobody with any sense would wish for a farmer king."

"That's what your people want. They want to see the gods' will carried out, and that means plantings and harvest. Their previous king was a warmonger, and you know better than anyone how that turned out for them."

Neither of us spoke for a moment. A red bird hopped from branch to branch on the winter cherry tree, a dry bit of wheat clutched in its beak. Somewhere up in the scarlet leaves his mate was probably waiting for him, working on her part of the nest in

49

preparation for winter. I bit the inside of my cheek, half-blind with envy of their perfect life.

The prince cleared his throat. "I thank you for your counsel, and I am sure it is wise in its own way, but I am afraid it will not make as the designated course of action. There are other kings out there, with much more experience than I, including my own family in Itomius. I must establish myself as a formidable sovereign who can hold his own land and take others in conquest, not a disappointing son who won a second-rate kingdom in a play battle."

"A play battle," I repeated, as nastily as I could. "So that's what you call it when hundreds of men and women and children lay dead in the streets." I nearly spat in outrage. "How lovely to hear your true thoughts, sir. Is that what you think of the people you swore to lead and protect? Is that what you think of me? Am I merely a second-rate princess you won in this play battle of yours?"

"For the love of the gods," he swore, "this is not about you, Alyce."

"You're right, it isn't about me. It's about your wretched pride. Tell me, sir, which of your nobles and lords first advised you to invade? Turius, I'm sure; he can't bear to be in the same kingdom with his wife for more than a fortnight, poor woman. He'd wage war against the Great Sea itself if it would take him away from her sight. And I notice your clever herdsman is curiously absent from these plans. Have you even spoken to him about this? Does he approve of your intent to butcher Myrilla from the inside out until we can bleed no more?"

"I have heard quite enough," he said, his voice a blade. Sharp and cold. "I bid you farewell, Queen. I hope you enjoy your flowers, perhaps you should stay with them until you learn their sweetness once more."

I narrowed my eyes. "Sweet flowers only follow where strong roots lead. A farmer king would know that."

He turned away from me, disgust written on his face. I watched him march resolutely to the door, thrust it open, and vanish on the other side.

The prince did not come to our chamber that night; I did not expect him to. Alone in the great bed I glowered up at the ceiling, my belly filled with angry bile. Let him go to war, I thought. If Kore had any mercy she'd cause my fool of a husband to lose his precious campaign and forgo Myrilla to a king with more sense and decency.

The next morning I slid out of the sheets and broke my fast. At least, that is what I attempted. I had no appetite; I managed to swallow a couple mouthfuls of bread and left the rest on my plate, along with the apples and cheese. My back was stiff as the maids dressed my hair, my cavalier stubbornness replaced by chilly fear. My marriage to the prince was less than two months in length, but in that short time I had already forgotten the terror of living with a rage-filled king. Now the memories came flooding back, and I felt myself sinking into my former shell. Why must I be cursed with such an unfortunate pattern?

I knew of only one safe place. After my temple prayers I headed straight for my garden. A thin frost covered the ground, crunching beneath my feet and lending sparkle to the grass in the autumn sun. When I reached the garden door I slipped the heavy bronze key from my pocket and turned the lock. This time the garden stood empty; no princes to be found among the roses and heath. I closed the door and pressed my back to it, thanking the gods for small mercies.

I set to work, singing softly to the flowers as the sun rose in the sky. I pulled at weeds and cut down the thistles, readying the soil for winter. But somehow the tasks held little joy. My hands felt slow and sluggish, more than once I had to set down my trowel for a rest. Icy wind whipped through the garden, stirring leaves and chilling me to my core.

I pressed on, but instead of filling me with new energy the work only drained my strength. Clouds scuttled across the sun, cooling the air further, and when I pulled my cloak tight around me I could hardly do it for my shaking hands. The garden was so quiet I could hear my rattling breath. I wanted more than anything to climb into my warm bed and pull the downy covers over me, but I didn't feel I could walk ten paces, much less the distance back to the castle. From the corner of my eye I spotted the bench, waiting invitingly beneath the rosy arbor. The trowel fell from my hand as I pushed myself to my feet and staggered toward it. Each step sent a blinding pain from the crown of my head to the backs of my eyes. Shivers racked my body and when I reached the bench I didn't sit as much as fall onto it. I pulled my knees up to my chest, sweating from the effort in spite of the cold, and closed my eyes. If I could rest, only for a moment, I knew I'd feel better.

I can't tell you how long I slept, but it must've been hours, for when I opened my eyes the sky was as black as pitch and peppered with thousands of stars. The thinnest sliver of moon hung over me as though suspended by a string. My head hurt so badly I could scarcely lift my eyes to look at it. I was lying on my side, desperately cold and wondering how I would ever walk to the castle, when I heard a pounding at the garden door.

"Alyce! Are you in there?"

The prince's voice rang through the clear night air, but there was no chance of me answering. Each harsh knock sent a lightning bolt of agony surging through my head and tears into my eyes. With monumental effort I burrowed further into my cloak just as the door swung open.

"Is the queen there?" I heard one of the guards say.

"Give me a moment to look," said the prince. Several pairs of feet shuffled and the prince ordered them to halt. "This is the queen's garden. I'll go alone."

His feet fell softly on the stone path, pausing here and there as he searched. I knew I should call to him, but my body ached and my head was swimming. For all I knew his presence could have been the product of my addled imagination. He drew closer to the corner where I was lying, and when his footsteps came faster I knew he had spotted me.

"Alyce!" he called sharply. "What are you still doing here? The castle is in uproar; no one's seen you all day. If this is your idea of revenge for yesterday it's petty and childish—"

He stopped in front of the bench, and even though I couldn't see him, I felt the wrath and frustration disappear from his body. His boots scuffed against the stone as he knelt and gently pulled the cloak away from my face. He took in my glazed eyes, shivering form, and beads of sweat glittering at my hairline, and swore under his breath. I flinched as he pressed the back of his hand to my forehead; it felt so cold that it burned.

The prince swept his cloak from his shoulders and wrapped it around me. Then, as if I were nothing more than a child, he lifted me from the bench and bundled me into his arms. His touch was agonizing, and tears seeped from beneath my eyelids. My head throbbed with every step he took, though his chest was warm and solid beneath my cheek.

Somewhere in the distance I heard the heavy garden door creak on its hinges. The prince's voice thrummed in my ear; the last thing I heard was him telling his men that the queen was ill with a raging fever, and then everything went dark.

VII

Weak light flooded my eyes and I smelled the remnants of a fire. The stiffness in my body told me I had slept for a long time, a very long time. Days, perhaps. It took me a moment to recognize my surroundings. I was in bed, suffocating beneath a pile of blankets and sheets, and the room was so stifling with the heat still pouring from the hearth that I attempted to throw the covers off me, if just to get some air. But I couldn't lift them. I could barely lift my head.

"Good morning, Lady Queen."

I gave a start—at least, as much of a start as I could give in my sluggish state. A woman sat in a chair near the bed, hemming a shirt. She turned to look at me and I recognized her at once. It was the woman from the temple. Up close she was so old and frail I had a difficult time believing she could even see her stitches. Her mouth was full of pins, which she removed and stabbed into the shirt before rising to her feet. I wanted to tell her not to bother, she had no reason to bow to me, but my confusion trumped my courtesy.

"How long have I been asleep?" I asked her, lifting my hand to push my hair out of my eyes. The weakness in my arms astounded me; it took heroic effort to simply move my fingers.

She saw me struggling and put down her sewing. "Don't fuss, Lady Queen," she said, adjusting the pillows against the headboard and helping me sit up. She took a ribbon from the table and tied my hair back; her hands were much gentler than I expected. When she finished, she bowed again, as if to apologize for touching me, and

54

stood by the bed. "You've been asleep for four nights, since the king brought you in with the fever."

I breathed deeply, trying to recollect any of that time, but it came up blank. "What happened? And please, sit," I added.

She took her seat with a grateful nod and resumed her sewing. "They had to break the fever first, so they put hot stones in the bathing chamber and poured cold water on them to make you sweat. Then they brought in river water—ice cold, it was—and filled the tub to the brim for you to bathe in. The bottom was lined with cold rocks from the river, too. That's what knocked the fever. You've done nothing but rest since."

I nodded, thankful I couldn't recall any of the treatment. Helpful though it was, it sounded like absolute torture. The woman crossed the room and spoke to a servant outside the door. "You're meant to eat now," she explained. "I was told to alert the kitchens as soon as you woke up."

Again, I nodded, though I couldn't imagine performing an action as complicated as chewing and swallowing. So I was quite relieved when, a few minutes later, a servant arrived bearing a tray laden not with food but wine and a bowl of steaming broth. She placed it carefully on the table and departed. I was just wondering how I would find the strength to lift the spoon when the elderly woman dragged her chair closer to the bed.

"You're a brave woman, Lady Queen," she said. "But it'll be at least tomorrow before you can feed yourself again." She lifted the crystal cup to my lips and let me drink a long draught of wine, then took up the bowl. I felt humbled and oddly comforted to see her spoon up the broth, then blow on it to help it cool before feeding me, as though I were a small child.

I drank all the broth and desperately wanted more, I was so hungry, but the woman shook her head. "It's a long while since you last ate, Lady Queen. It won't do to bring you back from fever only to sicken your belly on too much food too fast."

I conceded and fell back on the pillows. My stomach was warm and full, and I felt quite refreshed. The woman stacked the dirty dishes on the tray and returned it to the servant waiting outside. I looked over at the other side of the bed, wondering for the first time about its usual occupant. "Where is the king?" I asked casually.

She didn't look up from her work. "I believe he has business in the throne room."

It took all of my willpower not to roll my eyes. I had no doubt that as soon as he'd ferried me back to the castle he had no trouble leaving me to the care of physicians, hoping to distance himself from my illness as much as possible. He was, after all, a coward with no regard for any life but his own. "I'm sure he's quite busy," I said lightly. "And it's important he preserve his health. It wouldn't do to have both the monarch and his consort out of commission."

The woman lowered her sewing and gave me a look so cutting it was almost as if she'd glimpsed my thoughts. "The king has been at your side day and night, Lady Queen," she said, though it sounded close to a scolding. "He has scarcely slept these four nights. He's the one who oversaw your treatment and made sure your fever had abated before allowing you to be put to bed. He halted all official business so he could be sure of your health. He only made an exception for today because the foreign messenger he summoned arrived before he had a chance to postpone the meeting. He left just before you woke, and assured me he would return before midday."

My cheeks flushed and I dropped my gaze, ashamed. Not only had I underestimated this surprisingly well informed woman, but I had doubted the prince. He had taken every measure in ensuring my wellbeing, when I knew I wouldn't have lifted a finger to help him if our fortunes were reversed.

"May the gods forgive me," I whispered. "I've mistreated him as well as you."

She watched me for a moment. "You've not mistreated me. You're young, and still new to queenship. You will learn."

The confidence in her voice lifted my head. "Will you please tell me your name?"

"Lilianne, Servant of Kore."

I nodded. I had met very few Servants of Kore. These were women who devoted their lives to studying Kore in order to emulate her better, choosing never to marry or bear children so that when they met the God of Souls they would know him as she had. It was not a path chosen by many, certainly not one I had ever considered. Not that I had a choice in the matter. As a princess of Myrilla, marriage was required.

Suddenly shy, I swallowed and glanced at the door. "Would you mind, Lilianne, if you helped me to bathe? The king probably won't be much longer in coming, and I'd like to be fresh upon his arrival."

Lilianne nodded approvingly and called for the bath to be filled. I didn't have the strength to even walk to the bathing chamber, so I submitted to letting Lilianne lead me in and then bathe me like a little girl. She scrubbed my back and combed perfumed oil through my hair with the gentleness of a veteran bathmaid. When she finished, she wrapped me in a warm sheet and placed me before the fire to dry. As I watched the dying flames she hunted in my wardrobe for a bit, and then dressed me in a simple blue gown. I felt quite spent from the bustle of activity; I was just letting her help me back into bed for a rest when the door opened.

The prince appeared in the doorway. He looked neither happy nor disappointed to see me awake; his face remained thoughtfully blank as Lilianne bowed to him. I remained seated on the edge of the bed, trembling slightly from the efforts of bathing and dressing. The prince shut the door behind him and stood a little distance from me. He clutched a sheaf of papers in his hand and looked as though he hadn't slept properly in days.

"How do you feel?" he asked, with no preamble.

I eased back against my pillows. "Quite well, thank you. Lilianne has been a tremendous caretaker. I daresay she could outperform the most skilled nurse in Myrilla. I am very grateful for her presence."

Lilianne bowed. "You are too kind, Lady Queen. It's an honor to serve a sweet lamb such as yourself." With a sly wink, she slipped through the door and vanished into the corridor.

The room suddenly felt much smaller, with only the prince and me remaining. My nerves tightened as I remembered the unkind thoughts I'd had about him and in that moment I wanted, for the first time, to be friends. "Thank you," I started awkwardly, "for finding me in the garden and bringing me back to the castle. Lilianne said you were responsible for my course of treatment, so I owe my recovery to you."

He shifted uncomfortably. "It was no trouble, I'm just glad you're better." He looked like he wanted nothing more than to flee the chamber. "I just stopped by to see if you were awake yet. I'll be in the throne room with the dispatch messenger from Warkenland for the rest of the afternoon; if you need anything have Lilianne send a page."

"Wait," I said, pushing myself upright. "Why is the messenger from Warkenland here?"

"I sent for him earlier in the week and he arrived late last night. Of course, he understands that in your illness you were unable to receive him."

I narrowed my eyes. Any tender feelings I'd had for the prince withered further with each sharp word I spoke. "Forgiving the fact that you denied me the opportunity to welcome him as befits my station, I cannot see why you'd summon him here. Unless, of course, you're planning to proceed with your mad schemes."

"My 'mad schemes' have nothing to do with you, Alyce. You've made your views quite clear."

"I want to know why he's here," I demanded. "Is it war talk? Are you and Warkenland deciding between the two of you which nation will lay victim to your folly? It's madness. You cannot honestly hope to rouse an army. The people here won't stand for it. Not now, not at this fragile time. Did you hear nothing I said the other day?"

"Of course I heard you!" he nearly shouted. "Everyone on the castle grounds probably heard you." He paused and rubbed his brow, then began in a quieter voice, "Alyce, you've been ill for days. This is hardly the time or place to discuss such weighty matters. We can talk about it later; for now you need to rest. Lilianne will have my head if she sees all her hard work undone."

I ignored his attempts at sympathy. "I'm not a halfwit," I snapped. "My body may have been ill but my mind is perfectly sound."

He smirked. "Then I suppose I shouldn't ask you to take my cause to your precious temple and ask Kore's blessing?"

I was nearly shaking with anger now. "No, you shouldn't. And don't ask for mine either because you won't get it."

"Then I'll leave you to your recovery," he said, accompanying his words with a mocking bow. "Shall I tell the messenger you send your greetings? Or is your belly too full of bile?"

I unsheathed my falsest, most sugary smile, all offerings of friendship forgotten. "Yes, please greet him for me," I said sweetly. "Tell him I send my love. Tell him to please excuse my absence. Tell him I look forward to watching you and his king tear our little corner of the world into shreds."

VIII

I saw very little of the prince for the rest of that day, and several days after. I'd sit alone on the little window seat in our chamber, wrapped in blankets and watching the grounds turn increasingly cold and barren. It seemed that everything was cast in a dull grey light, with winter hurtling quickly toward us. I tried very hard not to think about what plots and battle plans the prince was drawing up in the throne room with his messengers coming and going, choosing to concentrate my worry on my flowers instead. I was eager to get out of the confines of the castle and into the fresh air once more.

As I won back my strength I learned to eat and bathe and walk again without Lilianne's help. The fever had torn through my body, leaving me weakened and frustrated, but it wasn't long before I was able to venture out to the temple again each morning. I'd wrap my thickest cloak around my heaviest gowns and walk up the hill, bent against the wind. The few bare wheat fields left in the kingdom had been sown while I was in my sickbed, so there was nothing for me to do but wait and pray that they would yield a generous harvest. Every morning I knelt at the altar and poured my paltry handful of grain into the fire as a sacrifice to the gods. The smell of burning grain filled the temple and I found myself wondering how it could be helpful to burn up the very thing I was hoping to save, but then I'd look at the pictures carved into the walls and my questions would dry up, quenched by fear. It wasn't my place to wonder; the God of Souls would have his way.

In spite of the weather, there was still much work to be done in the garden. I trimmed and pruned and covered exposed roots. I cut away wilted flowers and broke off every dead branch I could spot, all in preparation for winter. Most of the plants had slipped into dormancy, with the exception of the heath and juniper and a few other winter flowers. But the garden didn't look dead or depressing, just peaceful. The days grew shorter and the air was so bitingly cold that I didn't stay out nearly as long as I had in those early days of autumn.

One afternoon I knelt at the foot of a winter cherry tree, its pale blue blossoms just starting to open, when a sharp knock on the door shattered the silence and sent the birds flitting to the highest branches. Annoyed, I glared at the door, then turned away again, determined to ignore it. I had no desire to see anyone, and I knew if it were the prince he'd simply vault over the wall whether or not I invited him in. But the knock came again, louder this time, and accompanied by a voice.

"The king commands you to come back to the castle."

I recognized the speaker. It was Starten, chief guardsman to that oaf Turius. For my life I could not understand the prince's friendship with Turius. I knew they had fought battles together since boyhood, and Turius was renowned for his fierce loyalty to my husband. From the little I'd seen of him I'd found him far heavier in fierceness than loyalty. It was no surprise that his guardsman should display similar characteristics.

Moving deliberately slowly, I disposed of the uprooted weeds and made my way to the door. When I opened it I saw not just Starten, but a handful of other guards as well. I looked at them, bewildered. "Why are you here, and not the king's men?" I asked.

"My lord volunteered us," Starten said, and in that instant I knew something terrible must be at hand. Turius hated me; if he had sent his men to collect me it could be for no other reason than the prince was angry with something I had done, and Turius wanted a hand in my discipline as well. My skin clammed up and my eyes fell on the sword hanging from Starten's belt. So great was my terror that I didn't even protest when Starten took me by the arm and started toward the castle. The guards closed in around me, as though I were a dangerous murderer being led to her execution. Through the gaps between the men I could see merchants and farmers and minor nobles on the palace steps, waiting for their audience with the king. For a wild moment I wondered why they looked so puzzled—I was their queen, they knew my face well—then I remembered how I was dressed. My skirt was weighed down with dirt around the hem and lashings of mud marred my apron. My hands were nearly black with earth and when I caught a glimpse of myself in a merchant's glass I saw a streak of dirt on my cheek from where I'd absently brushed my hair out of my eyes. Horrified, I looked up at Starten.

"I can't go into the presence chamber looking like this," I said. "Please, let me wash first."

He kept his eyes straight ahead. "The king wants to see you immediately, my lord says. You're to come to the council at once."

I trembled as the castle doors opened before us. More nobles and lords moved aside to let us pass; I lowered my face, ashamed they should see me in such a state, and a few cherry blossom petals fell from my hair onto the carpet. Finally we reached the throne room. The first guard opened the great bronze door behind the dais, frowning slightly at me as we entered the presence chamber. Starten dropped my arm; he and his men stood slightly behind me, leaving me to face the council on my own.

They sat at a long table, the prince at the head, with a stack of rolled parchment before him. I saw not only the great lords of Myrilla seated at the table, but men dressed in clothes from neighboring kingdoms as well. The bull of Warkenland trotted across a bald man's chest, stamped into his leather armor. A cruel-faced man with a dark, silky beard sat a few seats away from the prince, the banner of Sophria draped over the back of his chair. I could just make out the wing of a silver owl embroidered on the heavy blue fabric, the symbol of Sophria's goddess. Even the Sea's Arm had sent an envoy, a wizened man with thinning white hair and gnarled hands folded over his ancient bronze armor. When the door closed they all turned silently to look at us. I breathed deeply, knowing I should at least appear strong and dignified, as a queen should, but my hands still shook violently, destroying my pathetic façade of poise. I brushed anxiously at my apron and sent crumbs of dirt scattering across the polished stone floor.

The prince stood; any fool could see he was less than pleased. I drew a deep breath, ready to defend myself, plead for my life, assuage his anger or say whatever it took to calm his wrath. But when he narrowed his eyes they were not aimed at me.

"What's all this?" he said, rounding on Turius. "You volunteered your men to escort my wife, your queen, to the council. Not drag her in like a criminal."

Turius inclined his head, though he hardly looked remorseful. "I apologize, Lord King. Sometimes my men misinterpret my tone when I'm delivering important instructions. I assure you they meant no disrespect. I simply tried to convey the urgency of the message."

The prince was not amused. He turned back to the guardsmen. "And was it in your urgency that you did not permit the queen to so much as wash her hands before bringing her? I thought not. Bring a basin of hot water and a cloth. Now." No less than three guardsmen jumped to perform the task. When they were gone the prince sighed. "Alyce, if you would be more comfortable in fresh clothes, we will wait for you."

I shook my head, more confused than ever. "I'd much rather find out what's happening," I whispered. "Why have you sent for me?"

"Come rest your feet and I'll tell you." He took my filthy hand and tucked it into the crook of his arm. His sleeve felt especially rich and soft beneath my skin, which was coated in dry, cracked dirt. The prince led me to the table and seated me to his right. I felt the others looking at me, some with curiosity, others with derision, all no doubt wondering why I should be present at the king's council, much less seated in the place of highest honor. Once more I tried to look like a strong queen, one who belonged in the world of men and war, but I couldn't meet any of their eyes for more than a second. Thankfully the guardsmen returned with a stone basin full of water, so hot that steam billowed and curled from the surface, and a soft cloth. I took the cloth eagerly and dipped it in the water, grateful to have something to do with my hands. Some of the lords wrinkled their noses, appalled that a queen would wash in public. I paid no attention; my uncle was known to wash his feet at the table before royal banquets. As long as I kept my shoes on I saw no shame in it.

I wiped the dirt carefully from my fingers as the prince began. "My lords," he said, "I thank you for attending this council on such short notice. Some of you rode all night to be present on behalf of your kings, and for that I am very grateful. I hope you will accept two nights' lodging here at the castle to recuperate before returning home. Tonight we will hold a banquet in your honor, and it is my hopes you will all join." He turned to me. "And I pray my beloved queen will attend, though considering how little notice she received before this council, she may choose to abstain. A beast such as myself doesn't deserve the blessing of her company."

A few nobles laughed, not unkindly. At the prince's left hand Turius rolled his eyes and muttered something to his other neighbor. I ignored him; my hands and face clean, I draped the cloth over the lip of the bowl and a servant instantly whisked it away. I knew I should make some jest or perform a charming act to show the prince my forgiveness, but I still wasn't sure why I had been summoned to the council. Coy acts had never come naturally to me anyway, only frankness. And it was with perfect frankness that I sat quite still in my chair, waiting to hear what else the prince had to say.

But it was the old man from the Sea's Arm that called out next. "Look at your queen, Lord King. She has flowers blooming in her hair and breath sweeter than any fruit. Persephone, Flora, Kore, call her what you like. She walks among us again. Your queen is the goddess of spring, I doubt it not."

The table grew quiet. I flushed and lowered my eyes, desperate for the talk to return to business. The prince must have heard my inward plea, because he reached for a roll of parchment and opened it on the table.

"Perhaps you are right, sir," said the prince. "Though I daresay she rivals Sophria's goddess of wisdom for her title. It was the queen's wise counsel that inspired me to invite each of you here today."

The Sophrian envoy was not impressed. I too would not have appreciated the comparison of an inexperienced queen with dirty hands to my principal deity. Kore certainly would not tolerate such nonsense. The prince continued, "Each of you went to considerable lengths to attend today's council, so I will not waste your precious time. Some of you are under the impression that this is a council of war. I am pleased to tell you it is not. It is a council of trade."

Bemused looks shot around the table. "Trade?" scoffed the Warkenlander. "Are you mad?"

"Not at the moment, Lord Thaine," said the prince, with a smile. "I've heard Warkenland beef is the finest in the world, and I'd love to taste it with a loaf made from Myrilla's best grain and a cup of salt wine from the Sea's Arm. I have trade agreements written here." He indicated the pile of parchment that I had wrongly assumed contained maps. "Please, take them to your kings and have them review the terms. If anyone feels unfairly compensated they are free to suggest alternatives."

The lords each examined their parchment. I held my breath, praying to the gods that at least one lord wouldn't find my husband's proposal utter folly. The rustling of parchment was muffled by the rug-covered walls. I studied their faces as they read. Some looked perplexed, some amused, still others gave no hint of their thoughts. Turius looked equally irritated and entertained, as though he wasn't sure the prince was serious with his plan. Finally Lord Thaine cleared his throat.

"I cannot speak for my king, sir," he said slowly. "But I do believe he will be interested to discuss the prospect. He has often said he regrets that the roads closed for trade between our land and Myrilla."

The Sophrian was not so keen. "The trade routes were abolished for a reason," he said, his dark beard glinting in the afternoon light. "What if the Sea's Arm loses its vineyards to fire, or their fisheries dry up? What if the mines in Ironfort yield no ore? What if your gods withhold rain and your fields produce nothing but brush? The others will pay out more in goods than they'll receive. There's no way to guarantee equal provision."

"You are correct, Lord Flynt," said the prince. "There can be no such guarantees. All harvests fail at one point or another, whether it's in cattle or grain or precious stones. That's one of the reasons I called this council. So that we may see each other face to face and hopefully establish the first roots of trust. If I simply wanted to trade I would have dispatched a rider with the agreement to request an audience with your king. I am not suggesting we reach an immediate conclusion; I am not as foolish as that. My hope is that over the coming months, whoever is willing to participate may reach a common goal for our kingdoms to exist cooperatively, each applying its own strengths to the common good."

"Well said, King Admetus," said the elderly man.

Others nodded in agreement. I clutched my hands together under the table, not daring to believe they might come to a peaceful solution. Perhaps Myrilla would flounder no longer. If Kore would only grant a plentiful harvest, the dark days of my uncle's reign would finally reach a blissful end.

"This is only a proposal," said the prince. "I thank you for your indulgence, my lords. I would consider it a great personal honor for you to let your kings look over the agreement. We will come together again for further discussion as necessary. For the moment, let us look forward to dining tonight as friends. The queen and I bid you a good afternoon."

He stood, dismissing the council. Chairs scraped stone as the lords and nobles rose to their feet and rolled up their parchment. Each greeted me and kissed my hand; to their credit not one flinched at the sight of my still dirty fingernails. Some names sounded familiar, from the wraith days of my childhood when Myrilla hosted dignitaries from our neighbors. The old man from the Sea's Arm gripped my hand with surprising strength, though his other rested on an elaborately carved cane for support.

"My name is Lord Daltena, my queen. First Man to King Noleman of the Sea's Arm," he said. "The last time I saw you, you were a babe in your mother's arms. I remember when your family visited the Sea's Arm just after your first year. The king presented you with a sapphire tiara and you cried at the sight of it. You wept until one of the servants brought you a little cotton doll to play with. For the entire visit, you refused to put it down, even when you slept." He touched my hand. "Your grandmother was as dear to me as a sister. She would dance with joy to see you as a queen today."

I bowed my head in thanks. "Your faith in my abilities is the picture of generosity, Lord Daltena. I am ever grateful for your confidence."

"It is yours for the taking. Myrilla will bloom under your watch." He turned to the prince. "You are a blessed man, King Admetus. I would keep an eye on my queen if I were you. The gods may decide they want her for their own."

The prince's eyes twinkled. "Wise words, my lord."

Lord Daltena departed, revealing a thunder-faced Turius. "I thought you were summoning a council of war, not inane talk of cheap peace. Please tell me this was a joke."

"It is certainly not a joke," said the prince, his voice equally hard. "And I expect you to have a word with your men about the way they treated the queen."

"Of course," said Turius, ever the gracious courtier, even when angry. He turned to me and bowed. "If my men harmed you in any way, Queen Alcestis, say the word and each will have their right hand cut off and thrown to the dogs while you watch."

I tried not to roll my eyes. "There's no need for such drastic measures, sir. Though I'll ask you to refrain from volunteering your men to deliver messages to me in the future."

"Of course," he said again. He turned back to the prince. "Admetus, I still don't understand this plan of yours. It's madness to reopen the roads."

"We'll discuss it tomorrow. Go to your wife and rest."

"But—"

"Tomorrow, Turius."

Sighing with exasperation, Turius stalked away, leaving me to depart the presence chamber with the prince. Servants appeared from the hidden corridors as soon as we shut the door behind us, polishing the throne and sweeping my mud from the floor. The throne room was bright with deep orange light pouring through the narrow windows. Another autumn day coming to a close.

"I apologize again," said the prince. "Turius is fond of you, truly—"

"He isn't," I cut in. "If he is, his fondness has a strict resemblance to anger. He hates me for breaking up your brotherhood."

The prince shook his head. "If he's angry with anyone, it's me, Alyce. Turius has always prided himself in being involved in my personal business. The day you and I were betrothed he was tired and delirious from battle. The events moved much too quickly for his liking. He's like family to me; as odd as it may sound, we've always sought the other's opinion for important matters, especially marriage. I chose you as my queen without any of his help or advice, and he still resents me for it."

"So he's a spoiled child. That's not much of an improvement on hatred." A servant bowed to us as he passed, lighting the torches in the dimming corridors. "I should be the one apologizing," I admitted. "You meant to present a queen to the council, and what you got was a dirty kitchen girl with mud on her face."

He laughed; the sound rang off the stone walls. "No, I got something even better than a queen. Didn't you hear Lord Daltena? You're the goddess of spring."

I allowed myself a small smile when I remembered the compliment from the Sea's Arm, though his later words troubled me even in memory. *The gods may decide they want her for their own.* I did not know what that meant, and I did not wish to find out. "So you wouldn't mind if I dressed this way every day?" I said aloud. "I must say it's a good deal more comfortable than court clothes."

"Certainly," he said. "You give new meaning to the word beauty." His eyes studied me with warmth, and I felt my cheeks redden beneath his gaze. Itomians are famous for their courtly speech, and even though it's shallow and frivolous and means nothing, it's still flattering if you aren't accustomed to it. When we reached the door to our chambers, he paused. "Do you think it will work?" he asked me, his voice heavy with doubt. "Tell me truly, Alyce, do you think the other kings will consider the plan?"

I drew a deep breath. "I don't know," I confessed. "I certainly hope they will, but there's no way of knowing until the papers are signed." When he still looked troubled I stepped closer to him. "Either way, Myrilla will know you tried to make peace. You looked to protect the best interest of your people, and they will remember that. If the time comes to fight again, they'll flock to your side more readily, knowing you wished to spare them." I hesitated. "If I may ask, what made you change your mind about the invasion? You seemed so intent on it when we spoke in the garden."

"When I stormed off, unwilling to listen to reason, you mean," he said, rubbing his brow. "I am sorry for that, Alyce. I was a perfect beast to you. I went to the mountain, to see my herdsman as you suggested. Well, after a while I did. First I wandered through the stables, stalling for time. I was afraid he would tell me I was acting the fool, as you did. By the time I left for the mountain it was nearly dark, so the climb was more difficult than I've ever remembered. He was waiting when I arrived, and we argued about it for ages. To be frank, he never really argues, though he certainly knows how to drive his point home. When I got back to the castle it was well into the night but I began writing up the plans immediately; I knew I'd lose my nerve if I didn't act quickly. While you were ill I stayed in our chamber working on them. The first envoys began arriving a few days ago; Lord Flynt rode up less than an hour before the council opened. You know the rest of the story." A yawn escaped his mouth.

"Begging your pardon, it seems my fatigue is finally catching up with me."

I rubbed my arms, feeling small and ashamed as I recalled the unkind thoughts I'd entertained about him over the previous days, without the faintest clue of the work he'd produced in such a short time. "Not at all," I said quietly. "If anyone in this castle has earned his rest, it's you. I'm honored that you thought to invite me to the council this afternoon. It was a privilege I will treasure always."

"It remains your privilege, if you will accept it."

"What do you mean?"

"There is always room for a wise queen when discussing matters of state," he said slyly. "That seat at the council table is yours, if you wish. I would be honored to have you at my right hand whenever matters are to be decided."

My mouth opened, but no words came out. Never had I imagined he would offer me such a position. No queen in Myrilla's history had ever sat on the king's council.

The prince's face grew uneasy. "Of course, I understand if you need some time to consider it. You have many other responsibilities and I don't want to impose my wishes on yours—"

"No—no, I'm very grateful," I stammered. "I'm happy to do it."

He nodded, though his face remained drawn. In the torchlight his weariness showed itself more plainly than in the sun. My uncle was wrong; the prince wasn't a monster. He was just a man trying to be a good king. Very slowly, I laid my hand on his arm. He looked down at it, surprise flashing across his face. It was the first time I had ever touched him unbidden.

"I'm honored," I said carefully. I started to say his name, Admetus, but when I tried to pronounce it, found I could not. The strange sounds felt foreign and clumsy in my mouth. "Thank you," I said again, slowly, in his dialect. "Thank you, *Adam*."

IX

Adam. It was the closest I could manage. If he minded he gave no sign; for his part he did not call me by my new royal name of Alcestis. That name would be reserved for official ceremonies and state visits. Instead, my husband continued to call me Alyce as he always had.

Later that evening the prince and I hosted a banquet for our visitors, where everyone dined on braised lamb and toasted the new treaties. Adam (it felt so strange to call him a proper name) sat to my left and gave me the finest pieces of meat from the tray. The musicians played lively music and by the end of the night even Turius looked like he was enjoying himself. When the last of the ambassadors had either begun their homeward journey or poured themselves into bed, I bid everyone goodnight and made my way to our chamber. A fire was lit and waiting in the grate to stave off the chilly night air. The day's exhaustion struck me like a hammer when I shut the door behind me, so instead of changing for bed I sank into a soft chair.

I had nearly dozed off when I heard Adam slip into the room. "I thought you'd be asleep already," he said, lighting a second lamp.

"Nearly," I replied. "It's been an eventful day."

"It certainly has. Thanks to you."

I didn't know what to say. I gave him a little nod and glanced around the room. My gaze settled on his bow, hanging from two hooks in the wall. The dark wood gleamed in the orange light from the dying fire. Its shine didn't surprise me; he polished it every day.

I couldn't help admiring its beauty, though when he saw me studying it, I looked away.

"Something wrong, Alyce?" he said, the corner of his mouth twitching.

I reached for my woolen wrap hanging near the hearth and draped it around my shoulders. "Oh, nothing's wrong. I just—"

Adam swept the bow from its place on the wall and sat before me. "The wood is from a blood oak near my family's castle in Itomius. It was a colossal tree; the biggest on the grounds. My brother and I used to dare each other to climb it when we were boys. Syrano fell from it once—off the lowest branch, mind you—and broke two bones in his arm." He smiled, unwinding the bowstring. "Five years ago, lightning hit it during a storm; the entire tree split in half from branches to roots. When it finally cooled I went out to look at the trunk, to see if any wood could be salvaged. Father told me burnt wood meant ill fortune for a bow, but in my opinion it's brought me nothing but luck. You can hold it if you'd like."

I held out my hands, carefully cradling the bow. It was heavier than I expected, and the wood was smoother than bone. Even the grain was lovely. The red lines swirled and curved under my fingers, leaping out in stark contrast with the deep brown wood. Any object carved from blood oak was a rare sight in Myrilla; it was considered too expensive a material even for luxuries. "I've heard blood oak can be temperamental under a carpenter's knife," I said. "Your craftsman did his work well."

He shifted in his seat. "I made it, actually. But you're right, blood oak is notoriously difficult."

I stared at him, amazed. "You made this?" At his nod, I gaped at the bow. "I can't believe it. This is…" I ran my fingers over the grain once more. "Adam, it's wonderful. I've never seen such a beautiful thing. You are truly gifted."

He mumbled his thanks and lifted the bow from my hands. "I'll show you how to string it. You put your foot here, and draw the string toward this notch. The knot slides right in place…and there you have it." He plucked the string and a bright *twang* shot through the air. He held it out to me again. "Try it."

I took it; incredibly, the bow felt different than it had before. It was poised and pulsing with energy, ready for battle. I plucked the string gently at first, afraid I might break the wood. After a few tries

71

I grew more confident, though when I started to draw the string Adam stopped me.

"Careful, Alyce. You'll get a nasty welt if you release it without mail or an armguard." He gestured to my forearm, dressed in wool. "If you'd like, I can teach you how to use a bow. This one's too long, but I'm sure I can find one to suit you. What do you think? I know Myrillans aren't particularly fond of archery."

"No, I'd love to learn," I said, breathless with excitement. "My uncle never liked me to participate in sport." Actually, his exact words were that it was a foolish risk, and that if I injured myself and failed to produce heirs with whatever foreign ruler he secured in a marriage contract, I'd shame the whole kingdom.

Adam watched me for a moment, something like pity in his eyes. "I'd be honored if you came shooting with me," he said. "Not to sound boastful, but I'm quite a good teacher." He took the bow and notched an arrow to the string, drawing it close to his ear. He did it so easily I wondered at his strength; I'd struggled in the simple act of pulling the string, I couldn't imagine how much less skilled I'd be at holding an arrow in place at the same time. Widening his feet to the perfect stance, he tightened his aim on his imaginary target, then lowered the bow without loosing the arrow. With quick, deft movements, he slipped the arrow back into his quiver and hung the bow on the wall once more.

"I want to thank you again," he said, resuming his seat before me, "for your help. What we achieved today could not have been done without you."

I blushed and shook my head. "You're the one who drew up the papers, made the arrangements and summoned the envoys." I dropped my voice in shame. "My only role in this was to shout at you and call you a child."

"Yes, and that's precisely what I needed," he said, to my surprise. "You did just what I should have done all along: kept the welfare of our people as the highest priority. You've done a much better job as queen than I have as king. I would do well to learn from your example."

I narrowed my eyes, unsure of his sincerity, when he left his chair and added another log to the fire, sending a flurry of red sparks up the flue. "It is no question that Myrilla is still very much a foreign land to me," he said. "I think I've proven quite well that I know little about its history or policies or traditions, and that's a fault I wish to remedy. I don't want Myrilla to be an extension of Itomius, a small offshoot that copies my homeland exactly. For one thing, it isn't practical. There isn't room to raise livestock, not with so much of the land devoted to crops. Not to mention the fact that the new treaties solidify Myrilla's role as the primary producer of wheat for ourselves and our neighbors."

"That's true," I said, growing suspicious. It wasn't like him to speak so kindly of my homeland, not when I'd listened to him muttering under his breath about its multiple deficiencies for the past two months.

"I'd like to learn about this place," he said, gesturing toward the darkened windows. "The last thing I want is to be a mindless conqueror, charging in and changing everything to suit my own needs. Especially when I know such action would be ill received. Many kings would have swarmed your land and torn down the temple, replacing it with one to their own gods. But I chose not to do that. Not only because we don't build temples where I come from—we believe the gods are everywhere, and aren't bound by stone or walls—but because I didn't want to disrupt the people's daily lives more than necessary." He paused. "Though I'm starting to realize your temple stands empty more often than not."

I nodded, thinking of how many people had abandoned their practice of visiting and sacrificing grain to Kore, knowing that nothing would make any difference. They had seen too many failed harvests to still hold onto hope.

"I want Myrilla to be a happy, peaceful kingdom, Alyce. I want people to raise their families here knowing they're safe and secure, and able to work and provide for themselves without fear. I'd rather history forget I were king than be remembered as a warring tyrant. And I believe you can help me with that."

"How? I'm in the same position as you."

"You're not, you're in a better one because you know this place. You know the rites and the traditions. You visit the temple each day and know the gods. Not to mention how dearly the people love you. Haven't you noticed how whenever someone makes a request in the throne room, they ask it of me but direct their thanks to you? I want to learn from you, Alyce. In a proper way, not by climbing garden walls and holding secret councils. You may not believe this, but I want to be a good king. To the people and to you."

I bit my lip, pondering his request. He watched me closely, as though willing me to agree and take him on as a pupil. A selfish part of me wanted to say no, to leave him to fend for himself in this great mess he'd created. But I forced down my pride and nodded.

"Very well. We'll start tomorrow."

When I woke the next morning I'd half expected the room to be empty, as it was every other day. Instead I saw Adam standing at the window, pink-cheeked and dressed warmly, peering out over the grounds. He heard me stirring and turned.

"Good morning," he said quietly. "I hope you slept well."

I propped myself on one elbow. "I did. You must've gotten up earlier than usual." I looked at his muddy boots and burr-studded cloak. "Have you visited your mountain already?"

"It's the herdsman's mountain, not mine. But yes."

I eyed my gown hanging on the wardrobe door and clutched the covers around me. I had never dressed with Adam in the room, or anywhere near the room, for that matter. Sensing my reticence, he turned to the window once more, so I could only see his back and none of his eyes. I slid out of bed and padded barefoot across the icy stone and grabbed the gown, carrying it to the bathing chamber. I scrubbed my face with cold water and arranged my hair before dressing quickly. The boiled wool gown wrapped me in warmth, though the thick stockings felt itchy against my legs. I returned to the bedroom and took a roll from the tray, already drizzled with honey and thick lashings of butter.

"Take your time," Adam said, easing into a chair. "No need to rush."

It was difficult to relax with him in the room, but I managed to eat my breakfast without wolfing it down. When I had licked the last droplet of honey from my fingers I reached for my cloak. Adam followed me down the corridor; every servant we passed bowed to us, though their startled expressions did not escape my eyes. I couldn't blame them. It wasn't exactly common to see the two of us out together.

Adam ordered our horses to be groomed and saddled, and informed the guards that we would be touring the nearby farms. It wasn't long after that Adam and I were riding out, side by side, into the cold morning air. We passed through the gates and left the castle grounds, with the guards a few paces behind. The royal standard snapped and fluttered in the wind: three ears of wheat encircled with rosemary, all gilded and set upon a pale blue field.

The apple orchards were first; I halted my horse and the rest of the party stopped. Adam leapt from his saddle and motioned to the guard that he would help me down himself. I hesitated, then reached for his arms, not wanting to seem ungracious. His hands gripped my waist firmly and when my feet touched the ground he kept his hold, ensuring I was steady before letting me go.

The orchard workers saw us approaching and removed their hats. A heavyset man dressed in green, whom I took to be in charge, bowed deeply. "King Adme—Admetus—" he stumbled over Adam's formal name. "My name is Wallyce, and it's an honor to have you here. And Princess—or Queen, I should say…." His whole face turned red. "I beg your pardon, Majesties. Forgive my stammering. I am unprepared for such a surprise. Such a *welcome* surprise," he hastily added.

"We don't mean to be any intrusion," said Adam. "We simply decided to take some air this morning and see how you and the other farmers are preparing for winter. What's that they're doing back there?"

He craned his neck and the rest of us looked with him. "They're pruning the trees," explained Wallyce. "They attach their blades to long poles so they're able to cut through the high branches without risking a fall."

"That's quite clever," said Adam, and Wallyce's face brightened at the compliment. "I'd very much like to try that sometime. Is it difficult to maneuver?"

"It's a challenge at first, but once you find your rhythm and the right pressure anyone can do it. We've been using this method for the past two winters, and there are fewer injuries than ever. All thanks to your Lady Queen," he said, with a humble nod to me.

Adam looked at me. "You arranged all this?" he said, pointing to the trees.

In his excitement, Wallyce answered for me. "We'd had the idea for ages, Majesty, but it was the queen who saw our needs and sent her maids out to give us the equipment. The trees were gnarled and

75

refused to produce any fruit. For the past two years we've worked to restore them. We're praying next autumn's harvest will bring the rewards of our work and the queen's ingenuity."

"I see," said Adam, still looking at me. "Very good then. Thank you for educating me, Wallyce. We must be on our way now; we'll not delay you any longer."

Riding once more, Adam shot me a wry glance. "You've kept your vested interests very quiet, Lady Queen."

I frowned. "What do you mean?"

"I knew you had Kore's ear and the hearts of the people, but I had no idea your hands were so active in the kingdom. That man said you'd ridden out to the orchards before."

"He was right."

"Well, I was under the impression that your existence under the previous reign was one of cloistered isolation."

"It was," I said, a little crossly. "But I had to learn to ride, after all. My uncle only permitted me to leave the castle walls a few times a year. And then only during winter, dressed as a servant. He didn't want anyone to accidentally recognize me and associate my face with the harvest, or springtime, or high summer. He wanted them to forget I was supposed to be queen, to forget I was ever born. Because of that, I took pains to help the people I encountered out here. It all had to be kept secret, of course, but I never stopped because I knew that if I helped just one person I wasn't a mere ghost haunting the castle."

Neither of us spoke for a moment. The horses' hooves clopped pleasantly along the road, which had turned from paving stones to dirt long before. The orchards gradually melted away into blank, endless fields. Without the protection of trees the wind felt stronger than ever, and chill after chill raced down my spine. I wished for the sun to break through the clouds and warm me, if only for a moment.

"Well, Alyce," said Adam suddenly, "that's two days now."

"Two days…what?"

He smirked. "Two days in a row you've reminded me what a complete fool I am. A complete, blessed fool."

Our tour continued well into midday. We paid visits to the vineyards and heard the attendants' plans for reviving the shriveled vines. We examined the empty cereal fields, newly turned and ready for barley and oats come spring, and acres of failed vegetables that had refused to produce. Each farmer promised again and again that next year would be better and give more crops, and every time he heard it, the alarm in Adam's face rose. I believe that up until that day, he had thought his mere presence would set the kingdom on proper footing. That his riding in on a charger to free Myrilla from her previous torment would automatically cause the gods to smile on us. But that was not the case, and he saw it. The ink had scarcely dried on his new trade agreements and now he stood faced with the challenge of pulling an entire kingdom up from its knees.

When we reached the wheat fields, home to the most sacred of all crops in Myrilla, we fell silent. Even the guards dropped back, as though they could feel Kore's presence among the black earth. Adam lifted me down from the saddle and we stood at the edge of the field, gazing out over the pristine rivets cut into the soil. A handful of birds darted overhead, black spots against the flat grey sky. The icy breeze returned and I drew my cloak closer around me.

Adam noticed. "We can go back now if you're too cold."

I shook my head. "I'm fine. Better than, actually. I could look at this all day," I sighed.

"I suppose it is beautiful, in its own way."

I couldn't help smiling at the veiled skepticism in his voice. "I know it's not what you're used to. A landscape that looks so flat and dull and dead. But it's not dead. Not really. The wheat's there, sown and alive; it'll be months before we see any signs of growth, but that doesn't mean they're not there. Beneath the soil there's new life forming every day."

He nodded. "That's very profound."

"It's the truth. As long as we're blessed with enough rain this winter and sunshine in the spring, I see no reason why we shouldn't have an excellent harvest. I once heard the last priest say, 'The gods do most of their work away from prying human eyes.' I don't think there's any better example of that than the fields."

"You are confident of the harvest, then?"

I didn't answer right away. It was easy for him to talk of confidence, when so much of his experience lay with livestock. Disease or unsuccessful breeding might hurt a population of sheep, but you could always buy more elsewhere or try different pairings. Farming was not so simple. You couldn't force wheat to grow in fields the gods had long forgotten. "I'm confident we will receive our allotted portion," I finally said. "Whatever that means."

"I suppose that's good enough for me, though I hope the members of the treaty are as openminded as you." Adam turned and led the way back to the horses, where the guards were holding them for us. He cupped his hands to receive my boot and helped me up once more. "Your Kore must require a great deal of patience to accomplish her work."

"Patience, yes," I said gravely. "And blood."

X

Indeed, the Blooding was only a few months away. The most important of Kore's ceremonies. I feel your discomfort, Reader. I feel you wincing, bargaining, denying the possibility that any decent god would require blood. Or perhaps pity has taken up camp in your heart. You read my words and think, Oh, those poor barbarians. Their intellect was so dim, they were so uninformed, they knew nothing of the true metaphysics of the universe. They misunderstood cause and effect, and placed all their hopes on ritual and superstition.

Do not judge me so quickly. I wager many of your gods demand blood, the same as mine.

We then entered the time of year when the days grow short. Each morning I woke to darkness or a weak sun rising, and Adam called for hotter fires in all the rooms. Even that didn't warm me; I had never been one to gracefully withstand the cold. Thankfully, Adam had no shortage of wool and furs and animal skins, so it wasn't long before the seamstresses turned out new bedclothes for the whole of the castle. Many mornings I sat before the fire in our chamber, wrapped in a heavy wool blanket and clutching a mug of hot, spiced wine. I visited the garden less frequently; in its dormancy there was little help I could offer. Instead I did something I had never been allowed in the time of my uncle: I explored the castle.

I know how pitiful it must sound, but it hadn't occurred to me that the option lay before me. The grounds were as intimate to me as my own chamber; the rest of the castle remained a mystery. The idea struck one morning when Adam returned from his visit with the herdsman and began sorting through a small pile of books.

"Where did you get those?" I asked, watching him.

"The library."

"We have a library?"

He laughed. "You jest, surely." When my confusion did not lift, he gave me an odd look. "Of course we have a library. Where did you think all these books came from?"

"I didn't know. I thought you might have brought them with you from Itomius." I knit my brow, feeling terribly ignorant. "I had no idea, truly. There's so much of this castle I've never seen."

He didn't speak for a moment, just studied the books in his hands. With a sigh, he sat on the foot of the bed and knocked the books together. "You can go anywhere you like," he said firmly. "This castle is as much yours as it is mine, so you should know what it contains. It's no good for a queen to be a stranger in her own home. I want you to leave this room"—he gently pulled me out of the chair and nudged me into the corridor—"and don't return until you've opened at least twelve unfamiliar doors."

I smiled shyly, unwinding the fur I'd wrapped around my shoulders. "If you insist."

"I do. In fact, it's an order, Alyce."

My hesitance didn't last long. Once I realized that no one was going to scold or punish me for poking around the castle, I began to enjoy myself. I had no inkling of how greatly I had been restricted during my childhood—and afterwards restricted myself. The few rooms in which I had been allowed held unpleasant associations; the very act of peering through new doors stirred hope in me. I could appreciate the beauty of the castle for the first time, and imagine new possibilities. New memories, *happy* memories, the likes of which I had never known.

Each room was more silent and still than the last, as though waiting for my presence. The heavy dust told me that many had remained empty during my uncle's reign. This did not surprise me; most were merely decorative and provided no function besides hosting foreign visitors. In one room the heavy stone walls were painted pale blue, with white clouds sponged onto the ceiling. Musical instruments—harps, lyres, horns, and others I didn't recognize—

lay scattered on the chairs and carpets, as though their owners had abruptly laid them down with every intention of returning later. One room on the ground floor reminded me of a workshop of sorts, with building plans and tools and great windows covered in shutters that could open and shut. I found an old sketch for a park just behind the south wall, featuring a gilded fountain and birch trees. The plans were beautiful, and as I placed the brittle, rain-spotted paper back on the table I wondered why the project had been abandoned. Other rooms were bare, without even a carpet to warm the stone floor. Still more contained antique sculptures and paintings, or swords and pieces of armor belonging to Myrilla's ancient kings.

The library was one of the few rooms to show any signs of recent activity. It was in the center of the uppermost floor, dark and free from windows. I lit a lamp and closed the door behind me, stepping forward as I inspected its furnishings: two tall shelves against the back wall housing modern books, and a dusty table in the corner stacked with parchment scrolls. Old almanacs, military records, things of that nature. Nothing of particular interest to me. Instead I was drawn to the books; I had no idea the castle possessed so many. Bound in different shades of leather and bulky in size, there were at least three dozen, covering a variety of subjects. I could see where Adam had wiped the dust from the front covers in order to see the titles clearly; the books completely free of dust must have been the ones he'd read. Two on philosophy (one written in the strange characters of the Greeks), one religious history put down by a priest a century ago, and one slender volume detailing Myrilla's wheat production over a ten-year period.

I set my lamp on the floor and pulled out book after book, glancing at the titles and carefully turning the pages. I eventually chose a book containing Myrilla's royal history and toted it back to my chamber; the volumes were so heavy I couldn't have carried more than one even if I'd wanted.

Later that evening I sat on the carpet, studying the book in the pale glow of the fire. I had nearly finished the chapter on Queen Mychaela, who planted Myrilla's first golden rose tree, when Adam burst into the room, his eyes bright. "Alyce, come look out the window." Before I could reply he rushed to pull back the heavy curtains. I pushed myself up and stood next to him, a smile spreading over my face. The air was filled with millions of tiny snowflakes, drifting slowly down from the grey sky. Even with the moon's absence the landscape was eerily bright.

"It's only a dusting," said Adam, leaning out into the icy night air. "But by morning I imagine it'll make quite a thick covering."

I stepped back as he lowered the curtain. "How beautiful," I breathed. "With Myrilla laying in a valley we don't get snow here often. I'm sure the farmers will be thrilled; an early snow promises a rich harvest." The fire beckoned me back to the hearth rug and I sat with my book once more. Adam pulled off his boots and sank into his chair with a pleased grin.

"I see you took my edict seriously," he teased. "Tell me, Queen Alcestis, are you now the true lady of your house?"

I turned the page. "Not entirely, but I think I'm well on my way."

There came a knock at the door. Adam leapt up to open it; a servant bearing a tray stepped cautiously into the room. "Your dinners as requested, Lord King."

Adam directed him to place the tray near me on the carpet. Steam rose from two earthen bowls filled with thick stew, accompanied by hard rolls and a little flagon of wine. I looked at Adam, puzzled. "We're not having dinner in the hall?"

"We've dined in the hall every night since we wed. I thought we might enjoy a change for one evening."

"I suppose." I hesitated, watching him pour a cup of wine. He held it out to me and my fingers curled around the stem. "But where will we eat?"

"Right here is just fine." He dropped beside me and reached for the bread. "So, what have you learned in your adventures?"

I told him all about the rooms I had discovered and showed him the book I had brought from the library. He seemed intrigued, especially by the chapters on Myrilla's ancient kings.

"I must have missed this book," he said, glancing through the pages. "I wouldn't mind reading it when you've finished. There's still so much I don't know." He stopped at an illustration of a young woman standing alone in a wheat field. Flowers covered her gown and fell from her hands, illuminated in gold. "Is this Kore?"

He said it in the Itomian fashion, with the *e* long, as in the word "see," which I am told is similar to the Greek pronunciation. I touched the edge of the drawing, rough and worn from age. "It is," I said.

"She's beautiful. Though I suppose that could easily just be the artist's rendering."

I studied the picture. "No, every story says she was lovely beyond compare. But that's not what drew the God of Souls to her. It was her kindness and joy, her virtue, that made him seek her as his own."

I closed the book and picked up my stew before it could turn cold. We ate in silence, broken only by our spoons scraping the bowls and the crackle of sparks when Adam placed another log on the fire. The room was dreadfully cold; I drew my fur around me and watched Adam sop up the last of his stew with a hunk of bread.

He gazed at the flames, chewing thoughtfully. "Do you think it's all real?" he asked.

"What?"

"That story." He gestured to the book. "Kore and the God of Souls."

"Of course it's real," I said hotly. "It's the very foundation of Myrilla's existence."

He set down his bowl. "I'm not questioning your beliefs, don't misunderstand me. I'm talking about Kore. She's Myrilla's goddess, yes, but she wasn't always. According to your story she was a mortal, just like you or me, and one day when she was out in the fields the God of Souls took her away. She simply vanished, gone forever, until her descendants took up the Myrillan crown. Do you truly believe that's how it happened?"

His face was earnest, not taunting, and I could tell he wanted an honest answer. My brow furrowed as I thought; it wasn't something I'd ever considered before. Perhaps you think me naïve, but in my kingdom gods and politics were interwoven so tightly that separating the two was unthinkable. You could not have one without the other. It was the reason I visited the temple each day, praying that the gods would shape me into a queen deserving of the title.

But as much as I dedicated myself to scholarship and ceremony, I had never seen Kore with my own eyes. No one had. Even the priest of my childhood had performed his rites based on what he had been taught, the legacy of his predecessors. The closest I'd come to encountering Kore was standing at the edge of the barren wheat fields.

"I don't know," I said simply. "I can only hope it's true."

He wrapped his arms around his knees, still watching the fire. "Just think if it were," he said thoughtfully. "If the God of Souls could take a common man and fashion him into a god. How extraordinary that would be."

"Extraordinary," I echoed, thinking of the picture of Kore. The strength and wisdom in her face, and the courage she must have held in her heart, in spite of her fear. If someone so perfect had indeed walked the fields as a mortal woman it's no surprise the God of Souls took her. After all, nothing less than perfection would ever satisfy him. I smiled to myself and sipped my wine, bitterly aware that my endless catalogue of flaws would keep me safe from the gods.

XI

Several days after our discussion about Kore, Adam and I were sitting side by side in the throne room receiving visitors when he leaned toward me and said, "I spoke to Lilianne earlier today. Just outside the temple. She hardly ever leaves the place, does she?"

I turned to him, taking advantage of the break in supplicants. "You saw her? When?"

"After you'd left to go work in the garden."

"Oh." I felt oddly betrayed. Part of me was pleased that Adam had taken such an interest in my kingdom's gods, but I hadn't yet grown accustomed to it. "What did you talk about?"

"The solstice takes place in two weeks and I wanted to discuss plans for the celebration."

My irritation grew. "Adam, we're still trying to balance the larder from when we celebrated the new treaties, and that was ages ago. How are we supposed to feast the whole kingdom with a bare pantry?"

He smiled as a woman approached, towing three children and holding a baby on her hip. Her dark hair had come loose from its plait and her face was shadowed with exhaustion.

"We won't feast the whole kingdom," he said to me. "Just a small portion."

I did not understand his riddle, and since he deemed it unnecessary to provide an explanation, I didn't ask for one. I was perfectly content to live in denial while he orchestrated his grand vision with

Lilianne. His spendthrift habits could not bother me if I behaved as though they didn't exist. Besides, I had the castle to attend to.

Accompanied by feasting or not, the solstice is one of Myrilla's most important days of the year. Light is crucial for the crops' growth and the return of the sun calls for celebration. Myrilla hadn't prepared for the winter solstice in the years of my uncle's tyranny, so under Adam's new reign I had decided a proper transformation was long overdue. I'd ordered evergreen boughs to be cut and brought indoors, and stayed up many nights by the fire sewing them into long garlands, trimmed with white holly berries, to be draped around the castle or given to any citizen who would like one. I'd painted long, flat leaves silver and fashioned them to look like huge laurel wreaths—in honor of Adam's heritage—and hung them from every door. Thanks to the beekeepers we had no shortage of wax, so hundreds of candles burned in the evenings, filling the castle with a fragrant glow. The activity kept my mind occupied; I was determined to make Myrilla look beautiful, a joyful spot of light on the darkest day of the year.

My curiosity about Adam's plans got the better of me, though, when I walked into the hall a few days later and saw him speaking with the master carpenter, their backs facing me.

"I believe the benches I've made will be high enough," the master carpenter was saying. "How many are you expecting, Lord King?"

Adam scratched his chin "At least two hundred—" He stopped when he noticed my shadow on the stone floor. "Hello, Alyce. You look lovely this afternoon."

The carpenter bowed to me and I greeted him warmly before cutting my eyes back to my husband. "Thank you, how kind of you to say. You are always so thoughtful and considerate. Now, as for these benches. You are expecting at least two hundred…what, precisely?"

"Guests. For the solstice."

I stared at him, certain I had misheard. The carpenter shifted uncomfortably. Behind me in the kitchen I heard a metal tray drop with a crash, accompanied by angry shouts from the cook. The racket must have stirred something inside me, for in the next moment I felt my hand reach for Adam's arm.

"Would you excuse us, please?" I said to the carpenter, smiling at him with blank eyes as I drew Adam away. My fingers gripped his arm like a clamp. "Now," I said through my clenched teeth. "What is this business about two hundred guests?"

"They're coming the eve of the solstice," he said, his excitement unaffected by my tone. "I can't tell you any more, it's meant to be a surprise."

I closed my eyes, willing him to adopt logic into his response. "Adam, I want to trust you, I do." I drew a deep breath and looked at him. "But how do you plan to feast two hundred people? We can't even feast the court, and that's a mere fraction. We cannot afford it—"

"These guests don't expect a feast," he said with confidence. "They'll be thrilled with whatever we provide."

"And what will that be?" I demanded. "Corncakes and bacon?"

He nodded thoughtfully. "That's not a bad suggestion. Economical and nutritious. Soldier's fare. Served with fresh milk you'd have quite a hearty meal." He managed to extract his arm from my claw-like grasp. "Now, Alyce, don't ask me any more questions. I don't want to spoil it. You must simply trust that I would do nothing to damage your reputation as a great queen and charming hostess."

With that, he left me at the hall doors and returned to the master carpenter, who had nervously turned his hat in his hands all through our argument. I frowned at Adam's back, desperate to know his plans, then made my way to the grounds where the tree men were waiting to cut whichever boughs I still needed.

When the morning of the solstice arrived, I woke with a strange sense of dread. Out of habit I glanced over at Adam's side of the bed, but of course it was empty. The air in the room felt wet and heavy and when I pushed back the curtain I saw nothing but grey skies and barren land. The cold seemed to seep into my bones; I pulled on two pairs of stockings and dressed in my thickest clothes. Even then I still couldn't harness any warmth.

I walked downstairs, eager to feel the heat of the great hall's fireplace, but when I reached the great double doors I stopped, causing two servants to nearly collide with my back. There, at the end of the hall, stood a fir tree so tall it nearly touched the ceiling. Teams of men hoisted it upright with ropes while Adam directed them. I watched, mute with amazement, as they secured it to the rafters. Several of the men noticed me and bowed; only then did Adam turn from his task.

"What do you think?" he asked, bounding toward me. "You've done beautiful work all over the castle with your garlands and wreaths. I thought you might enjoy unleashing your talents on an entire tree."

I gaped at him. "I wouldn't even know where to start."

"Well, there's no shortage of holly berries," he said, leading me closer. "And I think it'd look lovely if it were lit with candles. Small ones. We don't want to burn down the great hall. It's only a suggestion, of course," he said when I didn't respond. "Do you like it, Alyce?" he asked, suddenly worried.

"Of course I do," I murmured, unable to tear my eyes from the tree. It looked grand and joyful, like an evergreen giant standing proudly in our humble castle. I closed my eyes and breathed in the lovely smell: wintry and spicy and sweet. "I'll send for the candles," I said, unable to quell my enthusiasm. "Though if it's all right with you, we'll use winter flowers instead of holly berries. I've got a few ideas…" I trailed off dreamily.

He grinned at me, then returned to his work. I called for servants to collect candles and as many laurel branches as they could carry in from the grounds. I threw on my apron and vanished into the garden, clipping rosemary sprigs and winter flowers. My bag bulged upon my return and I set up a temporary workshop of sorts in the great hall, where I passed a few happy hours with the ladies of court, stringing together garlands of laurel and rosemary to wind around the tree. Servants climbed ladders and secured short candles to the branches while I tucked flowers of white and gold and blue among the boughs. When the whole tree was decorated from top to bottom, I stood admiring it with my hand over my heart. I had never seen such a lovely sight.

Not long after we'd finished did Adam return from yet another mysterious errand. His eyes brightened when he saw the tree and he clapped his hands like a boy.

"It's wonderful, Alyce. Everything you touch turns to beauty." He reached for my hand, and I thought he was going to say something else when Turius suddenly appeared.

"They're gathering at the gates," he said, removing his cloak. "Are you sure about this, Admetus? It's a gracious gesture, but they're only—"

"Don't say another word, you're sworn to secrecy, remember?" Adam cut him off in high spirits. He gently pushed me toward the door. "Now, Alyce, you go change for dinner while I welcome our guests."

"But I should be here too," I protested. "I need to welcome them alongside you."

"Propriety is of little importance to these particular guests," he said lightly. "Go along, Lady Queen. Dress for warmth and comfort. No need for your diamonds and jewels tonight."

At that, I laughed. He knew perfectly well I had none. "Indeed, I'll make sure the treasury is guarded and secure before I return," I joked.

"When you return, you'll bring all the treasure of Myrilla with you." He nudged me again. "Quickly, now. I'll send word when it's time."

I couldn't keep my excitement at bay as Trina, my maid, arranged my hair. No one had ever organized a surprise for me before, and I found the anticipation thrilling. I watched my reflection in the glass, enjoying the tug and pull of the brush and trying to imagine what Adam had planned. Trina twisted my hair into a soft knot and dressed me in an ivory wool gown. As Adam had instructed, it was comfortable and warm and fairly plain, apart from a few roses stenciled in gold thread around the waist.

Trina had barely finished when there came a knock at the door. A servant stepped into the room, breathless and cheerful.

"The king sent me for you, Lady Queen."

I followed her down the corridor and to the winding staircase. From what I could hear, a raucous party was already well underway in the great hall, though the voices sounded oddly high-pitched. Happy shrieks carried down the stone corridors, and the servants guarding the doors were so intent on peering into the hall that it took a moment for them to realize I was standing there. Embarrassed, they bowed in apology and swung open the heavy doors.

When I stepped into the great hall I received my second surprise for the day. Adam's two hundred guests were all present, but they weren't nobles or dignitaries. They were children. Children from the farms, accompanied by their parents. Happy cries filled the hall as they ran to admire the beautiful fir tree, decorated in all its splendor.

Wine circulated for the mothers and fathers while servants passed out cups of frothy milk to each child. When I saw the trays of food spread across the tables I laughed aloud.

Adam joined me and handed me a cup of hot mulled wine. "And what is so funny?"

"Corncakes and bacon," I said, shaking my head. "I can't believe you're serving that. I was joking when I suggested it."

"I know," he replied. "Which makes its perfection all the more amusing. Look at them, they can't get enough."

I watched the children descend upon the trays with the enthusiasm of veteran gourmands. The older boys and girls dished the hot food onto the little ones' plates, biting their lips in concentration as they maneuvered the long spoons. Servants stood at the end of each table with pitchers, ready to refill the milk cups proffered by pudgy hands. Empty trays were whisked away and replaced by fresh, steaming ones. Crumbs littered the floor and the great hall was louder than I'd ever heard it, but every child appeared to be enjoying themselves.

"What do you think, Alyce?" said Adam, stepping back to avoid a collision with a little girl whose face was smeared with bacon grease and milk. "Are you pleased?"

I nodded, wondering how I could have ever doubted him. "Yes, it's perfect."

"I'm so glad you think so. Now, I have one more treat planned." He clapped his hands three times. "If I could have your attention, everyone," he bellowed. The hall fell silent—at least, as silent as possible while occupied by two hundred children. "It is nearly sunset. If you will join me near the tree, we will light it."

Benches scraped against the stone floor as everyone left their plates and cups and jockeyed for a position near the tree. Some of the smaller children perched on their siblings' shoulders while others climbed onto the tables for a better view. Adam lit the wick of a tall candle and handed it to me, then nodded for the servants to extinguish all the torches. Soon the only spot of light in the whole hall was the flame on my candle; in its orange glow I could see just Adam's face, surrounded by darkness.

"You hold the only light in all of Myrilla," he said quietly. "Welcome the sun back to us, Queen Alcestis."

I knelt at the foot of the tree, shielding the flame with my cupped hand. Slowly, so as not to risk losing the flame, I touched it to an unlit wick and waited for the fire to catch. When I pulled it away the hall burst into cheers. I plucked the candle off the tree and handed it to Adam, and together the two of us lit as many wicks as we could reach. The hall glowed from the light, growing ever brighter as the servants lit the candles near the top with aid of long, slender torches.

The children returned to their plates, but I stood back and admired the tree. It was the loveliest thing I had ever seen. The scent of fir and rosemary and winter flowers, all illuminated by candlelight, swept over me like a wave of beauty. I touched my face and found my cheeks wet with tears. From the corner of my eye I saw Adam watching me, so I wiped them quickly away.

"Shall we call for some music?" I asked him, sniffling slightly. "It's the only thing this feast is missing."

He had the grace not to comment on my weepy eyes. "I thought the very same thing." Following a quick word to a passing servant, the court musicians appeared and played such cheerful tunes that most of the children abandoned their plates once more and danced.

The rest of the evening passed in a blur of happiness. The court and the commoners mingled as one, drinking hot mulled wine and watching the children dance with indulgent smiles. I spoke with women and men I had never met, many of whom praised me for my generosity on this blessed night. I told them it was all my husband's doing, and assured them we would hold another celebration soon. Such merriment I had never known; we talked and sang and laughed until our sides were sore.

We only called an end to the evening when children began falling asleep at the tables. Each guest was presented with a bag of sugared nuts on their departure, though sleepy yawns soon turned to rejuvenated delight when the children stepped out into the courtyard and saw heavy snowflakes swirling down from the grey sky.

Once the last family departed, Adam and I returned to our rooms, discussing the celebration's success as we made our way through the dark corridors. When we shut the door behind us my feet felt heavy and my face hurt from smiling. I pulled off my shoes and sank to the carpet before the fire, too tired to climb into the chair. Adam joined me, his eyes glazed with happy fatigue.

"Truly, it was wonderful," I told him. "I've never attended such a lovely solstice. Thank you for all your preparation. It can't have been easy, keeping such a great secret."

He unlaced his boots. "No, it wasn't. Not with your sharp eyes watching me," he teased. "Then when your clever mouth started firing questions last week I thought all was lost. That's why I had to bring in the fir tree. To distract you."

"Well, it certainly worked."

We sat quietly for several minutes, until the last of the snow had melted from my clothes and my hair had dried in the fire's warmth. Suddenly, Adam stood up and walked to the bed, rummaging underneath it for a moment. He returned with a long, slender wooden chest, which he placed on the carpet before me.

"What's this?"

"A little token I made. It's a tradition in my homeland for a husband to present his wife with a gift on the eve of the solstice," he explained. "To remind her that to him, she is the sun. That she brings warmth and hope and illumination to his life. A life that would be dark and cold without her."

"A pretty sentiment."

"And a true one." He drew a long, slim object from the chest. It was wrapped in green silk and when he placed it in my hands I recognized the shape at once. My heart raced as I unwrapped the silk, eager to see what lay within but not wanting to rush. I let the wrapping flutter to the floor in a soft green puddle.

It was a bow. An ivory-colored bow cut to fit my arm precisely. Carved into the smooth wood were dozens of tiny roses, wrapping the bow from end to end like a ghostly vine. My fingers closed around the grip; it felt vibrant and alive in my hands, the same way Adam's bow had all those weeks ago.

"Adam, it's stunning," I breathed. I ran my fingers over the intricate carvings. "How did you find time to make this?"

"I've carried it to the mountain with me for the past several weeks. My herdsman coached me a great deal. He's a master archer himself; he's the one who honed my skill and taught me to craft my own bows and arrows."

"Well, his coaching is matchless. It's truly wonderful." I admired the bow awhile longer, then wrapped it in the silk once more and laid it carefully in my lap. "Thank you. This is the most perfect gift I've ever received."

His eyes shone; I could tell he was happier than he let on. "I'm glad it pleases you."

"I wish I had a gift for you," I said sheepishly, "but I'm afraid I'm unprepared."

He stood up and held out his hand. "You're the sun, remember? The sun is a gift in itself." He pulled me to my feet and hung my new bow on the wall next to his. "Now, Queen Alcestis, I know you're burdened with many crucial duties, but when would you like your first archery lesson? Let's say, early next week?"

"That won't do at all." I shook my head and beamed at the gorgeous white bow. "I insist we begin in the morning."

XII

I wish I could tell you that every day of my first winter with Adam was devoted to fun and sport, but that would be misleading. He did set up archery butts on the grounds, where he taught me to use my beautiful new bow, and we entertained the court with a few cold weather picnics of roasted pheasant and hot mulled wine. But there was little time for merriment. While it did not snow very much that winter it was still bitterly cold. A dry, cutting cold that cracked your skin and burned your lungs when you drew breath. Many evenings we opened the great hall to anyone who wanted a warm place to sleep. Mothers brought their children in hopes that a night beside our hearth would help soothe their whimpering babies, and the men and women who tended the fields spread their cots close to the fire to thaw their frozen hands before returning to work. It broke my heart to see their suffering. Adam ordered the court physician to make daily rounds, checking the farmhands for blackened fingers or wheezing lungs. Every seamstress employed by the castle was instructed to stop hemming shirts and gowns in favor of weaving blankets from Adam's stock of Itomian wool. The castle larders reached their lowest levels and the day finally arrived when even Adam and I had nothing to dine on but cabbage stew flavored with pig fat.

We sat on the floor of our chamber, as close to the hearth as we could without sparks flying at us, and gripped our bowls with both hands for warmth. We hadn't taken a meal in the great hall for several days. There was simply no point. The court had practically disintegrated in the weeks following the solstice; many were paying visits to our neighbors on Adam's behalf, while others simply requested release because of the dismal state of the pantry. I stirred my soup halfheartedly, the tension in my stomach leaving no room for hunger.

Adam tapped my bowl with his spoon. "Eat up, Lady Queen. You're dining on the finest feast Myrilla has to offer."

I looked at the stew, gobs of stringy cabbage in a watery broth. "That's what's so troubling." I sighed. "Adam, what happens if Myrilla starves?"

"It won't. We have hunger, not famine. When I returned from the mountain this morning I rode out to the vegetable farms to see how they're looking."

I swallowed a wet, salty bite. "And?"

"The greens will be ready before long. A few days at the most. The farmers on the south end have a promising crop of winter vegetables. It's encouraging, you should go tomorrow and have a look around. The people are holding up fine. Winter won't last forever."

Silence fell as we resumed our dinner. I clenched my jaw, unable to chew any longer. Not because of the taste—I'd subsisted on unpleasant food throughout most of my life—but to stop myself shouting at Adam. It was all very well for him to talk of winter's end and the promising crops, but he hadn't witnessed years of disappointment in Myrilla's fields. He didn't know of the hatred my uncle had stirred in his failings to gain the ear of the gods. He didn't know the crippling defeat that came with looking out at the wheat fields to see that once again nothing had grown. To my horror, hot, angry tears pooled in my eyes and dropped into my stew.

"Alyce, what is it?" said Adam in alarm.

I shook my head. "Let's say the vegetables come in fine, and the orchards and vineyards produce, too," I said, my voice trembling. "Even if we're overflowing with apples and pears and lettuce, that doesn't help the wheat! Our portion of the treaty depends on the wheat production."

"I know that, Alyce. There's still plenty of time—"

"The wheat is *everything*," I said, as though he hadn't spoken. "Otherwise we'll be indebted to our neighbors for the rest of our lives, perhaps longer. True, the people of Myrilla will have food for

95

their tables but the kingdom itself will shrivel and die. I don't care about feasting or the court or showing off for the world, none of that matters. All I care about is the harvest. The gods have forgotten us for so long, I can't bear it."

The words rang in the air long after they left my lips. Adam said nothing, and I didn't have the courage to meet his eyes. I wiped my cheeks with the palm of my hand, warm with humiliation. I hated myself for crying in front of him, especially when he was just trying to comfort me with good news.

The silence lengthened. I waited for him to snap back, to call me foolish for doubting or to make some snide comment. But he simply took the bowl from my hands and set it on the hearth.

"Alyce," he said quietly. "You and I have the same worries. When I'm awake, there isn't a moment when I'm not thinking about the treaties and wondering if the wheat will grow. I can't even escape at night because I often dream about it. As much as I'd like to reach into the dirt and force the wheat to sprout, you and I can't do that. The seed is in the ground, and the fields are being tended. That's the extent of our influence. You said so yourself, remember?"

I nodded. "You're right, you're right. I know it." I managed to dry my eyes. "Though it's not out of our hands entirely just yet. There's still the Blooding."

Until that evening, Adam and I had not discussed the Blooding in great detail. He knew very little about it and, due to my anxiety over the food shortage, I hadn't begun the preparations. The Blooding and the harvest were the two most important events in Myrilla. You could not have one without the other. If no Blooding took place, a harvest was highly unlikely. And without a harvest you had no reason to Blood the fields in preparation for the next. During his years of power my uncle had neglected both of these practices, to the point where I wondered if the fields weren't so cursed that the soil itself carried rot.

"We still have a few weeks to get ready, don't we?" asked Adam, passing me the stew once more.

"Yes, though the precise timing depends on the temple." I gestured to the books piled on the table. "That's what I've read, anyway. I've spoken to Lilianne about it; she'll act as priestess during the ceremony. As a Servant of Kore she's qualified to lead the rites. When the gods call for the Blooding we'll have a full day's notice, but everything will have to be ready before then. There's time yet, it won't take place before the ground starts to thaw. I'll talk with Lilianne to prepare my part. You don't have to worry about anything except the slaughter."

He grimaced at the mere word. "I don't mean to sound ungrateful, quite the opposite," he said, "but shouldn't it be one of your responsibilities as queen, too? You know so much more about all this than I. I've slaughtered plenty of animals in Itomius, but never for sacrifice."

I raised my eyebrows. "I'm afraid it's the king's duty. You're representing the God of Souls, presenting his gift to Kore."

"What beast will have to give its life?"

"It depends on what the gods ordain," I explained. "When Lilianne gives us the date she will name the offering, too. In the past the priest has sacrificed deer or rabbits, depending on how much is needed. There are stories where the gods call for human blood"—I held up my hand when his eyes widened—"but everyone says that's just legend."

Shuddering, he swallowed the last of his stew. "I should certainly hope so."

"It has to be." I frowned and lifted my bowl to drink the broth. "I can't imagine the gods asking for such a barbaric tribute."

The weeks leading up to the Blooding balanced on a blade's edge. While Myrilla was in no danger of overabundance, the winter greens did ripen and the weather gradually relented. It was still cold, make no mistake, but the frigid, biting wind from the north had weakened and the air grew soft with moisture once more.

I met with Lilianne in the temple each day to practice my role for the Blooding. Acting as Kore, I would take a cask filled with blood meal and ground bones from the slaughter and walk the length of a wheat field, sprinkling the mixture over the ground. It sounds very simple, but I assure you it was not. It was more of a dance than a stroll, with specific footfalls to mimic the way Kore had run and danced to the God of Souls when he called her. I had to convey joy and strength and the gravity of Kore's fate all at the same time. I suppose there are some people who might enjoy the challenges of such an activity; I found it profoundly frustrating. It seemed grossly unfair that the wheat's outcome should fall to me, and the fear of a failed harvest gnawed at my mind. If the wheat didn't produce, I'd have no one else to blame.

Looking back on that first Blooding, I believe I could have handled the stress and uncertainty much better had I been permitted to discuss it with Adam. But we were forbidden to divulge any detail of our roles. I'd return from the temple, exhausted from dancing the length of the narrow chamber behind the altar over and over again, unable to mention a word of it to Adam. It was the same story when he'd come back from a rendezvous with Lilianne. What should have been an exciting mystery with anticipation heightening every day only deepened the gulf between us. All the secrecy was a shadowy reminder of our early weeks together, when wariness and suspicion had reigned. Even casual conversations stalled into quiet gaps, a glaring reminder that while Adam and I were firm friends, this man was only my husband in name. We had not yet learned trust in the midst of silence.

Even with all my practice, I felt overwhelmed with fear when the morning before the Blooding finally arrived. I knew as soon as I opened my eyes that something was different. The air in the chamber felt icy and clear, charged with life. I pulled on my dressing gown and drew back the curtain to be greeted by the sun for the first time in days. A strange sensation settled in my stomach as I dressed, and I wasn't surprised when a servant shortly announced the arrival of Lilianne. She appeared at the door carrying a skein of water and a bundle of white silk under her arm. I'd never seen her look so stern.

"It's the eve of the Blooding," she said, stepping into the chamber. "Are you ready, Lady Queen?"

I swallowed. "I-I suppose."

"Is the king here?"

"No, he's not returned from the mountain—"

At that moment Adam slipped into the chamber, rubbing his hands and stamping his feet for warmth. "Breakfast smells wonderful; I'm famished. The weather is gorgeous, Alyce—" He stopped when he saw Lilianne and some of the color drained from his face. "Is it time?"

"The queen must go to her place first," said Lilianne. "You will join me at the temple later for the slaughter." She looked at me. "Everything is ready, we must depart immediately."

"I understand." I looked longingly at the tray of steaming eggs. "Do I have time to eat first? I'll be quick."

She shook her head, as I'd known she would. "You'll dine again when the land is fed. Bid the king farewell. You may join him after the ceremony."

"Wait, Lilianne." Adam held up his hand. "Even if the slaughter happens tonight, the ceremony still won't take place until tomorrow. Where are you taking her?"

"The queen must prepare, just as Kore did before she joined the gods. No other place is more appropriate than the gardens. They are the most sacred place on Myrilla's royal grounds, second only to Kore's field."

She gestured for me to follow her, but I had trouble moving my feet. She'd never mentioned any of this to me. I felt terribly deceived. Adam must have shared my thoughts, because he blocked Lilianne's progress toward the door. "Now wait just a moment," he said, trying very hard to stay calm. The suffering of the kingdom during those cold months had worn hard on him, and frustration seeped through the cracks of his usually regal façade. "It's still the dead of the winter. You cannot expect me to allow you to take the queen and make her stay in some garden all day and all night, without so much as a scrap of food."

For all of Adam's stifled anger, Lilianne's cool voice never changed. "It's the way of the gods, Lord King, to ask us to give them everything. Kore understood that, and the queen is learning as well. She will know it even better by morning."

"She's already been ill once," insisted Adam, as though he hadn't heard her. "I don't see why it's necessary for her to stay out in the cold for that long."

"It is the way the gods intended it."

The simplicity of her answer only enraged Adam. The veins in his temple stood out as he nearly shouted, "I will not let you risk my wife's health. I don't care what the rituals call for. I've had enough secrets and hiding, it's bordering on foolishness now. I respect your traditions, Lilianne, but not far enough to jeopardize the queen's wellbeing. I do not see why it must be done this way, just to appease your country's cruel gods—"

"You are knocking on a dangerous door," cut in Lilianne, her face bruised with anger. "Perhaps Kore will forgive you yet for such ignorance. The Blooding is the only way to seek the gods' favor for a blessed harvest. No blustering or argument can change that. When you took the crown of Myrilla as your own, you swore to uphold the laws of our gods, did you not?"

Adam said nothing, he only glared at Lilianne with the same contempt he'd reserved for my aunt and uncle. His nostrils flared and he clenched his fists at his sides. Outside the window I could hear the gardeners greeting each other as they prepared for their morning of work in the courtyard.

"Since you have made your scorn quite clear," said Lilianne, "let us look to the queen to decide."

They both turned to me. Lilianne calm and still once more, Adam nearly purple with rage. I didn't relish the thought of upsetting either one of them, but I licked my lips and said to Adam, as steadily as I could, "I understand your concern, truly, but the gods know my purpose for being in the gardens, and they will keep me safe. I don't believe they would ask such a thing otherwise. It's the way Kore came to them, remember? The better I emulate her, the better our chances for the harvest." I reached out and touched his hand, just barely brushing his fingers with mine. "Think of the wheat," I whispered. "We have no other choice."

He said nothing else, just stood silently as I followed Lilianne from the chamber. Every servant we passed scuttled out of our path. The Blooding was no secret; the few Myrillans who were old enough to remember the event had probably caught on during the past few weeks as the air began to change. No doubt they had spread the word. What remained of our small court lined the entrance hall, bidding me a wordless farewell with solemn faces.

The guards opened the heavy doors before us and Lilianne led me into the brilliant winter sunshine. The twisting garden paths were deserted; I assumed she was taking me to some sacred, hidden grove separate from all the rest that was specifically used in preparation for the Blooding. So you can imagine my surprise when she stopped before the worn wooden door to my own garden.

"What are we doing here?" I asked, breaking the silent spell.

Lilianne produced her own key and turned it in the lock. Without a word she stepped into the garden and walked the path as though she knew them as well as I did. I was too shocked to even look around for new growth or admire the ripe winter cherries. I simply followed her down the path to the far wall, where she stopped before the iron gate. She rested her hand on it and gave me a knowing glance.

"The garden you chose to work, Lady Queen, is the garden of all true Myrillan queens," she said. "It's handed down from generation to generation. Your mother worked it the same way you have, before her death."

A hard lump rose in my throat. I never knew during all this time, from my pitiful escape attempt to the day I had collected the winter flowers for the solstice, that I had been working in the same place of my mother and grandmothers. That all the queens before me had stood in that very spot, just as I had, fearful of Kore and desperate to lead wisely. "I knew this place was special," I said, my voice shaking. "But I had no idea it was sacred to the gods."

"It's more sacred than you realize." Lilianne's gnarled fingers lifted the latch on the gate and opened it to reveal the black field, framed by trees. "After all, it contains the only gate to this wheat field. The very place where the God of Souls found Kore and claimed her for his own." She looked over her shoulder at me, her face a picture of triumph. "Give thanks and be joyful, Lady Queen. You're standing on the threshold of Kore's field."

XIII

I wish I could describe the spectrum of emotions that washed over me upon Lilianne's revelation. First, I felt foolish, wondering like a petulant child why no one had *told* me I was working in the garden that opened to Kore's field; it would have provided endless comfort in my early days of marriage if I had known I was sharing in such a legacy. Shame and ignorance followed, though by the time Lilianne left me in the garden with nothing but a flask of water and an entire day's solitude laid out before me, my nerves stretched to a new limit. I felt as though I'd already failed a test I had yet to begin. The whole thing seemed a cruel joke, orchestrated for the purpose of raising my hopes and then dashing them to pieces.

Unlike every other time I visited, I didn't work a bit in the garden that afternoon. I walked the paths many times, picturing how it would look in the upcoming spring when everything was new and green and bursting into bloom. The slender, dark blades of crocus leaves had already begun poking out of the cold earth, along with the snowdrop buds and hare's ears. I studied the cherry and plum trees, looking for branches that had turned a flat, ashy grey and needed pruning. The roses looked well, and as I sat on the bench beneath the arbor I tilted my chin up and looked at the tangled brown vines over my head, covered in thorns.

I found myself pondering things I'd never before considered. About Adam, in particular. I knew little of other countries' religions at the time; it was common to learn the names of the gods and goddesses of one's neighboring nations, mostly out of politeness, but their rituals and traditions were unfamiliar to me. I found it both appalling and fascinating that the man I shared a bed with at night came from a country with no temple. That he could honor his gods without offering burnt sacrifices of grain or blood or whatever else they might require. I could not conceive of a world without a temple dedicated to Kore.

His herdsman intrigued me more than anything. Who was this man who tended sheep and goats and dispensed advice to kings? Adam didn't speak of him often, but when he did, it unsettled me greatly. He talked like this herdsman was much more than just a simple shepherd. He made it sound like this common man was a god who had walked alongside the God of Souls himself and then stepped down from the heavens. I had always thought that a god cast out of his home would be a shameful creature, but Adam spoke of him with nothing but pride.

I turned these thoughts over and over in my mind, reaching no conclusion, until the sun had long sunk in the sky and given its place to the moon. I drew my cloak tight around me and curled up on the bench, and before long I was asleep.

The sky was still black when I felt Lilianne's hand on my shoulder, shaking it gently. She put her face close to mine and whispered, "It's time, Lady Queen."

I nodded and sat up, my joints stiffer than iron. Cold, wet fog surrounded me and frost glittered on the plants. The garden had never felt so quiet before. I could hear only the sound of my breath as I removed my cloak and bedclothes. I stood, naked and shivering, as Lilianne took a bundle of green silk from her bag and opened it carefully. Nestled within the folds was a summer gown unlike any I'd ever seen. It was pale and dirty and appeared to be little more than rags sewn together. Obediently, I held my arms out and stepped into it, though I couldn't help shuddering at the rough fabric's touch. The gown—if one could call it that—was ill-fitting to say the least. Its ragged hem didn't even reach my knees and one of the narrow sleeves kept slipping off my shoulder.

"This gown is crafted from the very grain sacks used in the first harvest of Kore," said Lilianne, fastening the last few buttons. "When she was taken by the God of Souls, he blessed the land so it

103

would always be abundant. Through you, Lady Queen, we honor her sacrifice today."

Dressed in the flimsy gown, I didn't feel much warmer than I had before Lilianne put it on me. I hugged my bare arms to my chest and watched her unfold another cloth bundle, this time revealing a wooden cask. It was small enough for me to hold in one hand, and intricately carved. I leaned forward to look inside when Lilianne opened it, but quickly withdrew. The odor emitting from the cask was revolting. I had known blood meal—dried blood and bones ground together into a powder—would not smell sweet, but I hadn't expected it to turn my stomach.

Lilianne seemed unbothered. She gripped the cask with both hands and looked solemnly at the dark brown powder inside. "To show Myrilla's gratitude, you must thank the God of Souls for his generosity in watching over your kingdom. I pray that Kore will be in your hands and feet and heart as you return thanks for the God of Souls' gift, and that he will see his beloved's likeness in you."

She held out the cask and I accepted it silently. Without another word of instruction, Lilianne crossed to the back garden gate and pushed it open. I swallowed at the sight of Kore's field stretched out endlessly before me. Lilianne stepped aside and I walked carefully along the cold stone path and through the gate. It swung shut behind me and suddenly I was alone.

I stood at the edge of the field, gripping the cask with stiff fingers. I couldn't even see Adam waiting at the opposite side. The air was wet and heavy; fog clung to the seeded dirt, pearly grey in the predawn light.

No one could tell me when to start, I had to decide on my own. I shivered and put out one cautious, bare foot. The dirt was frozen into hard clumps that felt like rocks beneath my tender skin. I let out a surprised cry and leapt back, suddenly furious. *It's only a ceremony*, I told myself. It wasn't real, it was a reenactment. The gods weren't going to take me away; in fact, they probably weren't the slightest bit interested in my pathetic attempts at the rites. Compared to them I was less than an insect, less than the dirt beneath my feet.

I drew a deep breath and tried again, but after three steps I simply could not take the cold and retreated once more. Frustrated tears sprang to my eyes. Why did I think I could do this? Why did I let Lilianne talk me into this madness? I glared down at the cask, tempted to hurl it away and forget it existed. If the gods wanted blood they could take it on their own time; I wouldn't be made a fool for their pleasure. My breath rose in white wreaths over my head and I half-turned, ready to abandon the ritual when the sky suddenly brightened. I looked over my shoulder and saw a burst of light, pink and gold, appear along the edge of the mountains. It did nothing to warm me—in fact, the breeze grew stronger—but now I could see Adam waiting, and Lilianne on her way to join him, both little more than pinpricks in the distance.

I shifted the cask in my hand and set myself square to the field once more. My foot automatically rose in the step Lilianne had taught me, ready to begin the walk. When I stepped forward this time the shock was still there, but I didn't jump back. Instead I took the next step, slightly unbalanced as my feet hardened against the rough ground. Only then did I remember the blood meal. I dipped my shaking fingers into the cask and drew out a small handful, sprinkling it in one swift, fluid movement just as I'd practiced so many times in the temple with Lilianne. The meal still smelled wretched, no brightening sky could change that, but I held it as carefully as if it were gold dust.

With each step I took, I noticed the hard earth less and less. My numb feet performed the dance with care and intention, and I scattered the blood meal as gracefully as I could. All my earlier reticence was gone. This may sound very strange to you, Reader, but for the briefest moment in that field, something deep inside me changed. Or perhaps 'changed' isn't the right word. I felt detached from myself, as though the feet that danced and the hands that spread the meal were no longer mine. It was the oddest thing. I imagine it's the same sensation that talented musicians and athletes feel when they perform in honor of the gods. My heart pounded and a sort of wildness rushed through me. For one glimmering instant I forgot about the rags and the harvest and the thousands of people depending on me. I even forgot about Adam, and I began to feel that I *was* Kore. I understood her; I knew the fear and excitement and curiosity that must have filled her heart that morning, ages ago, when she stood alone with the God of Souls.

I made my way across the field, spreading the blood meal until the cask was spent and I'd reached the far edge. I paused, gripping the cold dirt with my toes as if to imprint the memory on my very

105

skin. I did not want to forget this moment, this feeling of the gods holding out their hands to receive the blood Myrilla had offered. I couldn't stop myself smiling: a bright, strong beam that managed to be solemn and joyful at the same time.

Adam waited until I'd stepped onto the grass before spreading my cloak over my shoulders. Lilianne took the cask and said a few words, but I wasn't really listening. I stood close to Adam, letting the heat from his body warm me as Lilianne closed the ceremony and replaced the lid on the cask. Adam and I walked behind Lilianne, circling our way through the trees and up the road toward the castle gates. In the distance, the guards spotted us from their posts and rushed to escort us.

"So, the Blooding is done," said Adam.

My breath still hadn't fully returned, and my legs felt tired and shaky. "What did you think of it?"

He took a moment before answering. "It was...not what I expected," he finally said. "The slaughter last night was quick, though the roasting afterwards was not. I pitied the beast; it seemed almost disrespectful to grind his bones up the way we did. But to see how it was used today, the way you scattered it over the field...it was beautiful. You were beautiful, Alyce."

I flushed. "Thank you."

A sharp rock scratched the bottom of my foot and I stumbled. Adam caught my arm to stop me from falling. "Alyce, are you—" He stopped when he saw my naked feet, and glanced at my shoes in his hand. "I'm such a fool. I didn't realize I was still carrying these. Why didn't you tell me you were barefoot?"

A laugh escaped me, breaking the solemn air. "I'd forgotten."

"Well, we can't have this." He knelt down in front of me and slipped my shoes onto my feet, one at a time, as I held his shoulders for balance.

We had just resumed our walk when a small girl darted between the flanks of guards and ran toward us. She had dark hair and beautiful brown eyes, but her cheek was marred by a mottled birthmark, creeping down the side of her neck like a scarlet stain. In her tiny hand she clutched a bouquet of dandelions and purple weeds, which she thrust at me with great pride. It had no sooner left her fingers than one of the soldiers caught her and began pulling her back toward her father, who was shouting to her from his plow.

"Wait a moment," I said, touching the dandelion's petals. My fingertip came away smudged with yellow and I knelt before the little girl. "These are wonderful; did you pick them yourself?"

She nodded, her round cheeks spreading wide with a smile. "From my field, Lady Queen," she said carefully, with an unsteady curtsey. "I picked them just for you."

I looked down at the flowers again, my brow furrowed. Perhaps it was my stained hands grasping the stems or the scent of the meal on my grain-cloth gown, but that same deep knowledge of the gods rushed through me, touching a part of me I hadn't known existed. I couldn't explain or define it, and it vanished as quickly as it came. Tears welled in my eyes as I gripped the flowers tightly and drew the little girl towards me, kissing her forehead. She smelled like sunshine and freshly turned earth. I stood and wiped my eyes.

"What is your name?"

"Lamia, Lady Queen."

"Well thank you, Lamia. They truly are beautiful." I reached up and lightly touched her marked cheek. "Just like you."

The little girl dropped into another curtsey, biting her lip in concentration. Then she waved and skipped back to her father, still standing beside his plow. I studied my flowers again. They were picked with such affection and care even though they were just weeds. I felt eyes upon me and looked up to see more farmers peppering their fields, already working hard in the early hour. A swell of gratitude rose in me; Myrilla would be worth nothing but for them.

Just then, one of the workers in Lamia's field shouted something. He was so far away I couldn't make it out; I could only see his little hand reach up and snatch his hat from his head, waving it in the air. He shouted the words over and over, like a chant.

"What's he saying?" I looked at Adam in confusion, though his frown told me he couldn't understand the man either. It wasn't long before another farmer picked up the chant, and then two more, as it spread through the fields. Soon the chant surrounded us, so loud and clear the entire kingdom must have heard it.

"*Queen of Spring! Queen of Spring! Queen of Spring!*"

My body prickled with heat, though I managed to raise my hand and wave in what I hoped was a gracious manner. With a nod to the guards I signaled that I wished to resume our walk. Adam's feet,

107

however, stayed firm. I looked back at him, expecting him to make some wry comment about my unexpected new title. Instead he was watching me, wearing an expression of utmost tenderness.

"Queen of Spring," he murmured, in time with the farmers' chant. "Queen of Spring."

XIV

With the Blooding behind us and spring waiting just beyond the horizon, the castle became a much happier place. The coughing sickness that scourged Myrilla each winter halted its rampage after only a few deaths. Every day the ground thawed a little bit more, and we began the slow process of replenishing our larders. Supplies from neighboring kingdoms arrived in a steady stream, though whenever I saw a cart fresh from Warkenland or the Sea's Arm wheeling toward the castle, laden with goods, anxiety tempered my relief. The wheat simply had to grow.

The end of the Blooding brought a change in Adam, too. He seemed brighter, livelier somehow, but in an unusually quiet way. As though saving his newfound energy for an important task. He smiled more often; his smooth cheekbones lifting his cheerful eyes so they crinkled in the corners. The strangest new development, however, came about one dry morning when I arrived at the garden and heard a curious sound rising from behind the walls: music.

I slid the key into the door and turned it. Sitting on the bench with his back to me was Adam. He held a lyre in one arm and strummed it with the fingers of the other. I say "strummed," but he moved his hand so quickly that his fingers flew across the strings, plucking them individually or in pairs. It created a rippling effect, like water flowing downstream, and sounded unlike any music I'd ever heard. He kept his head down and focused his sight on the strings while I remained frozen on the edge of the garden path. I wondered if he'd heard the door, but I confirmed my presence was unnoticed when he began to sing. It was an old Itomian ballad—so he told me later—and while I'm afraid the translation won't be very good, I've written it here for you anyway:

Winter hid my love away
Cold and deep beneath the earth
May the gods give me the skill to wait
'Til the fingers of Spring bring her forth

Adam's rich voice filled the garden, startling a few birds from their roosts in the silver pine hedge. He sang with his whole body; I could almost see the words filling his lungs and racing up his throat before tumbling out of his mouth. Still, he didn't notice me, so I took a seat on a large urn, balancing on the lip. He sang a couple of other songs, and I do believe he would have gone on much longer, but then a gust of wind rushed through the garden and sent the door creaking on its hinges. His fingers stopped and he looked over his shoulder at me, paling in alarm. I kept still on the urn, unable to tear my eyes away. How had he kept this talent hidden for so long?

"Good afternoon, Alyce," he said, trying to smooth away his surprise. "I thought you might be in the mood for a visit today."

I couldn't reply; I was still taking in his presence. When I didn't speak, the smile on his face slipped a bit. "I came over the wall, but I didn't touch a single plant on my climb." He gripped his lyre and started to stand. "I'm sorry, I should have waited for you to unlock the door first, it was foolish of me—"

"No, no it wasn't." I leapt to my feet with my hands out-stretched. "Adam, I'm not angry, I swear it." Laughter bubbled from my throat. "I loved hearing your music, it was beautiful. I had no idea you were so gifted. Sit back down, please."

He did, obviously relieved. "Thank you, but you're too generous with your praise. After all, you're the one who inspired me to bring my lyre here."

"I don't see how."

"I think you do." His eyes shone, the way they always did when he was about to say something clever. "You know, Alyce, it could be argued that your daffodils and rosebushes are the luckiest citizens in all of Myrilla."

110

The corner of my mouth twitched, anticipating the rest of his riddle. "And why, pray?"

"They have the rare privilege of hearing you sing."

I stared at him. I'd never, not once, mentioned that peculiar habit to him. Or to anyone else, for that matter. "How do you know that?"

"I heard you. Back in the autumn when I watched you vanish through that door day after day. One morning I walked the outer length of the walls dozens of times, just listening to your voice."

I didn't know whether to feel appalled or flattered. "You never told me that."

He gave me a wicked grin. "Well, at first I wasn't sure it truly belonged to you. I had a difficult time believing such a sweet, gentle voice could belong to the icy woman I'd married."

With a cutting look, I folded my arms and raised a challenging eyebrow. "Perhaps if you'd given me more reason to be sweet and gentle you wouldn't have needed to sneak through the gardens like a prowler."

"Fair point," he conceded. "As always, your queenly logic triumphs." He looked down at the lyre in his hands. It was a magnificent instrument, carved from wood so pale it looked almost golden, the catgut strings pulled tight. An etched garland of laurel leaves graced the curved edge. Influenced by the herdsman, I felt sure.

Adam raked his fingers over the strings; the bright sound sent cold tendrils tickling my spine. "I'll be on my way, Alyce," he said, placing the lyre in a wooden box and snapping it shut. "I only wanted to stop by to give your flowers a different taste of music. Now that you've arrived my presence is superfluous. Enjoy yourself. I'll see you at dinner."

He gave me a little bow and walked to the door, but before he could vanish on the other side I called after him. "Adam, wait!"

He paused, and I was pleased to see a hopeful look on his face. "I'd like it very much if you stayed," I said. "If you have time. After hearing your music, the flowers will never be satisfied with my voice all on its own again."

I expected him to refuse, but he stepped into the garden once more and shut the door smartly behind him.

"Very well," he said. "As my muse commands."

111

At least once a week thereafter Adam brought his lyre to the garden. First he'd sit on the bench and spend several minutes bent over the instrument to tune it. He plucked the strings and adjusted their tightness in a way that must have made sense to him but that I, whom the gods did not deign to bless with musical talent, could not understand. Once satisfied he'd sit up straight, clear his throat, and begin to play. I recognized none of the tunes—they were all Itomian—but he played everything beautifully.

For all his confidence in other matters, Adam was strangely shy when it came to his music. The first few times he played I'd stopped what I was doing to watch him, devoting all my attention. But when I noticed his red face and clumsy fingers, and the way he flicked his eyes over at me if he happened to make a mistake, I found a way to subtly return to my work. Far from finding my inattention offensive, he actually played much better when I wasn't staring at him. Every now and then, however, my curiosity got the better of me and I'd study him from the corner of my eye. His fingers flew over the strings with precision and grace, the result of years dedicated to study. I marveled at his talent. Sometimes he asked me to sing while he rested his fingers, arguing that if the plants didn't hear my voice they'd forget to grow. I always obliged, singing either the familiar Myrillan melodies I'd practiced on my own, or attempting a new Itomian piece just so he'd laugh at my attempts to imitate his accent.

One warm afternoon Adam stopped playing his lyre and set it in his lap. I glanced over, expecting him to request a song, but he was frowning at the sky.

"What is it?" I asked. The last of the crocuses had bloomed in patches of gold and purple and white, accompanied by eager weeds. I'd worked for days to remove them and was ready to start clearing the soil around the silver knight's shield and yellow sunbird wings.

He sniffed deeply. "There's something different about the air today."

"I don't smell anything."

"It isn't a smell, precisely. It's the feel. I'm not sure, Alyce. Something isn't right." He plucked absently at the lyre. "When did it last rain?"

I opened my mouth to reply, then stopped. I hadn't the faintest idea. "I don't remember," I admitted. "It must have been weeks ago. Before the Blooding, even."

"I didn't realize it had been so long. How have the farmers watered their crops?"

"They irrigate from the river, provided it's high enough. And during the winter they collected snow for their underground cisterns, melting it as needed."

He nodded, though he didn't look satisfied. "I see." Then he resumed his playing, the lighthearted tune doing nothing to relieve the troubled heaviness in his face.

Adam remained quiet through the rest of the day. We had grown closer during the course of the past few months, talking and laughing like friends over our shared meals. But that evening we ate in near silence, just as we had in our first weeks of marriage. At that time I had welcomed his reticence, wanting nothing more than to delay any communication whatsoever. Now I found it quite unbearable. My attempts to draw him into conversation withered in the air between us and fell dully to the table. Even Turius couldn't provoke him into joining the spirited debate taking place around us, concerning the upcoming boar season back in Itomius and all their boyhood memories of hunts past.

When the miserable dinner finally ended, Adam was late coming to bed. I was nearly asleep when he slid under the covers beside me and murmured goodnight. I rolled to my side, ready to ask him why he was so disturbed, but I drifted off just as the words formed in my mouth.

It wasn't long, however, before I got my answer. It felt like mere minutes later that I was jolted awake by someone pounding very loudly on the chamber door. Adam leapt out of bed in a flash, dagger in hand, and tore it open.

It was Starten, Turius's head man. "I beg your pardon, Lord King," he said, with more grace than I expected from a man face to face with a naked king brandishing a blade. "Fire has been spotted in the mountains."

Fully awake now, I sat up in bed. "Where, exactly?"

"The second range," he said, still addressing Adam, to my annoyance. "In the east."

Adam dropped the dagger and threw on some clothes. "Show us at once."

I tossed the covers aside and pulled on my dressing gown. The cold stone floor nipped at my bare feet as I grabbed a candle and padded down the hall after Adam. He walked so fast I could barely keep up. Starten led us through the darkened corridors and up the winding steps of the northern tower. I felt slightly sick, unable to avoid the rush of memories from my uncle's reign. The nights I had slept in the tower opposite this one, terribly alone, looking up at the high windows in the hopes that someone would help me. The days of endless boredom and fear. Starten pushed open the door and I hesitated before crossing the threshold.

Adam looked back at me. "Aren't you coming?"

I nodded, forcing myself to enter the circular room. I forgot all about my reluctance, however, when my gaze settled on the opposite window. A bright red line shone on the uppermost mountain peaks, thin and distant. Harmless looking, if one didn't know any better.

"Can the people see it from below?" asked Adam.

Starten shook his head. "No. The valley is too low to view a peak that far away. This is the only spot in the kingdom high enough. We can't even smell the smoke down here yet."

"Good," said Adam. "We don't want to start an unnecessary panic, especially if the threat is legless. Let's agree to keep this quiet for now and concentrate on planning an evacuation if necessary. We'll stay put unless the wind changes."

Adam's confident voice did nothing to calm my racing pulse. For a farming kingdom like Myrilla, fire was devastating. We had just blooded the fields; we'd be left with nothing if the flames came down the mountains. The earth was so dry it wouldn't take more than a sneeze to spread the blaze. Stepping closer to the window, I licked my fingers and thrust my hand into the open air. The breeze was light and warm. "The wind's from the west," I told him, my voice thick with tension. "If it shifts to the south—even the slightest bit— it'll charge directly toward us."

Adam cleared his throat. "And what will that mean for Myrilla?"

We watched each other, neither wanting to admit the possibility that everything we had worked and prayed for, every stake in our treaty, every hope we had dared, could be devoured by flames. I looked out the window again. The red line seemed so far away, I couldn't imagine the ruin it would cause if it crept any closer. We'd have nowhere to go, no escape whatsoever.

I turned back to Adam, knowing he wouldn't want me to mince words. His open face asked for frankness and honesty, and I gave them to him.

"We would be destroyed."

XV

The gods know us better than we know ourselves, and in doing so, they can force us to face even our most secret fears. Sometimes it is for our own good, though at the time of the fire I thought it was only so they could exercise their power over us. When I went to bed that night after seeing the flames in the distance, I hardly slept. I was anxious and chilly with fear of the blaze, unable to stop myself picturing Myrilla reduced to ashes and rubble. It seemed inevitable to me. The gods would allow the fire to sweep over us, simply because they could. I was certain I had displeased Kore somehow, whether in the Blooding or in my interactions with Adam or the way I had cut short a few of my temple visits lately. And now she would unleash her wrath.

That's why I knew before I had even opened my eyes the next morning that the winds had changed. The smell of smoke poured into the chamber like an unwelcome perfume. It stung my nose and forced my eyes into slits as I fumbled my way to the window. True to Starten's words, the fire itself was not visible, but the dense haze that had blown down from the mountains certainly was. I could hear the confused and fearful shouts of the people crowding the courtyard below, waiting for answers. I splashed cold water on my face and dressed quickly. I reached for the door handle, rehearsing words of comfort and reassurance in my head, but the door opened of its own accord.

Adam stood on the other side. "Over a thousand people have gathered at the front gates," he told me, without preamble.

"There's more in the courtyard," I said, joining him in the corridor.

"They're terrified. We have to address them."

"I was thinking the same thing," I said, as a wide-eyed servant turned from the window to give a halfhearted curtsey, then immediately resumed her post. "I just don't know what to say."

"Do you remember any other time that fire threatened Myrilla?"

I shook my head. "The rains usually prevent such a possibility. But it's been so dry this spring…" I trailed off. "This has never happened before, not in my memory. Their whole livelihood is at stake; our words will be little comfort if we don't accompany them with a plan of action."

His brow furrowed. "You're right, though the fire's moving too fast to organize any kind of evacuation. With the number of children and the elderly it'll be on us before we reach the far edge of the kingdom. We'll have to open the castle and trust that the stone can withstand the flames. At its current speed, we might have a chance."

I nodded, not knowing any other suggestion to give. Once he had spoken to Turius and a few other lords about his plan, Adam stood on the upper terrace of the castle and addressed the now thousands crowded at the gates. I stayed by his side, trying so hard to smooth the worry from my face in order to look queenly and dignified that I barely grasped a single word that he said. I caught snatches of phrases, here and there:

"…great hall open to anyone desiring shelter…"

"…leave your things; possessions can be replaced…"

"…we have no room for panic, everyone must remain ordered and calm…"

He paused, and I thought he had reached the end of his speech, when he suddenly said, "The river is our only hope of defeating this fire. From what I understand there is a pump system, and while it hasn't been used for many years, I believe we can engage it to produce enough water to at least slow the blaze, if not snuff it out completely. Who among you will ride out to the river with me to try to save Myrilla?"

A surge of men pushed forward—a hundred, at least—pledging to remain by their king's side until the fire was defeated or consumed them all. Adam nodded, solemn but pleased. "Thank you for your service to our kingdom. Help your families to the castle and ready your horses. We'll ride out at once."

With a wave, Adam turned from the crowd and led me down the corridors to our chamber. I watched him gather his armor and a large white bedsheet, which he started to tear into wide strips.

"What are you doing?" I asked him, bewildered.

"Dipping the cloth in water will help keep my armor cool," he said over the sound of ripping fabric. "A little rust is a small price to pay to avoid a scorching."

"No, Adam." I picked up his helmet and turned it over in my hands. The black eye slit glared back at me, telling nothing. "The pumps at the river are ancient. If they fail, I don't see how your plan will work." Desperation crept into my voice. "What will you do instead? Charge the fire with water buckets?"

He ignored me and stuffed the fabric strips into a satchel. I watched, helpless, as he sat on the edge of the bed and pulled his boots onto his feet. When he was ready, he stood up and held out his hand. "My helmet, if you please, Alyce."

I gripped it tighter and moved in front of the door. "It isn't necessary for you to ride out. Let the others go."

"And do what, stay behind and cower in the great hall with the infants?"

My face grew hot. "It wouldn't make you a coward. You're the king—"

"Precisely," he cut me off. "I am the king. If I don't walk willingly into danger how can I ask others to do so in my stead? I was taught to lead by example, Alyce. The safety of Myrilla begins and ends with me. That's what it meant when that crown was placed on my head. I have specific duties, duties that are different from yours, and one is to ensure Myrilla lives to see another day or else fall in the attempt."

His face was so grave that I didn't argue. I simply passed him his helmet and stood back from the door. He studied me for a moment, saying nothing, then tucked the helmet under his arm. I wanted to tell him to be careful, to not do anything foolish or heroic, but he was already gone. The door closed slowly behind him, quieting the men's voices in the corridor. For a moment I stayed rooted to the carpet, but when I heard the gate opening I darted to the window. Far below I saw the column of volunteers passing through the court-

118

yard on horseback. They were so few in number I had no idea how they would ever fight the blaze. I lifted my eyes against the thick smoke and just managed to make out the fiery line in the distance. It had reached the peaks of the mountains, draped across the ridge like a red-hot snake. The fire was now in full view from the castle no matter where you stood, sending up clouds of hazy smoke that turned the sky purple. They could never contain it. By nightfall it would reach the vineyards at the foothills, and from there it would spread until it destroyed the whole kingdom.

I let the curtain fall back before any more smoke poured into the room. As much as I would have liked to hide in the chamber and wait for Adam's return, I couldn't. He was right when he said that we held different duties; as queen it was up to me to play hostess to the thousands of people filling the great hall. Not dignitaries, either, but restless children and worried mothers. I had to remain strong and emulate unyielding grace while my people watched me through their tears, inspecting my façade for any cracks of knowledge that might give away their loved ones' fates.

I slipped through the door and into the eerily silent corridor. There wasn't a servant in sight; many, I suspected, had ridden out with Adam. As I made my way toward the great hall I tried very hard to keep from locking my eyes on the windows. Hazy crimson light poured through the few windows that remained uncovered, though it did little to illuminate my path. None of the lamps were lit, I noticed in a burst of annoyance. Annoyance that quickly changed to shame. How dare I complain about unlit lamps when the whole castle might soon be swallowed by flames?

I was still silently scolding myself when I reached the great hall. Though, to be perfectly frank, I heard the chaos within before I saw it. Dozens of infants wailed in chorus, accompanied by the cries and whimpers of young children. I stood in the doorway, watching pale-faced mothers try to comfort their babes while the elderly kept their eyes fastened on the thick curtains covering the windows as though willing themselves to see through them.

It was a moment before anyone noticed me, but when they did a dreadful silence fell over the hall. Such was their distress that they forgot to rise upon my entrance. Not that it mattered. Propriety was the furthest thing from my mind. I wanted to reassure them, to tell them I was just as fearful as they, but the words refused to come.

Instead I searched their faces, each more anxious than the last, until I spotted a dark-haired youth seated on a bench and gripping a lyre with white fingers.

"What is your name, sir?" I asked him, painfully aware of how loud my voice sounded in the tense hall.

"It's Dagmar, Lady Queen." He tried to stand, but his legs trembled. "I was thrown from a horse last week. If my leg weren't lame I'd be riding to the mountain with my father, I swear—"

"No one condemns you here, Dagmar," I said quickly. "Myself least of all. We're all called by the gods to serve in different ways at different times. Please, sit. I only wanted to ask if you know how to play that lyre, or if you're keeping it safe for a friend."

He eased himself back onto the bench. "I play, Lady Queen, though not with the skill you're probably accustomed to hearing."

"No music is sweeter than that which is heard in times of trial. Would you be so kind as to grace us with a tune?"

Dagmar swallowed, clearly terrified at the prospect of performing for such a large audience. Then, just as I thought he was about to refuse, he bent his head and tuned his strings. The act looked so familiar, the very same as I had seen from Adam so many times before, that it sent a torrent of pain through my chest. The thought of him in the mountains surrounded by flames nearly sent me to my knees.

Finally Dagmar plucked at the strings, filling the hall with music. Almost at once the atmosphere relaxed. I knew the tune well—it was an old Myrillan lullaby—and I was not surprised to hear several mothers murmuring the comforting lyrics to their babies. From the corner of my eye I saw the ladies of court sitting at the high table, waiting for me to join them. But I couldn't force myself to climb the steps of the dais, not when I knew they'd fill my ears with endless questions and speculations on the volunteers' progress.

Settling on the end of a bench, I watched a group of small girls sitting in a circle nearby, playing with their rag dolls. They seemed to be organizing some kind of feast or ball for the dolls to attend. I listened to their meticulous plans, taking care not to show I was eavesdropping, and took great pleasure in the distraction. I was so charmed by their innocent play that I started when a small hand came to rest on my knee.

"Lady Queen?"

I looked up and saw the familiar birthmarked face of Lamia, the child who'd presented me with flowers after the Blooding. Her brow was drawn over her worried eyes and her clothes smelled strongly of smoke.

"My dear Lamia," I said as gently as I could, "tell me what's troubling you."

She sniffed deeply and tears spilled down her cheeks. "M-My Papa's gone to the m-m-mountain," she gulped. "I'm s-so scared he w-won't come back."

I didn't know how to comfort her, not when my fears so clearly matched hers. I brushed her hair back from her face; it was sprinkled through with flecks of ash that turned to powder on my fingertips. "Can I tell you a secret?" At her nod, I leaned close. "I'm frightened, too. All we can do is trust that the gods will take care of your Papa."

She contemplated this in silence, then looked up at me. "But what if they don't, Lady Queen?"

Again, I was stumped. Until that moment I hadn't considered the idea. But I found myself wondering what my life would look like if Adam met his end in the mountains. The loneliness, the absence of his friendship and encouragement. I'd have to remarry, of course. Under the laws passed by my uncle no queen was permitted to rule in her own right. Chances were I'd not be so lucky a second time, and I'd find myself bound to a fool or a tyrant or worse. My skin felt cold and I had to focus my strength on drawing breath.

Without responding to her question, I lifted Lamia into my lap and let her rest her head on my shoulder. Desperately I prayed for the gods to protect Adam. For his own sake and mine. I know it sounds selfish, but I considered him a friend, a dear one at that, and I couldn't bear the thought of rebuilding my life without him.

The afternoon passed slowly into evening, punctuated only by trays of cold meat and wine poured by the kitchen maids. No one ate very much; our eyes stayed fastened on the windows. Heavy canvas drapes covered every opening to block the smoke, so that when night fell no one noticed the change in light. More than once I found myself glancing around the hall for sight of Lilianne. I desperately wanted her counsel, but she wasn't there. She would never abandon the temple, even under threat of fire.

I was watching a cluster of little boys work out the guidelines for a game of cards when a deafening roar filled the hall. It was so loud and terrible it could only be the fire descending on the castle. Several people screamed or dove under the tables for shelter. I clung to Lamia and looked at the ceiling, expecting the rafters to collapse at any second and engulf us all in flames. Dagmar's music stopped, leaving terrible stillness in its wake.

The roar grew louder and an elderly man, hysterical and sobbing, threw himself at my feet. "Tell us what to do!" he shrieked. "We beg you, Lady Queen, save us!"

I have never been a heroic person, least of all in that moment. I wanted to tell him that no one was less capable of saving anyone than I. I wanted to tell him to pray for a painless death and ask the gods for mercy. I wanted to tell him that I was every bit as terrified as he, and beseech his comfort instead. But a small, quiet part of my mind remembered that I was the queen of Myrilla, and that even if the very castle where I was born happened to burn down around me, I could not let panic rule. Without a word, I placed Lamia on the bench beside me, and stood. I brushed the ash from my gown and stepped around the man. The hall, silent apart from the roar overhead, watched as I crossed to the far windows. I had to see the fire for myself; I couldn't give orders without knowing the enemy's whereabouts. I raised a trembling hand and, after the slightest hesitation, squeezed my eyes shut and drew back the curtain.

I expected a wave of heat to strike me or for a plume of smoke to fill my nostrils. Instead, I felt cool liquid splattering my face.

"Rain," I whispered. My eyes flew open, drinking in the silver sheets pouring from the heavens. I put out my hand to receive it, letting the cool relief stream through my fingers and drip down my sleeve. "It's rain!" I called, turning away from the window.

The windows immediately filled with people scrambling for a look. The same eyes that had studied the smoke in ghastly fascination since sunrise now widened in awe. Children climbed onto the sill and stuck out their tongues to taste the sweet downpour. Sorrowful weeping turned to tears of joy as men and women clutched each other in relief.

In the darkness we couldn't see the mountains, so there was no way of knowing when the column of riders would return. Still, there was no rush to leave the hall. I sent to the kitchens for bottles of tart cherry wine and made sure each child was given a hard roll smeared

122

with honey and jam. We toasted each other and raised our glasses to the gods, thanking Kore for sending the rain in our time of need. The celebration had barely begun when the hall doors burst open. The volunteers filed slowly in, drenched from the downpour but grinning like schoolchildren. They ran to their families and soon the hall was filled with dozens of happy reunions. When Lamia spotted her father she screamed out "Papa!" at the top of her lungs and flung herself into his arms.

Minutes passed; the steady procession slowed to a trickle, and I had yet to see Adam. I circulated the room, offering wine to the returned heroes and thanking them for their bravery, all the while keeping my eyes trained to the doors. Surely he was well; if the king was wounded someone would have told me at once. I drained the last of my own celebratory wine and set the empty cup on the table. Still no sign of Adam. Even Turius had returned and was busy consoling his wife, who continued to weep with relief. The last man entered and the hall doors shut with a heavy thud. A rock settled in my stomach. If something had happened to him—

"You don't have to look so worried," said a voice behind me.

I spun around and saw Adam beaming at me, his golden hair plastered to his forehead. He carried his helmet under his arm and dark streaks of soot covered his armor. Without a thought to my gown or my dignity or anyone watching, I ran three steps and suddenly his helmet clattered to the floor and I was in his arms, embracing him for the first time.

"If I'd known this kind of reception was waiting for me, I'd have returned much faster," he said into my hair. I felt his heart beating beneath the armor and I pressed my face into his chest, hardly daring to believe he was real, he was still with me. Only when I was satisfied that he had truly returned, unharmed, did I relax my grip. As I stepped back he frowned at the lashings of wet, black soot smeared across my front. "I'm afraid your dress is ruined. Sorry about that."

I didn't even glance at it. "It doesn't matter," I said breathlessly. "I'm just glad you're back and in health."

"You weren't concerned, were you, Alyce?" he teased. "Because there's nothing a man likes better than knowing there's a woman somewhere wringing her hands over his wellbeing."

"Don't be ridiculous, of course I wasn't concerned," I replied, as haughtily as I could. "Not for you, at any rate. I mean, if Turius hadn't returned, who else would criticize my every decision and spread nasty rumors about me behind my back?"

He laughed and accepted a glass of wine from a passing tray. Servants materialized to relieve him of his cloak and offer him bread and fruit. The celebration continued long into the night, and as every man, woman, and child praised Adam for his courage, he thanked them all and never once let go of my hand.

XVI

In the weeks following the fire, spring descended upon Myrilla in a whirl of color. New buds filled the trees, nestling on their branches like a green mist. Bursts of pink and gold and purple broke out in new places every day, and I could scarcely keep up with the work in the garden. The flowers seemed to bloom before my very eyes, and the air was heavy with the scent of apple blossoms. Long, trailing vines of sun bells covered the castle walls, their yellow and red blooms offset by their striking black leaves. Brambling dragonlace grew wild along the roads and paths all through the kingdom, white and pink and giving off a sweet, peppery scent. Daffodils in yellow and blue covered the meadows, providing endless nectar for the fat, droning bees, and lilies of every hue spread wide their long, elegant petals. Tangled curtains of wild roses and honeysuckle tumbled over the low stone walls surrounding the fields. The kingdom had truly transformed.

Every day the farms showed new promise. The river swelled from the warm spring rains and set the farmers to irrigating their fields with new vigor. Adam and I rode out to watch them carefully directing the thin streams of water with their spades, using the ancient methods passed down by their fathers and grandfathers. It was slow, painstaking work and absolutely mesmerizing to watch. It wasn't long before tiny green shoots peppered every vegetable patch.

Of course, the greatest joy of all came from the wheat fields. When I peered through the iron gate and saw the first flecks of green sprouting throughout the black field, I nearly wept for relief. It wasn't a guarantee—Myrilla had seen green wheat crops die plenty of times—so there was still much patience to be endured. Only when the wheat grew taller than my waist, golden and strong, with its heavy head of berries would we be assured of a harvest.

It seemed we took the air nearly every day. When we weren't receiving requests from the people, Adam and I spent hours together in my garden. Weeds sprang up as fast as I could clear them, especially following rain, and on those days Adam put aside his lyre and helped me. I'm sure the lords and ladies of Myrilla would have clutched their sides in mirth to see their king and queen crouching in the flowerbeds, arms and hands streaked with black earth. It was good fun, though, and Adam and I laughed together quite often. We took our bows to the archery butts and Adam continued to teach me; we rode out with the court to view the spring and early summer flowers; we spread rugs beneath the great oak trees in the courtyard and invited the servants to join us in a picnic of cold chicken, fruit tarts, and sweetened lemon juice.

One afternoon we were walking through the apple orchards, admiring the ripening fruit, when Adam pulled a roll of parchment from his pocket.

"My father and mother are hosting a banquet in a fortnight," he said. "They've invited us to attend."

"What's the occasion?"

"It's the beginning of boar season. They put on a great hunt every year for the court. Lords travel from all over Itomius to participate, and they bring their families. My parents will have all sorts of festivities planned, it's always a wonderful time. Would you like to come?"

"To Itomius?" Simply saying his home country's name left a sour taste in my mouth. "I don't know, Adam. I've never left Myrilla."

"Lord Daltena said your whole family visited him at the Sea's Arm."

"That's not the same thing; I have no memory of that journey." I took the parchment and studied it. Elegant Itomian script, heavy and black, covered the page. I handed it back to him. "If you wish to go, that's perfectly fine with me. But I don't think I should attend."

"Why not?"

"I don't have any particular reasons, just a feeling."

He smirked at that. "Right. You do have reasons, you just won't tell me."

I gently touched a small apple, saying nothing. It was pale green, but faint red streaks had started to appear along its skin.

"Alyce," said Adam, "my family would not have invited both of us if they didn't want you there. You're my wife, they see you as one of their own."

"No, they don't," I replied. "Do you not remember how much you talked about Itomius when we first married? It was your favorite topic of conversation. You and Turius discussed it nonstop. How the fountains are filled with wine and the palace walls are plated with gold. You told me yourself that when you were growing up your lowest servants ate better than the royalty here. You said Myrilla is a hole compared to Itomius. That your friends mocked you for even wanting to have it for your own."

He winced. "I forget what a good memory you have."

"It's easy to remember nasty jibes when they're aimed at your homeland. If that's the way your family feels about Myrilla, then that's how they'll feel about me. They're going to despise me. I won't go."

I started back to my horse but he caught up before I could put my foot in in the stirrup. "When I said those things about Myrilla, I was behaving like a spoiled child who's so caught up in what he used to have that he can't appreciate what's in front of him," he said, his voice warm. "Besides, we're both Myrillans now. If anyone there looks down their noses, they're looking down at both of us."

I glanced over my shoulder at the orchards and fields spread out in every direction. Each was a hub of activity, dotted with workers tending the crops. It made me terribly uneasy to think of leaving during such a critical time. I opened my mouth to say this, but then I saw the eagerness in Adam's eyes. He was aching for the hunt, and for me to refuse would hurt him deeply. I also couldn't help feeling curious about his family. He didn't speak of them often, and I thought that perhaps meeting them would help me better understand his ways.

"Very well," I said, breaking into an unexpected smile. "I'd love to come."

He nodded his thanks and lifted me into the saddle. "Itomius will never be the same for it."

◆ ◆ ◆

Because I had not traveled outside Myrilla since I was a young child, I had no inkling of the complexities involved in transforming a stationary court into a mobile one. Adam told me the feast would last a week; he did not deign to mention that the journey to his homeland would take just as long, including an overture in Warkenland to thank King Torbold for reopening the roads between our lands so quickly. The week of our departure I sat in the presence chamber looking at the maps while Adam and Turius—whom my husband appointed deputy during our absence—finalized the details of our train.

"I still don't understand how it'll take over twice as long to get there than it will to come home, even accounting the visit to King Torbold," I said to Adam. "It's the same road, is it not?"

"No, we're making a loop," he replied. "We'll take the western road to Warkenland, then turn north toward Itomius. When it's time to come home we'll go south."

I gestured to the map. "But there isn't a road through the mountains."

"Not on that map, there isn't." He joined me, leaning over my back as he traced his finger on the parchment. "We'll take the mountain pass, which opens straight into the fields. You'll be able to see the vineyards the moment Myrilla comes into view."

My ears rang with the words *mountain pass*. "That's how we're getting through the mountains? The road you and your men carved out when you brought your army?"

"Yes, I'm eager to see it again." He dropped his cheerful tone when he saw my face. "It's perfectly safe, Alyce, I promise. I wouldn't have let one soldier set foot in the pass without making certain it was sound. Scouts are there as we speak, inspecting it and making sure it's clear for our train. If there's even the slightest hint of danger we'll come back through Warkenland instead."

I nodded, though inside I felt sick. The thought of riding through those terrible mountains, mountains that had burned with raging wildfires only weeks prior, chilled my stomach. Still, I forced myself to praise Adam's plan. The list of supplies and courtiers Turius was putting together soon provided a distraction, however. I found it ridiculous and extravagant and, to put it mildly, utterly absurd.

"Do we honestly need to take *three* bakers with us?" I said, gaping at the sheaves of paper spilling over the table. "And what on earth will we need two ironsmiths for?"

Turius rolled his eyes at my question. "One of the horses might lose a shoe on the road and need a replacement." He pushed a scroll toward Adam. "Here's that boundary post dispute. You'll want to sign the new order before you leave or the farmers will be at each other's throats."

Adam leaned back in his chair to read the agreement. "It's common practice, Alyce," he said. "We must plan for any eventuality."

"Then bring a trunk of extra horseshoes and a groom who knows how to shoe a horse." I watched, annoyed, as Turius dipped his pen in the ink, then began adding even more supplies in his illegible scrawl. I turned back to my husband. "Adam, this is folly. We'll be gone three weeks, not three years."

Turius snorted. "I assure you, I wouldn't have you bringing anything you didn't absolutely need while you're away."

I snatched up one of the papers. "So you're saying we'll absolutely need thirty vats of wine, two dozen rabbits, and sixty pounds of cheese? You might as well uproot the castle and send it with us as well."

Turius started to argue, but Adam intervened. "This is what happens when a court goes on progress, Alyce," he said, prying the paper from my fingertips. "The way we present ourselves on the road is the impression we make on the world. We can't just think of Itomius, there's Warkenland to consider as well."

I scoffed. "Warkenland doesn't care how many courtiers and bakers we bring. They're so thrilled the roads are open that we could show up in sackcloth and they'd still feast us 'til dawn. And we're going to Itomius to visit your family. Surely they just want to see you, and not have to go through the whole production of entertaining your court."

"My parents wouldn't mind, but—" He stopped.

I folded my arms, waiting for him to continue. "Yes?"

He sighed and scratched his jaw. "My brother will be there, appraising and judging everything that passes under his eyes. Not to mention his wife's reaction—she's an utter snake. Everyone's always thought of Syrano as the prize of the family, being heir to Itomius and all. If I don't impress him…well, it doesn't matter what he says about me, but Myrilla's future may one day depend on a good relationship with him. I don't want to give any impression to make him doubt the prosperity of our kingdom."

I rested my elbows on the table, pondering his words. I wanted to tell him that any fool would know that Myrilla's lackluster train, no matter how abundant in quantity and supplies, would never compare to the glittering court of Itomius, but I bit back my tongue before I could snap at him. Instead I smoothed my dress over my knees and drew a deep breath. "What if we tried a simpler tact?"

Both he and Turius looked at me. Adam put down his pen. "What did you have in mind?"

"Well, if your brother is as difficult to impress as you say—"

"He can hardly help it, being blessed by the gods as he is," he said shortly.

I frowned, surprised by his bitterness. "Then he's probably expecting you to parade the whole court under his nose. He'll be looking for things to criticize, so don't let him. You said yourself nothing you do can match his success. I say don't bother to play his game."

Turius straightened his stack of endless lists. "With respect, Lady Queen, Admetus is aware of the proper way to engage with his family. I should know, having grown up in the Itomian court myself."

He started to pass the parchment to Adam, but my husband turned in his chair to fully face me and said, "I'm intrigued, wife. Pray continue."

I licked my lips, choosing my next works carefully. "Rather than create an opportunity for him to be unkind about what he sees before him," I said, "present a smaller picture of utter bliss and perfection for him to study, and he'll surely assume the rest of Myrilla appears the same way. So will everyone else, for that matter. A small, merry party of twenty horses is more likely to win approval than an exhaustive army of two hundred."

Turius shook his head dismissively, but Adam considered this. "That's very good. If nothing else, we'll be less of an imposition on Warkenland," he said thoughtfully. "King Torbold is the most practical man I've ever met. He won't miss the hassle of finding lodging and space for a large court. And it would drive any critics mad with speculation, seeing us blissfully happy amidst such quaint circumstances."

I smiled. "That it shall."

He looked at Turius. "What do you think, Deputy?"

Turius gazed at the elaborate list before him, then scored through the whole thing with an irritated sigh. Of course he was angry. Any triumph of mine was his defeat.

"Prudent as ever, Lady Queen," he said to me in a flat voice. "What a gift from the gods you are."

Three days later Adam and I set out for Warkenland, accompanied only by a handful of soldiers and even fewer courtiers. Turius, reveling in his new role of deputy, still could not understand why we had slashed our band to the bone. He saw us off from the courtyard, his eyes narrowed in suspicion.

"You're only taking two wagons, and one of them is half full of flowers and fruit," he said in a flat voice. "Do you plan to sleep on a bed of daisies and berries when you stop each night?"

Adam tightened his saddle girth. "Our trunks have everything we need. The pavilion will be a simple one."

"And the flowers are for gifts, and to ornament our train," I explained.

Turius didn't even glance at me; even then he still preferred to pretend I did not exist. "I think wine would be much more gladly received than flowers," he muttered.

I turned from my horse, which was happily munching a carrot, and glared at Turius. "They convey Kore's favor upon the wearer. Lilianne blessed them in the temple this morning. Just because you don't appreciate it doesn't mean other kings and queens won't."

Turius mumbled something under his breath, but before I could snap at him to speak up properly, Adam stepped between us.

"Enough," he said to Turius, then turned to me and put his hands on my shoulders. "Everything is accounted for. Are you ready?" At my nod, he lifted me into the saddle and clapped Turius on the back. "Try not to destroy the crops while we're gone. I expect detailed reports upon my return. Send your fastest riders if anything goes amiss."

With that, we rode out of the courtyard and through the gates. People crowded the road's edge, eager to glimpse their sovereigns.

131

It was strange to see Adam wearing his crown outside of the throne room, looking every inch a proper king as he smiled and waved. I did my best to mimic him, though all I could see was a crowd of endless faces, faces depending on Kore to deliver the harvest.

Once we left the gates far behind I felt much more comfortable. The crowd thinned to nonexistence; farmers tending their crops removed their caps and bowed as we rode past, otherwise we enjoyed solitude. The new stones in the road shone like a bright path before us, and the horses' hooves made a delightful clip against them. Dark clouds gathered in the south, streaks of blue fading to the earth and bringing nourishment to the fields. I closed my eyes and breathed deeply, invigorated by the scent of horse and leather, budding wheat and distant rain.

The skies remained fair throughout our journey to Warkenland. Adam was right about King Torbold's reaction to our party. He ushered us into his castle and offered us the choicest rooms for all our number. He praised Adam for a peaceful and just king and offered me the finest bull in his pasture as a gift. I could only stare at the menacing creature, which reached my shoulder in height, and stammer my thanks. Then Adam matched King Torbold's generosity by offering to buy the second-finest bull in the king's pasture, an offer the king of course graciously accepted. We danced and feasted and talked all evening. When I woke the next morning I was very sorry to leave. I suspected watching Adam try to impress his brother for a week would not be as pleasant as attending a banquet at Warkenland's royal table.

XVII

The closer we drew to Itomius over the coming days, the happier Adam looked and the sicker I felt. Gone was my reckless attitude from the presence chamber; I was certain I had entirely misjudged our presentation, and that our pitiful train would be the target of endless mockery. I had no experience with a court on progress; why had Adam even listened to me?

My husband, however, seemed utterly pleased with our decision to simplify. The morning we crossed the border to his homeland, his face grew brighter than the sun. Without the distraction of a great mobile court and all its inevitable problems of broken wheel axles and such causing delays in travel, he was able to enjoy himself. He grew increasingly talkative as we rode on; every rolling hill and fir tree seemed to have a story from his boyhood attached. On our journey's final night we camped near the northernmost fork of the Broom River and rose well before dawn to prepare for our arrival to the palace. The sun was just peering over the horizon when we set out with our train, festooned with Myrilla's finest offerings. Garlands of roses and ivory-colored moon ivy were wrapped around our horses' bridles and hung over our saddles. Adam's horse blanket glowed with fireflowers I had sewn into the warm crimson wool, matching the arms of his homeland. As a salute to his family's crest, he wore the wreath of laurel I had made him instead of his crown. I sported a similar wreath, though mine was interwoven with rosemary. Adam's armor gleamed in the dappled sunlight, and he rode with his bow strapped to his back and lyre hanging from his side instead of his sword, both of which I had adorned with laurel as well. My gown was dyed dark red, Itomian red, and trimmed with white and silver roses. Adam, his eyes alight with joy, looked like a woodland god as our fragrant party rode through the lush forest. "I swam in that pool when I was a boy," he said, gesturing through the trees. "Its waters never grew too warm, even in the hottest summers. After a long hunt I'd simply jump in with all my clothes on. And in the winter it was perfect for skating. The ice grew so thick you couldn't even break through it with an axe. Syrano tried once."

We reached the end of the trees and Adam leaned forward in his saddle. "There it is," he said, pointing. "Haddenford, seat of Itomian kings." He looked so happy I couldn't help smiling, though when I took a proper look at the palace my nerves grew taut. It was the grandest, most beautiful structure I had ever seen. It could have easily swallowed six Myrillan castles, and still had room to spare. The stone seemed to gleam silver in the early morning sun. The palace sat atop a sloping green hill, surrounded by a thin wall with a number of gates already open to welcome any guest. It seemed weak in terms of self-protection, especially when I considered the fortifications of Myrilla's castle. But then I noticed the troops spread out both inside and outside the fragile wall. Hundreds of soldiers, all battle ready and laid out in perfect order like pieces on a chessboard. And those were only the ones I could spot at a glance. I had no doubt dozens more stood interspersed among the massive crowd of Itomian citizens who had gathered to greet us.

Adam nudged his mount into a fast canter; the horse, sensing its return home, pricked its ears and snorted, tossing its head like a war charger riding in from battle. The other horses caught the scent of its excitement and raced happily toward the open gates. As we approached, the seemingly endless columns of soldiers turned toward us and saluted, welcoming their prince to his place of birth. The center column parted, its soldiers stepping aside in perfect rhythm and pressing the crowd back, to reveal the grand steps ascending to the palace. At the top I saw an elderly man and woman dressed in crimson and silver. I swallowed nervously as Adam dismounted and helped me down from my horse, though I did my best to look happy for the crowd. They seemed so pleased to see us; dressed in their strange Itomian clothes they shouted greetings in their foreign-sounding dialect and threw garlands of laurel onto the path before us. I held Adam's arm as we made the slow procession toward the steps, and gripped it more tightly when I noticed with great alarm that a number of people in the crowd were holding leads to cows, sheep, or goats.

I put my mouth near Adam's ear. "Why are there animals here?"

"The herders want blessings for their livestock," he practically shouted in reply.

I opened my mouth to ask why they didn't go to their temple to ask for a blessing, but stopped when I remembered Itomius had no temple.

The marble steps gleamed like ice as we ascended them. They were steep, and with the great weight of my train dragging behind me I was a little flushed and out of breath when we reached the top. Adam bowed to his parents and I curtseyed in the Itomian style, though for all my practice the result was still a little unsteady. All formal pretense vanished, however, for as soon as we straightened up Adam's father burst out laughing and pulled his son into his arms, and the queen kissed my cheek like we were intimate friends. She took both my hands and looked me up and down. "You must be Alcestis," she said, her voice somehow both grand and sweet.

"Yes, Queen Janelle. I was honored to accept your invitation," I replied, as Adam had instructed me.

Her piercing green eyes wrinkled at the corners. "For once, my son did not exaggerate in his letters. You are an exquisite beauty."

I didn't know what to say. I knew I should thank her for such a generous compliment, but my mouth couldn't form the words. Instead I sank into another curtsey, even lower this time, hoping it would please her. I guessed right, and when I rose up she nodded with approval. Adam turned to greet his mother, then stepped back to present me to the king.

"Father, this is my wife. Queen Alcestis," he said, his voice nearly trembling with excitement. I curtseyed once more on my tired legs and was rewarded with a small bow in return. "Alyce, I'd like you to meet my father. King Verian of Itomius."

King Verian gave me a warm smile. With his black hair and thick beard he looked nothing like Adam, apart from his merry eyes. Instead, Adam was a near-perfect copy of his mother. Her golden hair was flecked with strands of silver and she stood no taller than my shoulder, but she could have easily passed as his older sister. They looked so friendly and had such an air of kindness about them that my concerns diminished considerably. I almost felt happy when they nodded for the servants to open the great wooden doors. As we passed through I noticed that in addition to their impressive height, they were embellished with intricate carvings of livestock and birds. The pictures' edges had softened and worn with age, almost vanishing into blankness in spots where wind and rain had shown the least mercy.

Adam saw me looking. "Menuas, the first king of Itomius, carved those doors himself," he whispered. "The legend says they were made from a single piece of wood, cut from the center of the kingdom's largest tree. The gods told him to use the scraps to make his arrows, and they were so true to hitting their targets that he won every battle without losing a single man."

I found that particular piece of folklore very hard to believe, but nodded anyway. The entry hall opened up before us with dark wood floors covered with carpets dyed Itomian red. I expected to see candles and lamps lit on every surface, but there was no need. Instead, huge windows stood open straight ahead to a round courtyard, which I guessed served as the hub of the palace, with the rooms jutting out from it like spokes on a wheel. When the last of our servants passed through the great doors, bearing our trunks and gifts of goodwill, the doors swung shut with a very final-sounding bang.

Adam's parents led us through one room after another, each more splendid and lovely than the last. Servants dressed in white moved like pale shadows in the background, watching us pass. The very air was steeped in splendor and elegance; I had never seen any palace like it. For that is truly what it was: a palace. Our castle in Myrilla couldn't compare, with its boxy rooms built from ugly stone and stacked on top of each other to create the illusion of stateliness. Not to mention our penchant for walls: walls surrounding the castle grounds, walls encircling the castle itself, walls around the gardens and groves. At Haddenford everything was open. Great, airy rooms sprawled out before us, the high ceilings supported by slender pillars, and everything hewn from that lovely silvery marble. It reminded me of the stories I'd heard about the great palaces of the Greeks, though warmer and more welcoming.

We stopped in a large chamber, with a sweet-smelling fire burning on the hearth and plush carpets underfoot. One wall was nearly covered from floor to ceiling with an enormous tapestry depicting a hunting party in pursuit of a wild boar. I knew nothing about boar, but I'd never thought them particularly menacing until I saw the sharp tusks and fierce eyes stitched into the one shown in the tapestry.

The king and queen sat on cushioned chairs—the prettiest I'd ever seen—and invited us to join them, but Adam held up his hand.

"We will gladly take rest with you in a moment," he said in the courtly Itomian manner. "But first, if you would suffer us this one indulgence, my bride and I would like to present you with a few gifts. They represent our gratitude, both for your grand kingdom and your role as its monarchs and our royal parents."

He nodded to me; it was my turn to speak. Queens always handed out the gifts on foreign visits, according to Adam. I stood very straight and tried to smile graciously, though my heart was pounding at a furious rate.

"The first gift is for your kingdom's fields." I gestured to the servant holding the large sack. "This is our finest grain, used to sow the wheat fields of Myrilla. We present it in the hopes that it will nourish your people and livestock so that your kingdom's future will be hale and hearty."

The servant placed the sack before the king and queen. Next, a small sapling was brought forward, studded with pale green leaves and a few tightly closed buds. "For your castle and courtyard, we bring you a young rose tree, the very best selected from our gardens. It blooms with golden roses, native only to Myrilla, so that your people will always have grace and beauty within sight."

I licked my lips as they admired the young tree, and signaled for the final servant to step closer. I told myself it was going well, and that I had no cause to be nervous, but when they turned their attention to the last gift my voice shook a little.

"Our gift for your hearth and home is within this chest, which King Admetus"—I stumbled slightly over his formal name—"crafted from an iron ash tree, another of Myrilla's unique natives."

The servant placed the dark, gleaming chest in the king's outstretched hands. He and the queen spent a long moment admiring it, complimenting Adam on the panels' detailed designs. Adam thanked them graciously and winked at me, and I couldn't help smiling in return. The queen lifted the latch and opened the lid a crack; almost instantly a sweet perfume wafted from the chest, filling the great chamber. There was a collective intake of breath and the room fell silent. Even I smiled dreamily at the scent, I'd forgotten how lovely it was.

"That is the most delightful smell," said Queen Janelle, peering into the chest. "What is it?"

"It's a cutting of a snow lily root," I told her. "There is only one left in the world, and we have it in Myrilla. That piece will grow wherever it's planted, no matter how poor the soil, though it thrives best in complete darkness."

The queen closed the lid, though the perfume lingered. "This is a most generous gift," she said warmly. "Thank you both." Still smiling, she kissed my cheek and embraced her son, and then the king rose to do the same. The queen murmured something to a servant, who left and reappeared seconds later with two more in tow, all bearing trays. They placed them on the table in the center of the seating area, then slid into the shadows once more.

"Please, sit," said Adam's father. "Refresh yourselves and tell us all about your journey."

Adam did most of the talking, and I was grateful for it. The days of riding had left me famished and the spread of food was welcome. I enjoyed soft, ripe cheese spread on hard rolls, and clusters of candied figs and almonds. The sweet plum wine was almost as thick as syrup and so strong I had to sip it very slowly, lest it turn my tongue into a cumbersome piece of wool held captive in my mouth, causing me to slur and blurt out ridiculous things. Halfway through my glass I abandoned it altogether; I didn't want a telling flush to creep across my face.

When Adam finished his plate, he glanced around. "Where's Syrano? I thought he'd have made his grand entrance by now."

"He'll arrive tomorrow, sometime in the morning," said the king. "Just in time for the arms inspection." He stood and rubbed his hands together. "Now why don't you show your queen around the castle and grounds, while I escort mine upstairs for a rest before dinner?" With a farewell nod, he held out his arm for the queen, and they departed the chamber.

Once they had gone Adam turned to me with a wide grin. "Well, Alyce. What do you think?"

I couldn't begin to answer his question. Between the overwhelming reception at the palace gates, to the king's and queen's kindness, to the tangible majesty filling the palace itself, I couldn't articulate the flood of emotions rushing over me. "It's—it's wonderful," I finally stammered, gesturing at the rich tapestries, luxurious carpets, and gleaming columns. "All of it. Your mother and father are so gracious. And...*royal*. I know it sounds absurd, but I've never been around a king and queen like that. I'm terrified of saying something to offend them."

"You won't, don't worry. They're absolutely mad about you."

"I hope you're right." I crossed the room and rested my hands on the sill, looking out into the courtyard. A large fountain stood in the center, featuring a stone hunter pursuing—of course—a wild boar. The boar faced the hunter, poised for challenge, with water dripping from its tusked jaws. For his part, the hunter held an arrow fitted to his tautly drawn bow, his aim squarely fixed on the boar. A stream of water poured from the arrow's point, splashing into the dark pool below. "Tell me more about your brother," I said over my shoulder. "You don't speak of him often."

"I don't have much to say about him," Adam answered glibly. Just when I thought he was about to refuse me completely he joined me at the window. "It's not that I dislike him. While I have my moments of bitterness, I'm not usually jealous of him. You must try to understand, Alyce. Growing up, Syrano was always my parents' pet. Their favorite child. Everyone's favorite, really. Our nurse told us that when Syrano was born, he didn't cry, but laughed instead. The gods have favored him since birth, so everyone says."

I watched a brown speckled bird perch on the edge of the fountain, then bravely plunge into the pool for a bath. It washed itself for a moment, then shook the water from its wings before flying away. "And you think they favor him more than you?"

He rested his forearms on the sill, watching the bird too. "I used to think so." His eyes met mine and crinkled at the corners, as they only did when he was trying not to show how happy he felt. "Now I'm not so sure."

XVIII

Later that evening we dined privately with Adam's parents, eating in the family chamber, away from the great hall. They were warm and welcoming and asked us all about Myrilla and our lives at home. I had the loveliest time, though I was exhausted from the journey and doing a bad job of hiding it. After puddings Adam's father caught me yawning into my napkin and graciously suggested Adam escort me to our room. I don't even remember the walk to our designated chamber; I only recall a vague memory of stepping out of my gown and falling into bed, still wearing my stockings beneath my shift.

When I woke the next morning I experienced a brief panic. It took me a moment to remember I was not in my bed in Myrilla, but in the finest guest room Itomius had to offer. The great white bed was carved from ice laurel and large enough for me to forget I even had to share it with Adam. I glanced over and saw his side vacant, as usual. The downy covers were thrown back and rumpled, glowing pale blue in the morning sun.

A sharp knock sounded at the door and Silda, the maid assigned to attend me during our visit, entered the room and bowed. "We've drawn a bath for you, Queen Alcestis," she said quietly. "Your breakfast is just there on the tray. After you finish, if you like, we can help ready you for the day."

I rubbed the sleep from my eyes and sat up. Not since my illness the previous autumn had someone bathed and dressed me, but it seemed ungrateful to decline. I took the tray in my lap and ate fruit and cheese, followed by an enormous mug of fresh, foamy milk.

When I had my fill I let Silda lead the way to the adjoining bathing chamber, where I spent a luxurious hour learning precisely why Itomian baths are so famous. If you ever visit and have a chance to experience one, you will see what I mean. The massive tub was filled with ice, which was then melted and heated to steaming perfection. The result was water so clear that it appeared blue against the white marble.

Silda washed my hair and combed oil through it—a spicy, not-too-sweet scent I didn't recognize. Another maid scrubbed my body until my skin was as soft and smooth as the day I was born, and a third cleaned my teeth, fingernails, and toenails. They helped me out of the tub, wrapped me in a warm sheet, and instructed me to recline on a stove divan covered with cushions while I dried. Light poured through the tall, narrow windows as the sun rose in the sky, and birds flitted in and out of the chamber. Once I had sufficiently dried, Silda's helpers smoothed a cool, rich cream into my skin while Silda dressed my hair. I felt so relaxed that I couldn't stop smiling. Only when Silda mentioned I would soon be joining the other royal ladies did a small flame of anxiety flare in my belly.

"Has the queen planned an activity for today?" I asked, trying to sound nonchalant as I tied the sash of my dressing gown.

Silda's face lit up. "Oh yes, she has quite a treat in store. While the men are choosing their weapons for the hunt she's arranged for the women to take a pleasure cruise on the royal barge. The banks of the Broom are in full bloom and you'll be able to see all the kingdom's best pastures. The weather is perfect for it; I think you'll enjoy yourself immensely. When you return you'll join the men for a picnic on the lawn."

She opened my trunk and laid out my clothes. I chose a lightweight gown in blushing pink, thinking the sun would be quite hot on the river, and sifted through my flowers and greenery for a handful of gardenias. I sewed a cluster of the fragrant blossoms onto the waist of the gown, then tacked several smaller white flowers across the bodice to affect a windblown appearance.

"That's beautiful," Silda murmured, fingering the folds of the gown. "You truly have a talent for making things pretty, Queen Alcestis."

"You're very kind," I told her. I wanted to add that I hoped her countrywomen would agree, but that seemed tactless. Instead I held

141

out one more gardenia for Silda to pin in my hair. She obliged, and when I removed my robe she wrapped the feathery gown around my body and fastened it securely. With one last appraising look in the glass, I slid my feet into my sandals and followed Silda from the room. The corridors were already bustling with activity; servants dressed in white ferried trays to and from rooms, chatting amiably to each other. Each one stopped when they saw me and bowed deeply. Their sheer number amazed me; I had no idea one palace could house so many servants.

When we reached the rear side of the palace, Silda led me through a second pair of great doors. A lovely park spread out before us, green and lush and sprinkled with laurel trees, and cut through with a path of cream-colored paving stones. At the far end lay the Broom River. The royal barge was tethered to a wide dock; I had never seen such a beautiful watercraft. Painted Itomian red and trimmed with silver gilding, it looked like a gleaming jewel floating on top of the sparkling water. I followed Silda along the path, watching the rabbits play among the trees and dart to their burrows at the sound of our approaching steps.

Several women had already boarded by the time we reached the barge. Silda bid me farewell and said she would be waiting to help me change for dinner upon my return. Without her I felt a little uneasy; I knew none of these women apart from Adam's mother, and she was surrounded by courtiers. Each wore the same Itomian style of dress: richly colored gowns sewn from heavy brocades and velvets, with high collars and sleeves to the wrist. Precious stones glimmered from their fingers and ears and necks, and sometimes the gowns themselves. I lightly touched the gardenia tucked into my hair and forced my lips into a confident smile.

Adam's mother spotted me from within her throng. "My darling Alcestis," she said, coming forward to take my hand. She looked me up and down, a crown of golden laurel shining in her hair. "How gorgeous you look. You're as refreshing and fair as a warm spring breeze."

I felt my cheeks color. "Thank you, Madame. I'm so pleased to be here. Your royal barge is beautiful; I look forward to seeing Itomius from such a privileged view."

"I hope you find it satisfying," she said, squeezing my hand before releasing it. "Make yourself comfortable, sit anywhere you like. You see the refreshments under the awning there. Help yourself as you wish. We'll be casting off in just a moment."

I thanked her again and walked under the awning toward the stern of the barge. It was tremendously long; with over fifty women on board it didn't feel crowded in the least. A huge spread of fruit and cheeses and warm honey pastries waited under the awning, just as the queen had said, and nearby stood a table of morning wines. I was still full from breakfast, so I accepted a cup of cold, golden wine scented with lavender and wandered to one of the cushioned seats lining the inner edge of the barge. I was startled to see the landscape already creeping past; the castoff had been so smooth and subtle that I hadn't even felt it. A trio of musicians played quietly at the stern, their instruments complementing the music of the gently flowing river. And so the pleasure cruise began.

A practical, far-seeing queen would know that a dedicated block of time with the most powerful women of Itomius was the perfect opportunity for a fledgling such as myself to make a positive first impression. I am afraid, however, that I did not behave like a practical, far-seeing queen. Not because I didn't want to socialize, but because I was so enchanted by the view. I couldn't tear my eyes away from the bank. One moment it opened to softly rolling pastures peppered with black cows or little white bundles that could only be sheep. Then it changed to woodlands, so dense and green that I wanted to climb out of the boat and explore their shadowy depths. Then, sometimes, the bank vanished as a fork from the Broom opened up and wound its way into the distance. I saw tiny blue ponds and willow trees and wild roses climbing the ruins of old pasture walls. It was so peaceful that with the gentle motion of the barge I could have easily fallen asleep. An option that a few of the ladies had chosen, if the faint snoring at the other side of the barge was any indication.

Not wanting to disturb anyone's nap, I took my empty glass and left it on a servant's tray, then made my way to the bow. Here the breeze was strong and the sun shone brightly on the water. I sat on one of the cushions and glanced around to make sure no one was looking, then stretched my hand out to touch the clear river. I gasped and sat up straight; I hadn't expected it to be so cold. I took a deep breath, snickering at myself, and dipped my hand into the water and felt the icy rush flow between my fingers. I lifted my hand and let a few drops fall into my mouth, relishing the pure, sweet taste. I wanted to scoop up handful after handful and drink until I could stomach no more.

The barge cut quickly through the water, giving just enough time for me to catch a glimpse of the silver riverflowers below the surface. Brightly colored fish darted through the dense blooms, glinting like rubies, emeralds, and sapphires in the sunlight. I caught a riverflower by the stem and pulled it from the water to study it, but the exposure to air turned its gleaming petals to dull grey paper. Disappointed, I dropped it and watched the current carry it away.

"Who are you?" said a voice.

I turned and saw an exquisitely dressed little girl. She stared down at me, puzzlement scrawled across her face. But her expression was almost friendly compared to the hostility with which her companion regarded me. A young lady, not yet welcomed into womanhood, whose critical eyes swept over my prone form. I brushed awkwardly at my dress, painfully aware that even my finest court clothes looked like rags compared to these children's garb.

"Alcestis, of Myrilla," I said, gripping the edge of the barge. "And what are your names?"

The little girl curtsied in the Itomian style. Beautifully, I noted with envy. "I am Princess Norine of Itomius," she said without a trace of self-consciousness. "Youngest child of Prince Syrano, heir to the Itomian throne, and Princess Aveline, born of Lord Corneal of the Durwood."

I nodded absently, struck by her noble countenance. Here stood a child of seven or eight years, at the most, and she already possessed more regal grace and dignity than I could ever hope to learn in a lifetime. She wore her heavy satins and velvets like a second skin and the jewels around her neck could have paid for my entire wardrobe several times over. I turned to the older girl, waiting to hear her name and pedigree, but she merely wrinkled her nose and glanced at Princess Norine.

"That's the barbarian queen," she said, nearly spitting with contempt. "Mother told us she would be here, remember?"

My mouth dropped open, but nothing came out. I simply sat frozen on the cushion, smarting at being called a barbarian by some pompous child, when Princess Norine gave me a curious look.

"What were you doing, just now?" she asked. "With your hand in the water like that?"

I tore my eyes from the older girl's cruel face, wishing my cheeks weren't so hot with shame. "I was watching the fish, and looking at the riverflowers," I said hollowly. "The riverbed's covered with them. When you bring them to the surface they dry up like paper."

The little girl moved to the edge. "Can you show me?"

"I...would be happy to. Certainly." I motioned for her to kneel beside me and looked into the water once more. The flowers were thicker here; when the princess put her delicate hand into the river and pulled on one flower, two more came with it. She watched in amazement as the flowers transformed into their papery, ghostly form, then giggled. Water streamed from her hand and up her satin sleeve, deepening the Itomian red into a dark, blood-colored stain. Again and again she plunged her hand into the river. A green fish swam between her fingers and she squealed in delight until a sharp voice called out behind us.

"Norine! What are you doing?"

I turned and saw a spectacularly tall woman glaring down at us. She wore red and white and seemed to glitter in the afternoon sun. Dozens of diamonds and rubies were sewn into her gown; I had never seen anyone dressed so finely. I wiped my dripping wet hand on my skirt and rose unsteadily to my feet. Her eyes, much like the older girl's, ran from the top of my head down to my feet, and then back again. What she saw did not please her, from the way her brow drew together, wrinkling her porcelain-perfect forehead.

"You are the wife of Admetus." It wasn't a question.

I nodded too many times. "Yes, my name is Alcestis." I left off my title. It seemed ridiculous to call myself a queen in the presence of this flawless woman. "You must be Princess Aveline."

"Indeed." She gave me her scathing onceover a second time. I kept my eyes from meeting hers, lest I offend her. "How are you enjoying your visit?"

"Oh, everything's lovely." I tried to stand as still and perfect as her, with my hands folded daintily and my chin held high, but the barge's movement through the water made it difficult to keep my balance. I had to grip the edge. "Adam—I mean, Admetus—is so happy to be here. I've thoroughly enjoyed seeing his homeland."

145

Princess Aveline nodded absently. "Yes, Itomian hospitality is legendary. We're welcoming to all sorts of people. No matter where they're from or what they believe." Her eyes drifted to my bare arm. "Or how inappropriately they dress."

For a moment, I didn't understand what she meant. But then I looked around and saw all the other women dressed in layer upon layer of rich, heavy fabric, with sleeves hanging past their wrists and stays laced so tight I wondered at their ability to breathe, and I felt like a fool. I had taken such care in choosing my clothes for this journey, wanting nothing more than to present myself to Adam's family as an idyllic Myrillan queen, only to have that image wrecked by a flimsy pink gown. Normally I wouldn't care; if a foreign princess had visited me at home and said nasty things about me I'd have just ignored her. But what had this woman's daughter called me? A barbarian queen. That's what they would say about Adam, too. They'd see him as a capable prince of Itomius who lowered his value by marrying an animal who couldn't even bother to dress appropriately on a state visit.

One woman within earshot sniggered, while another disguised her faint laugh as a cough. My cheeks burned and I hugged my arms to my chest. "I didn't realize…" I began. "I'm so sorry. I have nothing with me that isn't cut in the Myrillan style."

Princess Aveline waved her hand, half-turned away from me as though bored of our conversation already. I looked past her and saw a handful of other ladies gesturing for her to come join them. "When we get back to the palace," she said to me over her shoulder, "you may borrow one of my gowns for dinner." She paused, then added, "After you wash, of course."

When the cruise finally ended I couldn't wait to disembark. Not long after my unpleasant conversation with Aveline the barge came to a particularly wide portion of the river. The captain turned the barge so we were sailing downriver and back toward the palace. Since we no longer had to fight the current the return journey was much shorter. During that time I spoke with Adam's mother and a few of her friends, all of whom were unfailingly kind and welcoming. They asked about Myrilla and had all sorts of questions about the planting season. I answered them the best I could; at the reminder of the upcoming harvest I prayed silently to the gods, asking their blessings on our wheat crop. All of our work would be worthless if it failed.

Thinking of home kept my mind occupied and helped the last stretch of the cruise pass quickly. I was eager to see Adam and find out how his preparations were coming. I found the hunt very intriguing; wild boar and other such game are in short supply in Myrilla. Hunting isn't a pastime for anyone, save the farmers fighting their garden's pests. If you ever come to Myrilla hoping to hunt for sport, you'll be gravely disappointed unless you want trophies of rabbits and crows.

The royal barge pulled close to the dock and the servants secured it with heavy ropes before helping us out. Adam's mother disembarked first, followed by Aveline and her daughters, and then myself. The green park stretched up the gentle slope with the palace sitting at the top of the hill like a gleaming white crystal. A large semicircle of white pavilions trimmed in laurel were pitched where the slope leveled out. Some housed food and drink—a silver fountain dispensing three different colors of wine stood out in particular—while others contained divans and daybeds for anyone who wanted to rest in the shade. The air smelled of roasted meat and the fresh, clean scent of the river, and suddenly I felt famished.

I walked up the hill toward the collection of pavilions and caught sight Adam, filling two crystal cups from the intricate silver fountain, which was wrought in the shape of horns piled on top of each other. Pale purple wine splashed from the rim of a trumpet and into the cups in Adam's hands. When they were full he left the shade of the tent and met me on the grass.

"Currant wine?" he asked, proffering a cup. "I think you'll like it. It's not as sweet as the plum from yesterday."

I took a long draught; it was crisp and cold and just the slightest bit sour. Precisely what I needed. "It's perfect," I said, wiping my mouth. Adam was grinning like a fool and hadn't touched his own cup. "You look awfully pleased about something," I said, eyeing him suspiciously. "Did you take all the best arrows for yourself?"

He chuckled, his face flushed from the sun. "No, I managed to leave a few for the others." With his free hand, he gestured to the tethered barge. "I hope you found the pleasure cruise sufficiently pleasurable."

"But of course." I paused, trying to summon a positive anecdote. "The river is beautiful, I see why you speak so fondly of this place." I followed his gaze down the hill and toward the Broom, which shone like a silver ribbon draped across a swath of green velvet. Sipping my wine, I marshaled my next words carefully. "I met your brother's wife. Princess Aveline. She's quite elegant."

"Much like a block of ice is elegant," he said bitterly. He frowned down at his cup. "She's not the friendliest sort; I'm sorry I wasn't by your side for your first encounter with her. Was she unkind to you?"

The heat of embarrassment rushed to my cheeks and I was about to tell him everything. The snide voice she used, the cutting words, the way she humiliated me before all those important women. But then I noticed Adam's mother under her own pavilion, reclining on a long divan laden with cushions. She caught my eye and paused in her conversation to lift her hand to me in greeting. A rush of gratitude swept through me and I forgot all about Aveline. Queen Janelle of Itomius—the most powerful woman in our part of the world, and my husband's mother—approved of me. That was all that mattered.

I handed my empty cup to Adam, who placed it along with his on a passing servant's tray. "How could anyone be unkind on such a beautiful day?" I said airily. "Now, why don't you show me what you've been up to all morning."

He offered me his arm, obviously pleased. "Excellent idea, Alyce. I'll take you to the armory. I believe Syrano's still there. You can meet him at last."

XIX

I am the first to say I know little of weaponry or anything to do with war. It isn't due to lack of interest; it simply was not part of my education. Since my uncle had intended to sell my hand in marriage to the prince or lord willing to pay the highest price, I was taught only that which he deemed necessary. And military matters were decidedly unnecessary for a Myrillan princess.

I did know the Myrillan armory during my uncle's reign was little more than a dank underground chamber with piles of rusty swords and shields scattered throughout. Its primary purpose was to serve as a hiding place for rats and roaches. Our army was famous for being ill-prepared and poorly outfitted; little did I know the extent of our impotence until I stepped into the royal Itomian armory. It didn't look like a place to store weapons; it looked like a museum. A long, narrow gallery, dimly lit by torchlight with a cool, stone floor. Polished shields hung on the walls, inscribed with ancient characters I couldn't recognize, interspersed with battle axes and swinging maces of every size. Full suits of armor stood here and there, as though filled with invisible bodies, and some held swords in their fleshless hands. Baskets of arrows and spears were clustered in groups organized according to length and purpose.

Toward the back wall a tall, dark-haired man was sorting through a rack laden with wooden bows. He heard us approaching and turned.

You may recall what Adam said about Syrano, that he was often deemed blessed by the gods. I did not know what he meant until I

149

saw Syrano myself. From the way Adam spoke about him I was almost expecting a male version of Aveline, endlessly sniping and critical. Or else a stodgy, humorless scholar who would find offense at my clumsy attempts at wit. But I was wrong on both counts. You never saw someone so peaceful and self-assured, as though he had no doubt of his place in the world. And it had nothing to do with his royalty. I had the feeling that even if he was born to a goat herder or a penniless beggar, he wouldn't be any different. He had the most gentle, quiet eyes, trustworthy yet full of fun at the same time. He wasn't your typical handsome prince—not nearly as handsome as Adam, I noted (to my own surprise). But there was something very different about Syrano. I could only stare at him, unsettled and perturbed, as his face broke into a wide smile.

"Queen Alcestis," he said, not waiting for Adam's introduction. "It's good to meet you at last." He bowed low and drew my hand to his lips.

I managed a stiff Itomian curtsey in response. "And you, Prince Syrano."

"I trust my wife and daughters welcomed you on the pleasure cruise?"

"They did, yes," I said, swallowing a little.

"Good. You'll meet my son, Claren, tomorrow. It's his first royal hunt so I'm making sure he gets plenty of rest. The hunting stories sure to be exchanged at the banquet tonight aren't ones to encourage sleep," he said with a wink.

His strange countenance affected me greatly; I could hardly think of anything to say. I gestured vaguely to the abundance of weaponry and forced myself to ask, "How are your preparations for the hunt coming along?"

"I daresay I'm as fit as I'll ever be, though not as fit as your husband. I've never seen him looking so robust and sound. Marriage seems to agree with you, brother. There's no greater gift from the gods than a loving wife." He looked from Adam to my mortified face. "And from what Admetus has told me, you surpass them all, Alcestis. He's talked of nothing else."

Adam's embarrassment mirrored my own. "If you don't mind, I brought Alyce down here to show her how I spent my morning, not to receive a discourse on marriage."

"Of course," said Syrano, but the glint in his eye made me suspect he'd figured out more about our relationship than he was letting on. "I apologize for missing dinner last night," he said to me, putting aside all the teasing. "I was attending to some business for our father. His health has given him trouble these past months. Traveling is much harder on him now. I'm sure my brother has told you."

"He hasn't." I turned to Adam. "You never mentioned that your father is unwell."

Adam seemed unbothered. "Syrano is always overreacting about these things, Alyce. Father is aging, yes, but he's perfectly fit. Why create distress where there's no proof?"

"But—"

"It's speculation," he said, a little sharply. "Nothing more. Now, where are the bowstrings, Syrano? I need to ready my replacements. Wait here for me, Alyce."

Syrano passed him a bundle of dried catgut and Adam stalked from the room, muttering that he would return in a moment. I watched the space where he had stood, suddenly cold, and rubbed my arms. Syrano replaced the bow he'd been handling and sighed. "Admetus knows his own mind, doesn't he? He's always been the stubborn one."

I nodded. "Almost as stubborn as I am."

I said it as a joke, but Syrano considered me. "I can see that," he said thoughtfully, then shook his head. "Don't misunderstand me, I don't mean to offend. It's probably one of the reasons you suit each other so well."

"I suppose," I said, not feeling much better. It wasn't the most flattering portrayal I'd ever heard of myself, but also not the worst.

"Alcestis," he said after a pause. "Alyce—if you prefer. I've never visited your home, but I know its history. Myrilla is famous for its struggles. I know your borders have been breached again and again, and that your fields have seen barren seasons more often than not." He hesitated. "I also know you've suffered a great deal, isn't that right?"

I ignored the lump rising in my throat. "Less than most," I said, my voice quivering. "I guess Adam's told you everything."

"Not everything, but some. You've seen where I grew up: endless fields and forests, all flanked by the glorious river. Not to mention calling this palace my home. You've met my parents, who have never

151

hidden their love from me. Believe me, Alyce, I cannot imagine what you've endured. To have lost both parents as a young child, only to be secreted away by an aunt and uncle who treated you with nothing but scorn and neglect...and then forced you to marry a perfect stranger. My brother or not, it still wasn't right. By the gods, it's a wonder your heart hasn't turned to stone." He watched me brush away the tears gathering my eyes. "But in spite of all those things, you're standing here today as the Queen of Myrilla. You're strong, Alyce. And your strength has strengthened my brother in endless ways. I hope one day you will see that for yourself."

I dried my cheeks with a swath of fabric from my skirt, sending a shower of gardenia petals floating to the floor. "Thank you, truly, Syrano." I tried to articulate the deep gratitude I felt, the comfort that his unquestioning acceptance gave me, but found I could not. "I... I thank you. Adam is a fine man, the best I've ever known. He's so generous and brave; I don't think anything in the world frightens him."

Syrano suddenly looked troubled. "Oh, he has his fears like anyone else."

"Like what?"

He looked to the doorway, where Adam's silhouette appeared in the light, carrying his newly strung bow. He seemed focused and cheerful, their earlier quarrel already forgotten.

"For as long as I can remember," Syrano said, "my brother has been terrified of death."

By the time we finished our tour of the armory it was late in the afternoon and dinnertime was hurtling quickly toward us. I knew better than to expect a private family meal that evening. With both Itomian princes present it would be a proper banquet, surpassed only by the celebratory feast once the hunt was finished. I had half forgotten about Aveline's offer to loan me a gown until we returned to our chamber and I saw a dark, velvet mass suspended from a hook. I called for Silda and asked her to help me dress early, certain I'd need a great deal of time to grow accustomed to wearing such a thing. She obliged, joining me behind the screen while Adam stretched out on the bed, testing the notches of the arrows against his bowstring.

"What did you think of Syrano?" Adam called to me as I stepped into the gown. It seemed to swallow my legs; the skirt alone must have been sewn from an entire bolt of fabric. With a slight grunt, Silda pulled it up so I could slip my arms into the long sleeves.

"He was very welcoming," I called back. "I thought he might have a low opinion of my background, but he spoke with nothing but kindness—" My words were cut off when Silda began to lace the gown. It was so tight it squeezed all the air from my lungs. I couldn't understand how it could possibly be so snug until I rested my hands on the bodice and felt long rows of bone sewn into the fabric. They chafed my ribs and pressed my breasts so firmly I squirmed in discomfort. Silda finished lacing the gown and tied the high collar shut, then stepped away so I could look at myself in the glass.

I studied my reflection. The gown was exquisitely made, without a doubt. Rich velvet brocade in midnight blue, studded with diamonds to look like stars in the night sky. But I felt strangled, as though the fabric was constricting around my torso and trying to impede my breath. Desperately, I slid two fingers under the collar in an attempt to loosen it, but to no avail. No wonder the Itomian women on the pleasure cruise moved so little, I thought. I could scarcely draw a deep draught of air, much less raise my arms. I stepped out from behind the screen, the gown's endless and heavy train puddling behind me.

"What do you think?" I asked uneasily.

Adam looked up from his bow. "Why are you wearing that?"

"Princess Aveline lent it to me. For dinner."

"Did you not bring enough clothes?" he asked, with a meaningful glance at my still very full trunk.

I rested my hands on the stomacher, stiff and immobile from the boning. My waist felt like it was encased in iron. "No, I have plenty. That's not…" I stopped, embarrassed. "Aveline made some remark earlier about the way I was dressed, and suggested I wear something of hers tonight."

Adam put down his bow and sat up slowly. "What sort of remark?"

I felt the color rising in my face. "She said my Myrillan gowns are inappropriate. Or indecent. I can't remember which word she used. And the other ladies agreed with her, I could tell from the way they snickered after she said it. Not your mother; she's been nothing but gracious. But the ones who were standing there…"

I trailed off, not meeting Adam's eyes. I heard him rise from the bed and only when he stood directly in front of me did I look at him.

"Alyce," he said steadily, "don't be angry with what I'm about to say." He drew a deep breath (I envied him for that). "But that is the most absurd thing I've ever heard."

I glared at him. "No, it isn't," I said, hot with indignation. "It may seem trivial to you, but these kinds of things are a critical part of state visits."

He burst out laughing. "State visits? Alyce, this is my family, remember? You said yourself we shouldn't be concerned about propriety. I'll agree with you that Aveline is not the most welcoming person when you first meet her—honestly, I wonder sometimes why Syrano ever married her—but you needn't worry so much. This is your first time outside Myrilla's borders since you were a child. I understand you're nervous, but I still want you to enjoy yourself. Don't let a bunch of whispering women ruin that for you. You're an excellent queen and they're fools if they can't see it."

I bit my lip and nodded. "I suppose you're right. And truly, I did enjoy the pleasure cruise," I said, the tension fading from my face. "I loved seeing where you grew up. It's a beautiful country, Adam."

"Thank you. I asked them to prepare it especially for you," he teased. "I had a fine time with you today as well."

He returned to the bed and picked up his bow once more. I turned around and kicked the heavy brocade train behind me, ready to ask Silda to unlace the gown and help me choose another from my own wardrobe. But before I stepped behind the screen, Adam called to me.

"Wait, Alyce."

I turned to him, pausing the act of gathering the skirts in my arms. "Yes?"

"Just one more thing," he said. "As for your Myrillan clothes, if you could have seen how you looked today, walking toward me over the lawn with flowers in your hair and that dress fluttering around your legs in the breeze…" his words died away, and I was surprised to see him blush. "Trust me, you'd never wear anything else."

154

XX

It was no surprise that the banquet Adam and I attended that evening was the most opulent I had ever seen. There are few places left in the world that still put on such extravagant affairs as the Itomians. The great hall—double the size of ours at home—was packed to the brim with the Itomian court and guests present for the boar hunt. Long tables buckled under the weight of stags and boars, roasted whole with their antlers or tusks set artfully in place, and enormous baskets of fish caught from the Broom River to be cooked over the fires to your liking. There were platters of beef, pork, and rabbit, interspersed with overflowing bowls of fruits and vegetables. Flagons of wine in every color were scattered along the tabletop so that if a servant didn't appear quickly enough to refill your glass, you could help yourself. Giddy laughter and good-natured arguments filled the hall, and when Adam and I paused on the threshold of the great doors, waiting for our introduction, we exchanged eager glances.

"King Admetus and Queen Alcestis, of Myrilla," announced the herald, and every head in the hall turned to look at Adam, their long-lost prince, and his new bride. My gown was the color of fresh butter, with forget-me-nots and cornflowers sewn into the sweeping skirt. Before Adam offered me his arm he had to brush away a few stray blue petals that had found their way to his sleeve. He led me through the gauntlet of tables, hissing names in my ear so quickly I could barely keep up.

"That's Prince Sabban, a friend of my father's. And Lord Hothpert and his wife, Lady Violette. Lord Ozias serves as steward to the northern half of the kingdom," he told me, gesturing to a young man with curly auburn hair and a distinct scowl. "I spent a summer with him when we were boys; his father tried to teach me to sail on Lake Windmast but I was a miserable disappointment. He told me I'd never make a seafarer."

"His son certainly looks miserable now," I whispered back. "I wonder what's the matter with him."

"Syrano told me his wife just gave birth a few days ago, so she couldn't join him here. He hates traveling without her. Now over there"—he nodded to a distinguished-looking woman, who gave him a rather cold glance in return—"that's Lady Prospera. She was desperate for me to marry her daughter. Kept shoving her toward me every chance she got."

"Poor girl," I said, amused. "And why didn't you oblige her?"

"She wasn't interested, I assure you. She said I was too loud and boisterous, and she was the stoniest prig you ever met. I could probably count on one hand the number of times I saw her smile. She's betrothed to a financier now, and quite happy. No hearts were broken."

We reached the high table and found our seats. Unlike our high table in Myrilla, where everyone sat facing each other, there were chairs only along one side of the table so that we could all see the hall. The arrangement enabled the servants to fill our plates for us without reaching over our backs, according to Adam. We stood behind our places until Syrano and his family entered (the cool look Aveline gave me when she saw my clothes could have frozen the sun), followed by Adam's parents. Once they were seated there was a great shuffle of chairs and the feast began.

At first I felt silly pointing out all the things I wanted to eat instead of taking the food from the great platters myself, but the young woman preparing my plate was gracious and helpful, explaining the contents of unfamiliar dishes. I soon found myself with a plate of spiced reed fish wrapped in silver fern leaves and baked, and a scattering of mushrooms stuffed with venison, blue peppers and goat's cheese. I sampled the latter with great skepticism, but quickly grew enamored with the salty, creamy tang.

The hall was nearly silent for all the happy eating, and only when I was on my second selection—thick black bread spread with the sweetest butter I had ever tasted—did Adam gesture to the man sitting to my right.

"You remember Lord Thaine, Alyce. He and his brother are here from Warkenland for the hunt."

Lord Thaine gave a satisfied nod, his dark eyes twinkling beneath bushy black eyebrows. "And greatly looking forward to it. May I have the pleasure of introducing my wife, Kassia." He reached for the hand of the woman beside him. She had fiery red hair and was heavy with child. "My brother Eroy's over there next to Prince Syrano. No doubt telling everyone in earshot how he plans to bring down the Caledonian boar tomorrow."

"With one arrow, I'll wager," Adam added, snickering.

I looked between them. "What's the Caledonian boar?"

"It's the king of the forest," said Lord Thaine, with a wide sweep of his arm. "Years ago, boars larger than warhorses used to fill the hunting grounds of Itomius. Nasty beasts, they were, and blood-thirsty. But over time their numbers have diminished, and now there's only one left. It's the ultimate prize for any true hunter."

"Boars larger than warhorses," I repeated, both fascinated and horrified by such a prospect. I turned to Adam. "You've seen one of these before?"

"I'm sorry to say I haven't," he admitted.

"And you'll be hard pressed to find anyone who has," said Lady Kassia, rolling her eyes in mirth. "I was born in Itomius and all my life I've heard how there's only one Caledonian boar left in the forest. I'm sure my mother heard the same story. And her mother before her. It's a myth, Queen Alcestis. The perfect quarry dreamed up by men to comfort themselves when they returned from hunts with empty quivers and no game."

"My wife is terribly practical," said Lord Thaine in a mock whisper. "Must be all that Itomian sensibility and work ethic hammered into her from birth. Not a drop of imagination between the lot of them. Impossible to live with, aren't they, Queen?"

Adam chuckled when he heard this. "Take care, sir," he shot back. "Else you'll find yourself imagining a new place to sleep to-night."

Spearing a roasted pheasant leg with his fork, Lord Thaine acknowledged the hit. "True, true. But really, Queen Alcestis, you must come with us on the hunt tomorrow," he said, gesturing for a servant to pour him another glass of wine. "None of this business of hanging back with the other ladies. You Myrillan queens are tough, the gods know that. Your grit is legendary, to have survived as many wars and invasions as you have—" Lady Kassia elbowed him swiftly in the ribs, cutting him off. He cleared his throat and lowered his head in apology. "No offense intended, of course, Queen."

The serving woman placed a bowl of thick rabbit stew before me. "None is taken, sir," I told him. "In fact, I'm flattered you have such a high opinion of my strength. I've never thought of myself as particularly formidable. Must be all those years of wars and invasions playing havoc on my confidence," I said, with a wink to his wife.

"Well, you're an example to us all, Queen," he said, lifting his goblet in a toast. I watched, amazed, as he drained the whole thing yet again and called for more. How he managed to stay upright in his chair escaped me completely. He looked past me at Adam. "What do you have to say about all this, King Admetus? Has your queen the nerve and skill to join the pursuit? Or will she be content to wait in your chamber, ready to warm the bed upon your return?" He paused. "Of course, that would take equal nerve and skill, being married to a beast like you."

Everyone in earshot laughed, appreciative of his bawdy jest. I didn't dare look at Adam; his embarrassment hovered beside me like a tangible cloud. The heat rose in my face and I tried desperately to think of some clever barb to toss back at him, but thankfully Lady Kassia came to my rescue.

"Don't tease them," she chided her husband. "They're still newly wed."

"The newly wed were made for teasing. The gods knew what they were doing when they designed the act of love. Nothing else could be so sacred and so amusing at the same time."

Lady Kassia shook her head. "A poet couldn't have said it better, good sir. But don't let him bully you into hunting, Queen," she said to me, "no matter how pretty his words are. I'd go myself, but not this year." She rested her hand on her rounded belly. Lord Thaine

158

beamed, and with tenderness that surprised me, placed his own hand on top of his wife's and kissed her.

"So, will you come?" asked Lord Thaine. "We need a woman's gentle hand to keep us monsters in line."

I swallowed the last bite of my stew and the empty bowl was instantly whisked away. The serving woman reached for my plate and began filling it with cuts of meat from the platters before us. I thanked her and held my knife and fork, considering Lord Thaine's question. "I never thought about going on the hunt. It certainly sounds like an adventure. I wouldn't want to be in the way, though. I haven't the experience the rest of you do. And the way you've all been talking it sounds awfully dangerous."

He nodded in agreement. "That's the thrill of it. Don't you agree, O wise King Admetus?"

Our eyes all turned to Adam, who was sipping his wine thoughtfully. "Yes, though there's a difference between doing something thrilling and something reckless," he said, with tact. "The boar hunt isn't a haphazard venture. It's full of sport and danger and good fun, but it's also a calculated undertaking. We choose our arms with great care and make sure our mounts are healthy in order to minimize accidents. We don't rush at the game like novice boys chasing a rabbit. Of course, accidents can and do still happen in the field, but not out of foolishness or neglect."

Lady Kassia nodded. "Well said. Sometimes when the gods call us home, they take away our weapons and leave us no choice, but other times we can fight our way out of their grasp."

A chill went down my spine. I inwardly squirmed at the way Itomians talked about the gods, without reverence or veneration. There was no fear in their voices, no respect or blood. It wasn't right, and I couldn't shake the feeling I'd be punished for it somehow. I felt the shadow of Kore looming over me, even in that banquet hall miles from the temple. I was almost eager to answer when Lord Thaine gave me an expectant look, still awaiting my decision about the hunt, simply to shake away Kore's disapproving presence.

"I must say each of you presents a compelling argument, and I'm quite keen on the idea. But I'd first like to hear my husband's honest opinion," I said, turning to Adam. "What do you think? Should I come?"

He studied me for a moment with an expression I couldn't quite read. I sat very still, certain he would dismiss me and say I'd be better off staying behind. Amidst his hesitation the servants brought out baskets of fruit and placed them on the table, accompanied by bowls of sugar and pitchers filled with honeyed cream. Adam chose a shiny green apple with a red blush on one side, cut it in two with his knife, and gave me one half. Finally, he answered, "Yes, I think you should come. In fact, it would make me very happy to have you there."

Lord Thaine's booming laughter filled the hall once more as Adam continued. "She's a fine rider," he said to Lord Thaine while he kept his eyes on me. "And she possesses both great nerve and skill"—he shot him a warning look—"so I believe she'd be a fine addition to our hunting party. We'd be honored to have you, Alyce."

"Thank you, Adam," I said, trying not to blush at his kind words. I spooned berries onto my plate and poured sweet cream over them, their red and purple juices swirling together in the white pool.

"Excellent. It's settled then." Lord Thaine cracked his goblet against mine and drank, then kissed his wife full on the lips. "Don't worry, Queen Alcestis, between me and my brother Eroy—and that husband of yours, of course—we'll make sure you return from the hunt in one piece. Just keep your mount near us and you'll be safe."

With that, he gave me a slow, heavy wink as only the very drunk attempt, and shoved his chair back to go speak with his brother further down the table. Next to me, Adam shook his head in amusement and reached for his plate of raisin cake and candied oranges. "What's so funny?" I asked.

He glanced up at Lord Thaine, who was now attempting to arm wrestle with his brother for the last sugared lemon. At least, what he thought was the last sugared lemon, since an entire bowl sat just to Adam's left. "Trust me, Alyce, if you want to be safe in the hunt you'll stay well away from Lord Thaine's and Lord Eroy's mounts."

Down the table, a great shout rose up when Lord Thaine won the precious lemon, lifting the prize over his head before he sliced it in half and squeezed the juice directly into his mouth. I couldn't help giggling, especially when Lady Kassia picked one up from the bowl next to Adam and tossed it at the back of her husband's head. I managed to look away from the spectacle long enough to scoop up the last of my berries.

"Why is that?" I asked Adam, raising my voice to be heard over the chaos.

He put his mouth close to my ear. "Because they don't ride horses," he practically shouted. "They ride bears."

XXI

I've never considered myself a particularly cosmopolitan queen; Lord Thaine may have been jesting when he hinted at my somewhat callous background, but he wasn't far off the mark. I did have a limited sphere of experience compared to other queens. Some experiences I could have gone without, such as the nastiness of Princess Aveline and her companions, with their insults thinly veiled and presented under the subtle guise of courtly Itomian talk that I found so perplexing. But I didn't know how far from home I had truly traveled until the next morning when I saw two great brown bears being led from the stables by a handful of very terrified-looking grooms, saddled and ready for a boar hunt.

Apparently, I was the only one unfamiliar with the brothers' mount of choice, because no one else seemed remotely surprised when Lord Thaine approached his bear and tossed it a whole silver trout, which the bear snatched out of the air with its frightfully sharp teeth. It chewed the fish for a moment before swallowing it in one gulp—an uncanny rendering of its master guzzling wine the previous night.

Since the hunt would take place throughout Itomius's extensive network of forests, everyone dressed in shades of green and brown in an effort to blend with the surroundings. I proved no exception; my dress was dark, the same green as a pine tree, with slender bunches of fragrant fir needles sewn into the fabric along the trim. I felt much too warm wearing long sleeves on such a sunny day, but Adam insisted, saying my pale skin would startle the game. Lord

Thaine, in his mud-colored hunting clothes with a quiver strapped to his back, nodded toward the bears. "Would you care for an introduction, Queen Alcestis?"

I swallowed, eyeing them nervously. "They look dangerous."

"I know how fierce they look, but if it comforts you, keep in mind that Eroy and I found them as cubs while out on a hunt very much like this one and have raised them since. The gods sent them to us as a gift, I'm sure of it. The poor motherless creatures wouldn't have survived without us. They're so accustomed to being around humans that they're as tame as your horse."

He offered me his arm and I accepted it mutely, wondering what I had gotten myself into. Talk of a hunt is all well and good when you're sitting at a banquet table, but it's quite different when you're surrounded by barking dogs and the stench of boar urine. As Lord Thaine led me toward the bears I spotted Adam in a cluster of men, all testing their bowstrings. He looked oddly tense, speaking with Syrano in a low voice that I couldn't make out in the distance between us. I didn't have time to ponder his strange mood long, however, for a moment later my heart nearly stopped when I found myself nose to snout with Lord Thaine's bear. Its clean fur looked silky and soft, but I wasn't fooled by its lovable appearance. Its legs were thicker than the columns back in the palace and one swipe from its paw could have easily crushed my skull. The top of my head barely reached its shoulders in height.

Lord Thaine scratched the bear behind its ear. "Queen Alcestis, it is my pleasure to introduce to you my hunting partner: Daisy."

I thought he was joking. Surely such a fierce animal would have more violent sounding name, like Killer or Destroyer. When I realized he was serious I let out a laugh, then quickly clamped my mouth shut for fear of startling the bear. Its ears pricked and it lowered its head, touching my forehead with its wet, rubbery nose. I froze in place, hardly daring to breathe as the bear sniffed my hair and my cheek. I closed my eyes as it smelled my neck, praying it wouldn't tear open my throat with the terrible white blades concealed in its maw.

After what felt like an endless inspection, the bear snorted in my face, its fish-scented breath blowing back the loose curls that had fallen over my brow. I could have sworn the bear looked almost bored as it blinked at Lord Thaine, clearly requesting another fish as payment for tolerating my presence. The other bear didn't so much as glance at me. I didn't mind at all.

"They both look well," said Adam, appearing beside me. He put his hand to my elbow and drew me backwards, away from the bear. "When's the last time you brought them on a hunt?"

"Oh, I take her out at least once a week." Lord Thaine reached out and patted Daisy's haunches, his hand disappearing into the luxurious carpet of fur. "But that's just the two of us. In a group like this? I'd say it's been a year. She'll behave, though. As long as those dogs don't get underfoot and annoy her."

"If they do, they'll be sorry," put in Lord Eroy, looking up from cleaning his bear's paws. "Dogs learn by example. It only takes one to suffer a broken back to set the others to right. I just wouldn't want to be that dog."

As if in response, the dogs began howling in chorus. I thought for a wild moment they might have understood Lord Eroy's words, but then a heavily bearded man lifted a bone-white horn to his lips and blew. The bright, vibrant sound echoed through the stable yard, sending the dogs into a greater frenzy. Even the horses caught the horn's energy, arching their necks and tilting their ears forward, eager to make chase. The bears snarled and growled, their paws stamping the dirt as the brothers—with two men boosting each of them—climbed into their saddles. They had utterly transformed from the docile creatures I had met earlier. Now I understood why Adam had advised me to keep my distance from them during the hunt. One false step and they'd rip you to shreds.

Amid the raucous participants I spotted one reluctant observer clinging glumly to his horse's reins. He was young, scarcely more than a boy; beneath his fair Itomian hair his face was nearly a perfect match to Syrano's, though considerably greener in color. I left Adam in his discussion with one of the dog handlers and led my horse toward the boy. "Hello," I called, not bothering to attempt an Itomian curtsey. "I believe you're my long-lost nephew."

I'd hoped he would at least smile, but he only nodded. "I'm Prince Claren, and you're my aunt, Queen Alcestis. I wasn't at the banquet last night. Father wanted me to rest. It's my first proper boar hunt."

"Mine too. I've never hunted anything, in fact."

His green pallor brightened with his astonishment. "You haven't? But you're a queen."

"I haven't been a queen for very long," I admitted. "There isn't much opportunity for hunting in my homeland. And this is my first foreign visit since I married your uncle."

His brow wrinkled as he considered this. "That's a good point," he said slowly. "Mother did say you grew up very poor. Poor people don't go on hunting parties."

He said it with the characteristic bluntness of a child, no malice intended, but it still sent a wince skipping across my face. Before I could begin to string together a response he looked me straight in the eyes and said, "But I don't care if you know how to hunt or not. You're a kind lady, Aunt Alcestis."

With all the grace of a seasoned courtier, Claren drew my hand to his lips and kissed it, then swept a low bow in farewell. I watched him make his way to his father, his posture much straighter and more confident than before.

"Hunters, up!"

The bearded man blew into the horn again, and the few hunters remaining on foot scrambled into their saddles. I looked around for Adam, a tiny flicker of anticipation coursing through my belly. He made his way to me through the throng and clapped his hands together.

"Ready, Alyce?"

I nodded stiffly. "I am."

Hunting calls and shouts went up all around, but I was too nervous to join in. Trembling with excitement, I gripped my horse's reins and gratefully allowed Adam to help me into my saddle, though as I moved my foot to fit it into my stirrup, he continued to hold my boot.

"There's something I want to make sure you understand," he said, suddenly serious. "Caledonian boar aside, these woods are teeming with dangerous creatures. You must stay with me; don't leave my side. If for any reason we are separated, find Syrano and ride with him. If you end out on your own I want you to ride back to the palace and wait for me there."

I bit my lip and nodded again. "Of course."

The horn blew a third time, and he grinned, bright-eyed with happiness. "I'm glad you're here with me, Alyce," he said, and swung himself into his saddle. I guided my horse beside his, and before I could blink, we were off.

Having never hunted before, I didn't know what exactly to expect. What surprised me most was how long the whole business took. After the initial bolt into the heart of the forest, the pace slowed considerably. The dogs had to stop time after time to reclaim the scent, and as they darted to and fro with their noses pressed to the ground the rest of us were left to wander idly. The bears lumbered along, pausing to sharpen their front claws on the odd tree trunk and frightening any roosting birds or nearby squirrels. As we progressed I found myself utterly enchanted by the beauty of the forest. The trees were enormous; their high branches entwined overhead to form a thick canopy shading the forest floor. Every so often we'd splash through a shallow creek bordered by cool ferns and flowering shrubs, with mossy boulders crouching nearby. Birds flitted past us, little more than black darts against the green ceiling. If it weren't for our noisy party the only sounds in the forest would've been trickling water and the rustle of leaves.

My joy in the hunt grew as the hours passed. My legs ached from riding and I grew so hungry that even Adam could hear my quaking stomach. When we dismounted for a little break he fished in his saddlebag for a piece of hard bread, accompanied by a strip of meat. He passed them to me, and I wolfed both down so quickly I found myself staring at my empty hand, wondering where the food had gone.

"Fine dining, isn't it?" Adam took a swing from his wineskin and passed it to me. "I'm afraid that's the life of the hunt for you. You can only eat what you carry or kill."

I swallowed a mouthful of the sticky-sweet wine. "Indeed. It's a good thing crops don't run off and hide after you plant them, else Myrilla would starve."

Adam pointed to one of the dogs. It had wandered slightly away from the others and was sniffing the roots of an old oak tree. "That one's about to catch the scent," he whispered. "Just watch him."

I did. The dog had wiry grey fur and moved methodically over the forest floor. "How can you tell?"

"He's the only one with the courage to leave the safety of the group. The others will be tripping over themselves for ages trying to find it, but it'll take them twice as long."

The dog lifted its head and I was startled to see its eyes were cast in milky white. "Oh," I gasped. "He's blind."

"And a better hunting dog for it," said Adam, lit up with pride. "He's older than all the others, with more experience than the rest of them combined. His nose could smell out a three-day-old trail."

I turned toward him and raised my eyebrows. "I have a feeling you know this dog."

"His name is Kingfisher. He's my father's. They hunted together every season until Father gave it up." He sighed. "It's a pity he didn't come today, don't you think, Syrano?" he asked as his brother rode up beside us.

"Father hasn't hunted in months, Admetus," he said gently. "It's too hard on him."

"That's absurd. He's always been an athlete of the highest caliber. He could ride rings around you and I."

Syrano shook his head and dismounted. "This past winter was unforgiving; his lungs took the water and he hasn't been the same since."

"Father's more fit than anyone else here and you know it," Adam argued. "Just because you think he's an old man—"

"That's precisely what he is, Admetus," said Syrano, in his voice of unrelenting calm. "In your mind he's ageless, but in reality he's quite elderly. He knows it as well."

Adam stopped walking, outraged. "How dare you say such a thing about our lord father? Are you going to push him out of the throne as soon as his seat is warm enough for you? It would shame him to hear you talk in such a way."

I watched Syrano, certain he would lose his temper now, but he merely shook his head again. "It has nothing to do with thrones or politics, and you'd know that if you'd listen to a word I've said. Not all men fear death as you do. Father has done great things in this life; it's no disrespect to wish him safe passage into the next."

The dog—Kingfisher—brayed. Adam was right, he had caught the scent first. I looked at him, ready to congratulate him on his accurate guess, but his face was so hard and far away in thought that I only reached out and touched his arm instead. He glanced down at my hand, then shook himself and threw his reins over his horse's neck. "What frightens me more than anything right now," said Adam, his voice calmer, "are those two monsters up there." He nodded toward the bears. "I know Thaine and Eroy raised those animals from cubs, but they don't have obedience in their blood. They were never meant to be tamed."

"I know what you mean," said Syrano. He waved for Claren to join us. "Keep good distance from them, Alcestis. I'm loathe to think how my brother would survive if the gods snatched you away."

I checked the tightness of my girth, ready to resume chase, but the cluster of dogs that had disappeared so eagerly into the trees a moment before now returned to the clearing in hasty retreat. The eager baying faded into shrill whimpers and cowering tails. I glanced at Adam, about to ask him what had happened, but he looked as confused as I.

Our silent questions were answered, however, when a horrific crashing sound echoed through the clearing. We all watched in mute terror as the giant Caledonian boar—indeed, taller than a warhorse—emerged from the dense trees with blood smeared on its tusks and its coarse fur dappled in the sunlight.

XXII

I know how foolish it makes me sound to admit this, but my very first thought upon seeing the Caledonian boar was that it couldn't possibly be real. I thought it might be an elaborate illusion drawn up for our amusement, like a play-battle in a court entertainment. The idea of a boar of such great size seemed mockingly impossible at the banquet; even Adam had admitted to never laying eyes on one. Now it stood before me, a mere stone's throw away.

I was not alone in my astonishment. It felt as though a full minute had passed before anyone moved or spoke. The boar scraped its bloody tusks against a tree, casually, ignoring our presence. I could only see the eyes set in its flat face when it turned its head to the side, and its cloven hooves pawed mildly at the leaves underfoot. Its tail switched back and forth like a whip, and it was so tall I wasn't sure I could have touched the top of its ears if I stood on tiptoe and stretched out my arms.

"By the gods, it's a monster," I heard someone swear.

From the corner of my eye I saw Lord Thaine notch an arrow to his bowstring. Adam spotted it too. "Don't shoot," he hissed.

Lord Thaine, his face pale, didn't hear my husband's warning. He drew his string and with a sharp twang the arrow struck the boar in its side. It snorted loudly, but instead of falling to the ground, dead, its eyes rolled in fury. Only its outrage kept it from charging immediately, and in that split second of hesitation, pandemonium ensued. Horses and dogs sprinted for the trees, leaving their human handlers chasing after them on foot. One of the bears let out an earsplitting roar while Lord Eroy scrambled onto its back. Somewhere in the chaos Adam grabbed my hand and pulled me toward my horse, which had wandered away without my knowing.

He caught the reins before the horse could bolt and shoved me up into the saddle. "The fool's angered it now," he shouted over the rabble. "It'll take a hundred arrows to bring it down, and that's if it doesn't kill us all first."

"Admetus!" I heard Syrano call. Gripping his son's arm, he pushed toward us. "Take Alyce and ride away from here. I'm sending Claren with Lord Farlow."

He set Claren on his horse and the boy picked up the reins. In the clearing behind him, the boar gored a man's leg and a red river poured onto the dirt. "But, Father," protested Claren, "I want to help."

"And you are brave for it, my son. But two princes cannot fight the same battle."

Before I could hear Claren's response Adam appeared on his mare beside me and, with a slap to my horse's hindquarters, we galloped into the trees. The ground was rocky and the horse stumbled several times, nearly sending me out of the saddle. Birds screeched high above, but nothing could drown out the screams behind us. They seemed to carry through the woods, fighting to keep up with our horses. Adam flew beside me, leaning over his horse's neck, urging it to run faster, faster. Leafy branches scratched at my face; I felt a cool trickle creeping over my eyebrow, I wiped it and my fingers came away bloody.

We reached the edge of another clearing and Adam abruptly pulled his horse to a stop. I followed suit, tugging on the reins so firmly my horse threw its head in protest. I watched Adam, breathing hard. I had no idea how far we had ridden or where we had ended up. Neither of us spoke for several seconds.

"Will the others come soon?" I asked, simply to break the dreadful silence.

Adam shook his head. "I don't know."

Another scream sounded in the distance. Buzzards had gathered and now circled overhead. I squeezed my eyes shut, trying to hold back my tears. "What did Syrano mean, when he said two princes can't fight in the same battle?"

170

"He was talking about the succession. If both princes fell there'd be no heir to the throne."

I nodded and swallowed a hard lump in my throat. "I see."

A rustle came from the cluster of trees to our left. Adam drew his sword and turned his horse toward the noise. I lifted my reins, ready to fly like the coward I was, but the shape that emerged from the bushes stood not on four legs, but two.

"Aunt…Aunt Alcestis," it called, pitifully.

"Claren!" I shouted. "How did you get here?"

"My horse threw me, I've been running as fast as I can. Then I heard your voice." Claren staggered and Adam leapt from his saddle to steady him.

"What about Lord Farlow? Where is he?"

"Last I saw he was still riding. My horse followed his."

Adam held him by the shoulders. "Did you see the boar?"

Claren nodded, his eyes wide with terror.

"Where?"

"Back there, sir. He's hideously fast."

"Indeed he is. Now, Claren, I can't give you my horse, but you can share my wife's." He lifted the boy onto the back of my saddle. Claren's arms wrapped around my waist in a vice-like grip; I was sure I'd have to pry him off me if we ever made it out of the forest alive. "The boar is fast, as you said, and clever. He'll follow our scent. If he doesn't find us himself the dogs will lead him to us without realizing what they're doing. I'll wait here and hold him off. The two of you ride back to the palace and tell them what's happened."

"I don't know where the palace is," I protested. "If you leave us we'll be lost—"

Adam cut me off. "Claren, you can find your way home, right? You know these woods. All Itomian princes do. Can you follow that creek to where it feeds into the Broom?"

Claren nodded. "Yes sir."

"Good. Now, it is time to be brave." He pulled a long knife from his belt and held it out to Claren. "I want you to carry this with you. You must protect your aunt; she's very precious to me." Claren took the knife and nodded gravely. "Good. Ride quickly, Alyce. I'll see you at the palace."

A horrible, sick feeling sprouted in my belly. "Adam, please don't—"

"Ride, Alyce!"

He struck my horse with the flat of his sword and she took off, stumbling slightly from the added weight. Birds flew before us, disturbed from their ground nests as we galloped across the clearing. Claren shouted directions in my ear and though I could barely hear over the rushing wind I obeyed the best I could. East, then north, always coming back to the creek. My only consolation was the absence of agonizing screams; at least Adam hadn't met the boar.

Once more we found ourselves in thick forest. The horse was slowing; I smelled the sweat foaming on her sides. I drove my heels into her again and again, still her pace continued to fall. I saw a dark flash of fur in the trees to my left and my pulse quickened. I opened my mouth to ask Claren if he was sure we were heading in the right direction, but before I could utter a word the dark thing crashed through the trees. It wasn't the boar, thank the gods, but one of the bears. Wild-eyed and streaked with foam, it carried no rider. At the sight of it the horse reared and wheeled around, sending Claren into the dirt beneath its hooves. I jumped down at once, terrified he'd been trampled, but the moment I left the saddle the horse went tearing into the woods and out of sight.

I pulled Claren to his feet and he drew Adam's knife with a shaking hand, his eyes round as he took in the bear. Blood dripped from its jaws, and it left wet black footprints where it walked.

"Don't make any quick movements," I whispered to Claren, keeping my gaze on the bear. Silently, I drew Claren closer to a wide tree, hoping the bear wouldn't notice us. But it sniffed the air and fixed its shiny eyes in our direction. I raised my hand very slowly, mimicking the motion I'd seen the brothers use when they mounted up earlier, in an attempt to calm the beast. If it would have worked, I'll never know, for Claren clutched the knife and raced toward the bear. He lifted the blade as if to throw it but didn't get the chance. The bear suddenly lunged forward, leaping higher than I would have ever thought possible. I dove to the ground and grabbed Claren's legs. He fell with a breathless thud; too late I realized with a jolt of horror that he could have fallen on Adam's knife and I would be to blame. But there was no time to think of that. I squeezed my eyes shut and waited for the bear to savage our bodies with its claws, or for its teeth to tear at my skin and hair, but nothing happened. I heard a roar behind us and looked up just in time to see the bear tackling the boar, only meters away from where I had stood.

In an instant I was up and had dragged Claren—thankfully, blessedly uninjured—to his feet. With only one glance at the boar my fear surged anew. "The horse is gone, we have to run," I breathed, pulling Claren after me. I looked over my shoulder, thinking I'd see the boar and bear still locked in combat, but they had crashed elsewhere. In my moment of distraction I tripped on a rock and stumbled. A hand caught my shoulder and I nearly screamed.

Thank the gods! It was only Adam. "Are you all right?" he demanded. I nodded, unable to speak for my joy, and he looked at Claren. "Well done, nephew. Come with me, we're almost to the palace."

Claren's green complexion had returned and the knife trembled in his hand. The three of us ran, and though I knew we were more vulnerable than ever, relief coursed through my body with having Adam at the helm once again.

We hadn't run far when I heard the now familiar hoofbeats and grunting of the boar. The palace was still nowhere in sight, and my legs ached from the hard riding. Claren, for all his effort, was fading fast. He slipped on the leaves again and again, and each time Adam or I helped him up he felt heavier. "Adam," I said, panting as I pulled Claren after me. "He won't make it much longer. We have to stop."

"We can't, Alyce. The boar is badly injured but he'll still kill us if he gets the chance."

My jaw clenched with rage. Never had I hated an animal so much. "Then let's climb a tree and wait for it to die."

He opened his mouth to argue, but when the hoofbeats grew louder he snapped it shut. He turned, searching, then sprinted for a maple tree.

"This'll do. Now hurry." He cupped his hands in a foothold. Sweat poured from his forehead. "Climb as high as you can. Quickly, Alyce."

I glanced back at the trees, we had only seconds before the boar would spot us. "No. Claren first."

Before Adam could argue, I put Claren's foot in my husband's outstretched hands, and between the two of us we heaved him into the tree. A branch snapped behind us and we both whipped around to see the boar breaking through the dense undergrowth. Adam gripped my hand, pulling me away. The only spot capable of providing any cover was a cluster of tangled holly bushes. We scrambled beneath it and flattened ourselves beneath the prickly leaves.

I fought to lay perfectly still, taking short, shallow breaths lest any sound give us away. Adam pressed close to me, his eyes locked on mine. My arms were folded and trapped against his chest; I couldn't move even if I had wanted to. I desperately hoped Claren had climbed out of sight and was keeping silent. I heard the boar approaching the holly bush from behind me and swallowed tightly. *Just lie still*, I told myself. *Just don't move and this will all be over in a minute.*

The boar's heavy steps came to a halt, and I heard a rustling sound as it sniffed the fallen leaves littering the muddy floor. The sound traveled closer and closer until I felt its rubbery snout prodding through the sharp leaves and brushing against my back. I squeezed my eyes shut, though no tears escaped. I was terrified to the point where crying wasn't remotely possible. The boar's bloody tusk grazed my ribs and Adam's hand closed around mine. Why wouldn't the horrible beast just die? It had to be close; the stench of blood and ruined flesh filled my nostrils, so strong I nearly gagged on my own breath.

Something else pressed against my back, and when I flicked my eyes upward I saw the boar's front leg raised overhead through the leaves. I realized with a lurch of horror that it was trying to step over the holly. My relief at not being gored was quickly eclipsed by the fear that it would stumble in its weakened state and crush our bodies into pulp. My fingers clung to Adam's as I felt the three remaining hoofs knock into my back before scraping the leaves above. Only when the final hoof touched the ground behind Adam did I let my body relax. The boar let out a strangled cry of agony, and then sank to its knees. Its body hit the earth so hard I could've sworn I heard the trees shake, and a handful of new leaves floated down from the high branches.

I started to edge my way out of the shrub, but Adam held me down. "Not yet," he murmured so quietly I could barely hear him. "It's probably dead, but we need to wait to be sure."

I nodded, not daring to speak. The cool breeze returned and I shivered, burrowing closer to him for warmth. Very slowly, Adam reached forward with his free hand and touched my face, brushing his thumb along my cheekbone. "Are you hurt?" he asked, barely audible. When I shook my head, he breathed deeply through his nose, satisfied.

The minutes passed slowly and the sun had shifted to a place high in the sky when we finally stirred from our hiding place. Adam slid from under the holly bush and helped guide me out. The prickly leaves caught at my hair and my hands were smeared with mud when I finally emerged, but I'd never cared less how I looked.

It took some coaxing before Claren left the safety of the tree to join us on foot. He clung to the branch, half-hidden by the leaves, until Adam finally convinced him the boar was dead and he was safe. The moment his feet touched the ground he threw his arms around my waist, trembling and pale. Then, as if he'd remembered the responsibility Adam had tasked him with, he frowned and said, "Are you well, Aunt Alyce? The boar didn't injure you?"

I resisted the impulse to brush his hair back and kiss his forehead as though he were a little boy. "Not in the least, Prince Claren. I am as well as I've ever been, thanks to you."

Adam reached for my hand. "The others are probably waiting at the palace. Let's start that way."

We didn't run, instead we walked quickly and quietly along the creek. It wasn't long before the woods opened into green fields and I spotted the river in the distance. The gleaming palace perched on top of the hill, perfect as ever, untouched by the turmoil of the hunt. Adam looked down at my hand, clasped tightly in his, and met my eyes with a soft smile.

Claren ran ahead of us, it wasn't long before he was just a colorful speck racing across the grass. I made no effort to hurry; I let my mind wander lazily, thinking of the delicious cold drinks waiting under the pavilion and the hot bath I'd enjoy later in the evening. I'd already half-pushed the hunt from my mind; the boar was dead and we had survived, nothing else mattered.

I pointed to a cluster of men under one of the pavilions. "It looks like they're getting help for the man who was gored. I hope he isn't hurt too badly."

Adam craned his neck to look as we ascended the slope. "If they act quickly enough he should be fine. As long as it's kept clean and infection doesn't settle in."

As we drew closer I saw that not only were the other hunters crowded around the man, but Adam's parents as well. Even Princess

Aveline and her daughters were heading towards the pavilion. I thought it was awfully decent of them to come out and visit the injured man, and nearly said so to Adam, but the words stopped in my throat when I saw not the man who had been gored, but a familiar head of dark hair and those gentle eyes, snuffed of all light.

I stopped walking, forcing Adam to stop too. He looked at me, puzzled. "What is it?"

"Adam—" I started, drawing him further back, but then Aveline's scream tore across the lawn like a razor ripping through silk. "Adam...Adam don't..." I nearly begged. "Please don't look over there—"

Without a word he shook me off and charged to the pavilion, but Lord Thaine stepped in front of him. His eyes were red and his hat hung limply from his hands. Blood poured from a deep cut in his cheek and stained his collar. "I'm sorry, Admetus," he said through thick tears. "I'm so sorry. Syrano is gone. Your brother is dead."

XXIII

There is perhaps only one thing that can feel as terrible as losing someone you love. And that is watching someone else learn of a loved one's death. You're frozen and helpless, little more than a sculpture standing sentry, unable to look away. There is nothing you can do to assuage the pain, to make it better. You are powerless beyond compare.

When Adam heard Lord Thaine's words, he became possessed with what I can only describe as a terrible surge of strength. It didn't come right away, though. It built like a tidal wave approaching a vulnerable beach. At first he could only stare at Lord Thaine, mute with disbelief. Then, as he studied my face, he furrowed his brow. "He's made a mistake, Alyce," he said. "Don't look so upset. They're all mistaken. That can't be Syrano."

"Adam." I fought to steady my voice while desperately trying to draw him away from the pavilion. "Come here for just a moment and sit down—"

"I don't *need* to sit. There's just been a mistake, everything's fine. I'll show you," he insisted, flinging my hand from his arm. When Lord Thaine tried to stop him, Adam shoved him out of the way and elbowed past the others until he was under the pavilion. I followed after him, my head throbbing from Aveline's continued screams; from the corner of my eye I saw Claren sitting at the edge of the crowd with his arms around his sisters as they cried quietly into his chest. My heart shattered into pieces; I wanted to go to them and kiss them and distract them and get them away from the pavilion,

177

but my mind was with Adam. He had forced his way to the center and was kneeling beside his brother's body, hysterically ordering the physicians to do anything, try anything, give him any medicine or perform any surgery that would help Syrano.

"It isn't too late to stop the bleeding," he kept saying. "Make a poultice and get him some wine to drink—"

"Adam—" I placed my hand on his shoulder but he threw it off.

"Send for the surgeon and get him inside," he ordered one of the servants. "Be careful not to move his head too much, his neck could be injured."

I crouched beside him, trying not to look directly at Syrano's lifeless body. "Adam, listen to me—"

"There isn't time, Alyce! Send for more bandages—" He pointed at one of the bewildered servants, but before he could spew out any more instructions I gripped both his hands in mine, forcing him to meet my eyes. He didn't seem to see me at all. "Let go, Alyce. I have to—"

"Stop, Adam," I begged. "Just…stop."

Slowly, realization seeped through his determined face and he finally understood what had happened. I felt his body relax and my tears began to flow.

"I'm sorry," I whispered, still gripping his hands. "Lord Thaine was right. Syrano's gone. I'm so sorry," I repeated.

Silently, he lifted his head and gazed around the pavilion, taking in the grief-stricken faces as though seeing them for the first time. He looked at his parents, little more than a lost child seeking an explanation—any explanation—and then his brother's body. He touched Syrano's cold hand and his shoulders heaved with silent, cruel grief.

I could only watch, paralyzed with despair, until Adam's father stood and told us to go into the palace, that there was nothing more we could do. At least, that is what I think he said. I could only hear Adam's sobs. But the next thing I knew I was walking up the palace steps, clutching my husband's hand so he wouldn't collapse to the ground.

We waited in one of the private galleries for some time; eventually Adam's parents joined us, drained from the terrible events of the afternoon. None of us spoke. Only later would I learn that Syrano had stopped to help a fallen hunter to his feet when the boar gored him in the thigh. The physician assured us he wouldn't have suffered long since the blood drained quickly from that particular spot in the leg. A small comfort in the darkness of his absence.

Aveline and her children were the last to arrive. I waited until the king and queen had spoken to them before I made my way toward Aveline. She looked absolutely exhausted, and underneath her flawless veneer I could see that she was a woman just like me, only she had just lost the most important person in her life. After all, Adam could have easily been the one killed in the hunt instead of Syrano. She sat in a carved wooden chair before the empty fireplace, staring into the dark space where the flames should've been. I approached quietly, wringing my hands and unsure how to start.

"Princess Aveline?" When she didn't answer I took a step closer and dropped my voice. "I want you to know…I am truly sorry for what happened to your husband. I know nothing I say will do anything to help, but if there is any assistance I can provide you or your family, please know that I am at your service."

Still, she never moved. I watched her profile—so perfect it could have been minted on a coin—and started to turn away. Just in time I remembered to curtsey, hoping to please her. Something about it must have caught her attention, because she rose gracefully from her chair.

"Pretty words," she said, with a wintry smile. "You are a poet and a sage, Alcestis."

I faltered. "I'm not sure what you mean."

"You're a poet because you always manage to say what people wish to hear. And you're a sage because you speak the truth, sometimes more accurately than you realize." Her lovely eyes narrowed. "It's quite true that you should be at my family's service. In fact, I'd wager most of the servants in this palace are of higher birth than you. Perhaps you should serve them as well. Only, they probably won't want you touching their shoes with your dirty Myrillan hands."

I said nothing. My heart pounded in my throat and my fingers turned numb. I was vaguely aware that everyone else in the gallery had fallen silent and was watching our exchange with morbid fascination.

179

"I'm sorry, Princess Aveline…" I started, flinching as she took a step closer to me. The emeralds and sapphires gleaming from her fingers and neck looked more like sharp tools for torture than objects of beauty.

"You have much to be sorry for. You are the very picture of injustice. It is new proof that the gods' cruelty knows no bounds," she went on, her words flying like arrows, "that my husband lies cold on that slab while yours will sleep next to you tonight. You," she spat, "a filthy farmer's daughter who has the nerve to call herself a queen."

A split second of silence followed. I felt as though she had slapped me; I even lifted my hand to my cheek, expecting to feel her blazing fingerprints on my skin. But she hadn't moved. I heard footsteps and from somewhere beside me I felt Adam's arm encircle my waist, attempting to draw me away. I somehow obeyed his entreaties and allowed him to guide me to a chair. Once I was settled he turned abruptly to face Aveline, his mouth already open and loaded with a livid retort, but his father stepped in front of him.

"Not now," King Verian murmured. "The children are present."

Adam's voice shook with rage. "Father, she can't—she can't speak to my wife that way—"

"I'm as angry as you, about all of it," said his father, and I was horrified to see tears welling in his eyes. "But this is not the place for angry words." He looked past Adam's shoulder at me. "Queen Alcestis, I believe your husband is in need of some fresh air. Would you kindly escort him to the courtyard?"

I nodded, not daring to speak. I pushed myself out of the chair and lightly touched Adam's arm. He needed no coaxing; he thrust open the gallery door himself and pulled me into the corridor behind him. Servants leapt out of his way as he thundered toward the rear doors, towing me along. I glanced back in the direction of the central courtyard, our intended destination. "Where are we going?"

He ordered two very alarmed servants to open the heavy doors. "You'll see in a moment," he said, not looking at me.

Outside, the air felt unusually frigid. I wrapped my free arm around myself, not sure if I was shivering from the temperature or the encounter inside. Adam kept up his relentless pace as he led me through the park and down to the river where a little boat floated beside the royal barge, tethered to the mammoth dock. When I realized he intended for us to take a journey in this strange watercraft I dug my heels in the grass and wrenched my arm from his grip.

"What are you doing?" I demanded. "I'm not getting in there."

"Get in the boat, Alyce. Please."

"I won't!" My voice trembled. "Not until you tell me what's going on."

He was immovable. "You're being ridiculous. It's perfectly safe."

"I don't care how safe the *boat* is, it's you I'm worried about." I took a step back. "You're frightening me, Adam."

Finally he stopped pawing the ground like a nervous stallion. He rubbed his forehead as the little boat knocked gently against the dock. "I'm sorry," he said quietly. "That isn't my intent, Alyce, I swear it. If you will please come with me, I'd like to show you something. It's not far up the river, but it's on the other side. We have no choice but to take a boat."

I watched him, still unsure, but I put my hand in his and allowed him to help me into the boat. It wobbled on my entry and I perched on the narrow seat, hugging my knees to keep warm. Before he untied the rope and joined me, Adam removed his cloak and draped it around my shoulders. When I asked him if he wouldn't be cold, he shook his head.

"I'll keep warm, don't worry," he said, picking up the oars.

Riding in this boat was vastly different from the royal barge. Here I was only inches above the water, and if I had liked I could have plunged my whole arm into the icy depths, not just the tips of my fingers. We skimmed the water close to the bank, close enough for me to spot several heron nests hidden amongst the tangled reeds. Adam rowed with veteran skill, perfectly slicing the oars through the icy water in almost lyrical rhythm. I wanted to enjoy it, to revel in its distraction, but I was too concerned about my husband. We didn't speak; the only sound was of him pulling fiercely at the oars, accompanied by the birds overhead.

The landscape opened into lush pastureland, and it wasn't long before Adam steered us to a low inlet in the bank and leapt ashore. I held the oars while he dragged the front of the boat onto the mud and lashed it to a sapling. He took my hands and pulled me up, keeping the boat steady with his foot as I stepped onto the bank. On this side of the river it felt warmer, and the sweet smell of hay filled the air. In spite of the mild breeze a chill raced down my spine. I gazed out at the green fields, sprinkled through with laurel trees, and scowled. To my eyes it appeared simple enough, but the stirring in my heart told me otherwise. Never before had I stood in such an odd place. It held secrets, I could tell instantly. The very air was charged with mystery. For some wild reason I found myself thinking of the temple at home, with its grain and stone and pictures. Except this field came without the security of walls. I felt small, exposed, just as I had during the Blooding.

My breath quickened and I nearly took a half step back, toward the safety of the boat, but Adam had started walking out into the field. I desperately wanted to leave, even the wind seemed feral in this place, but I gathered what little courage I had left and followed after him. My reticence grew when I fell in step beside him and felt no comfort. He was so lost in thought I might as well not have come at all; he didn't need me here.

When we reached one of the laurel trees I could bear it no longer. "What is this place?" I asked, not daring to speak above a whisper.

He touched the slim, low branches, and one of the leaves drifted to the ground. Just when I thought he wasn't going to answer, he said: "This is where I met the herdsman."

Suddenly the bad feelings inside me boiled to the surface. Of course this was the herdsman's field, what other place could carry such a haunting, unsettled mood? I knew it wasn't right. I knew it held some terrible secret. Every nasty thought I'd had about the herdsman over the past ten months threatened to spew from my lips. What kind of man claims to have seen the gods face to face, but conceals himself from other men? And if he is, in fact, one of the gods as Adam claims, why does he refuse to act? How could Adam trust him even in the face of tragedy such as this? Rage at the herdsman colored my cheeks and clenched my fists. It was only out of concern for Adam that I held my tongue.

Absorbed in his memories, Adam didn't notice my inner fury. "I was only a boy," he went on, "a little younger than Claren is now. Father had put me in charge of one of the small herds in the field just past that tree line. It's a rite of passage for Itomian princes. Syrano had cattle and I had sheep. One of the lambs wandered off and Father told me I couldn't lose any of them, not a single one. I was terrified of punishment, so I searched all morning and afternoon."

182

He curled one of the laurel twigs into a ring. "I couldn't find it. I thought it was dead, eaten by some wild animal. I sat on the edge of the river, right down there"—he pointed to where the boat was tethered—"and cried. And then, just as I'd resolved to return to the castle and confess my failure to Father, I heard a low bleating. The bleating of a lamb. I looked over my shoulder and saw the silhouette of a man walking toward me with a lamb in his arms. I couldn't see his face, not in the dying light. But I wasn't even looking properly, so relieved I was that he'd found the missing lamb. I took the lamb back without even thanking him, and returned to the other sheep. When I went to bed that night I was racked with guilt. I couldn't believe I had been so ungrateful. The next morning I rowed out here, unsure if I would even see him again, but he was here. And he was here every morning after."

He fell silent. I had never heard him say so much about the herdsman. My throat brimmed with questions, but I pressed them down except for one. "Did anyone else know about him?"

He nodded tightly. "Syrano. Syrano knew him too."

Whatever disquiet I had about leaving Adam's family for the afternoon was quashed upon our return to the palace. No one had even noticed our absence. Or if they did, they had the grace not to say anything. We found Adam's parents in the gallery where we had left them; both apologized to me for Aveline's outburst and while the memory brought a prickle of shame to my face, I told them not to trouble themselves on my behalf. Adam asked if we might dine in our room, and upon their agreement, said goodnight.

We walked slowly through the corridors, not speaking. My exhaustion grew with each step. The morning's hunt felt like it had taken place days ago, not hours. I still had dried blood on my brow and untended scrapes on my arms. Silda was waiting for me in the chamber and I could smell perfumed steam pouring from beneath the adjoining door. I desperately needed a bath. I craved to feel clean. But I didn't want to leave Adam when he was in such a fragile state.

He sensed my hesitation. "Bathe," he said. "You'll feel better."

"Adam—"

"Silda, you're not to let the queen out of the bathing chamber until she is as fragrant as a rose. Do you understand?"

Alarmed, Silda nodded. "Yes sir."

"Good." He looked at me, his eyes shadowed by dark circles. "Dinner won't be long."

I followed Silda through the door. "You can start without me. I'm not hungry."

"Neither am I."

In the bathing chamber I let Silda help me out of my clothes and into the steaming tub. The hot water felt like knives against my skin, and my tight muscles groaned in protest. The luxury was just the same as before, with maids to tend every fleck of my skin and scrub away the last traces of dirt. But it held little charm. My thoughts whirled with Adam and the herdsman and Syrano's death. I winced as Silda dabbed at the cut over my eyebrow, cleaning it with a foul-smelling liquid that stung terribly. When it came time to dry before the fire I stretched on the divan, gazing into the flames. Standing in the herdsman's field had unsettled me greatly. And when Adam said that Syrano had known the herdsman as well, it made me think that perhaps I was the mad one for disbelieving, and not he. I caught sight of my reflection in the glass and looked away, refusing to acknowledge such a possibility.

Silda dressed me in my nightclothes, then disappeared from the bathing chamber, trailed by her helpers. I slipped through the door, hoping to find Adam asleep in bed. But I saw him sitting before the fire with an untouched dinner tray growing cold on the table.

I sank into the chair beside him. "You were right. Bathing did help," I lied. "Perhaps you should have one yourself. I can call for them to draw it for you."

"No, I've washed already," he said, with a nod to the corner basin. He drew a deep breath, and after a pause said, "Alyce, I'd like to speak with you about something important."

I watched him carefully. "All right. I'm listening."

"When we return home I want to hold a coronation. I want you to be crowned Queen of Myrilla, in your own right."

"You...what?" It was the last thing I'd ever expected him to say. "Adam, that's impossible. My uncle's laws explicitly forbid any queen to rule in her own right."

"Yes, I realize that. I'm going to annul them."

I turned to look at him fully, and only when I saw his face did I realize he was serious.

"Adam, this has been a truly horrific day," I said gently. "Not only have you lost your brother in an awful accident, but your nephew—who is a child—is now the next in line for your father's throne."

"Alyce…"

"I understand you're worried about succession, but now is neither the time nor the place to discuss it."

"It has nothing to do with succession." To my complete shock he started to laugh. "Alyce, my darling wife, are you so unaware that you truly think I'm concerned about Myrilla's future sovereigns right now? I'm thinking of *you*. I'm thinking of what a wonderful queen you are, your kindness and loyalty and sense of justice. How you put the needs of others first, even when doing so means you're at risk. I want you to be my queen, not just in marriage, but in law. I want you to rule beside me as an equal. Look at Aveline, the woman Syrano was given for his future queen. What she said to you today…I will never forgive her for that. Never have I known such a poisonous beast." He reached for my hand, studying my fingers in the glow of the fire. "How thankful I am that the gods gave me you instead."

It was a moment before I could find my words. Even when I did, I didn't know how to respond to his proposal. "Don't say you won't forgive Aveline. She's the mother of your nieces and nephew. Her words hurt me, yes, but she's hurting much worse."

He touched my cheek, smiling tenderly. "You see? Even now you're all patience and grace. If the gods ever made a woman to rule in her own right, Alyce, it is you."

I kept very still. He had never spoken to me like that before. I took in his earnest face, searching for what strategy he had hidden there, but found none. "Thank you."

Satisfied, Adam put another log on the fire as I climbed into the snowy white bed. My confusion only increased when he slipped under the blankets and whispered: "You should also know, Alyce, that as great a queen as you are, you're an even better wife."

His heavy arm slid around my waist and the last thing I felt was his face burrowing in my rose-scented hair. I should have spent the whole night tossing and turning with worry, but I don't think I moved an inch. In fact, it was the best sleep I'd enjoyed in months.

XXIV

The funeral was held four days later, the very morning we were scheduled to depart. What looked like all of Itomius turned out to bid Prince Syrano farewell as his body was carried down to the river. I stood alone; Adam was part of the close band that placed his brother's body into the floating pyre before it was set aflame. My heart hurt for him. Without any siblings of my own I could not imagine his pain. And when I saw the weeping Prince Claren touch his father's lifeless hand one last time I selfishly thanked the gods for taking my parents when I was much younger than he.

Adam's father, bent over and broken with grief, held out a glowing torch and lit the straw at the edge of the boat. It wasn't long before the wind caught the flame, spreading it over the pyre as it drifted down the river. I wiped my cheeks and muttered a prayer under my breath, asking the God of Souls to give Syrano safe passage into his kingdom after death, and for Kore to lavish him with all her fruitful blessings.

When the pyre vanished from sight, the crowd dispersed. Everyone was dressed in yellow—the Itomian color of mourning—and peppered the grass like a field of daffodils in the sun. I made my way to Adam, who was talking with Prince Claren. He nodded as I came near. "Your favorite nephew has something to tell you, Queen Alcestis."

I looked at Claren. "I shall be glad to hear it."

The little prince cleared his throat. "I want you to know, Lady Queen, that you are a brave and valiant woman, blessed by the gods

186

in every way," he said in a rehearsed voice whose stiffness made it no less endearing. "I hope that we may live in love and friendship all our lives, not only as fellow sovereigns, but as nephew and aunt."

I nodded, in no danger of dismissing the young boy's earnestness. "That is my wish as well, Prince Claren," I said gently. "I dearly hope to see you again soon. Perhaps you can come to Myrilla for a visit this winter." I swallowed tightly. "Your mother and sisters would be most welcome as well. Our home is always open to your family."

"Thank you, Aunt Alcestis," he said, forgetting all dignity and throwing his arms around my waist in a crushing hug. I stroked his hair, as fair as his father's was dark, and a single tear fell from my eye onto the top of his head. When he finally released me, he bowed low to both me and Adam, then ran over the smooth lawn to join his mother.

"He's a precious child," I murmured, wiping my eyes once more. "He shouldn't have to experience this."

Adam moved closer to me and rested his hand on my lower back. I waited for him to make some platitude about the gods and their plans, as he'd done so many times before when I was upset, but he didn't. All he said was: "No, he shouldn't."

After luncheon we finished the preparations for our homeward journey. So many visitors and dignitaries had arrived for Syrano's funeral that Adam and I were able to slip away unnoticed before fruit and cheese were served. Adam made for the stables to ensure our horses were fit and ready and that the wagons were properly loaded, while I took a final sweep of our rooms to confirm we had forgotten nothing. Once I had double-checked the last corner I stood in the center of the great bedchamber for the final time, gazing around at the unabashed opulence. The midday sunlight streamed brightly through the windows, transforming every tiny gilded detail into a glimmering spectacle.

There was a knock at the door. "Come in," I said absently, thinking one of the maids had arrived to strip the sheets and blankets from the bed for washing. But the voice that greeted me did not belong to a maid.

"Alcestis."

I whirled around and saw Adam's mother standing in the open doorway. I curtseyed at once, but I was so caught off guard that I forgot to do it in the Itomian style, with my hand extended invitingly and that elegant turn of the neck. Thankfully, she didn't seem to mind my lack of grace, if the serene smile on her face was any indication.

"Madame," I said breathlessly. "How may I be of service?"

She stepped into the room. "I only wanted to see that you and my son were well set for your departure. Is there anything else you'll require for your journey home?"

I shook my head, flattered that she would come all the way to our room just to check on our packing progress. "Not at all, Madame. We are nearly ready; we wouldn't dream of imposing on your hospitality a moment longer."

Adam's mother said nothing, she just watched me with a curious look on her face. I heard birds chirping outside the window and the grooms shouting to each other in the stable yard. When I thought the queen was about to bid me farewell, she said, very gently, "You have much to learn about family, Alcestis, if you think your presence here is an imposition."

I lowered my head. "You're right, Madame. I thank you." Chastened, I kept my head down until I felt a cool hand on my arm. The queen was smiling at me, and she gestured toward the open door.

"Come with me," she said. "I have something to show you."

I obliged, following her through the curved corridors until we reached the other side of the palace. I had not seen these rooms before—of course the palace was so big it would take many weeks to visit and catalogue each chamber—but I soon realized we were in the royal wing where Adam's mother and father lived their private life. The queen led me straight through her bedchamber (four times the size of mine and Adam's) into a room full of trunks and gowns. Bolts of fabric lay in neat stacks, labeled meticulously and sorted according to their use. A handful of maids were scattered throughout the room, organizing and mending the gowns. They curtseyed upon our entry, then returned to their silent work. The room was bursting with beauty and Itomian style, but my memory of my brief time in Aveline's constricting clothes turned my admiration a bit sour.

The queen must have noticed. "Aveline told me you refused to wear her gown for dinner," she said. "You found it uncomfortable, didn't you?"

I bit my lip, searching for a tactful reply. At my hesitation, she smiled. "There's no need to be ashamed, dear. No one finds them comfortable. Even after all these years I've never grown accustomed to them. I much prefer your Myrillan style of dress."

The queen crossed the room and opened a polished wooden trunk, drawing out a large, folded bundle of cornflower blue silk. "My great-grandmother visited Myrilla when she was about your age. That was back when your kingdom was famed for its prosperous wheat fields and vineyards. She was from the Capelin Isles, just a little lord's daughter touring the great big world. Many courts did not welcome her kindly, including the Itomian court, I am sorry to say. But the Myrillan king and queen treated her as family. On the last night of her stay, Queen Bremeline presented her with this."

She unfolded the blue wrapping to reveal a gown sewn in the Myrillan style. A gown unlike any I had ever seen. The white silk flowed like water to the floor, cut to drape perfectly over the wearer's body. I looked closer and saw thin ropes of white satin sewn into the skirt and bodice, like hundreds of vines, sprinkled through with embroidered white roses.

"It's beautiful," I said, afraid to touch such a delicate garment. It reminded me of my aunt's finest court dresses, antique gowns with exquisite embellishment reserved only for the most important of occasions. As a young child I had naively yearned for the day I could wear such lovely clothes, but then my uncle sold the collection in one of his attempts to keep the kingdom afloat. I never thought I would see a true Myrillan gown again.

"Try it on."

I knew I should protest, but found I could not. I so desperately wanted to wear it, if only for a few moments there in the queen's chambers, that I nodded and let the maids undress me. I smiled as the cool silk poured over me, committing each fiber to memory so I would never forget the way it felt. The gown fit like it was made for me, draping and clinging in all the right places. A diamond clasp in the shape of a twisted vine fastened the fine fabric over my left shoulder, leaving my right shoulder naked and pearly white in the low lamplight. But there was nothing immodest about it; even Princess Aveline and her ladies wouldn't have dared accuse me of indecency, though any memory of their criticisms grew increasingly dim the longer I stood there. I glanced down and saw my bare arms

189

nearly glowing from the gown's radiance. Even my hands, still blistered and raw from the hunt, appeared fresh and renewed in their proximity to such beauty.

"Lovely," said the queen. She nodded to one of her maids, who brought over a small lacquered box. "And now, the finishing touch."

She opened the box and carefully removed a crown of laurel, wrought from white gold. Each leaf was hammered paper-thin and marked with veins, no two alike. "I wore this at my coronation," she said. "It's always been a personal favorite. I'd like you to have it. My gift to my son's new wife."

This time I had no trouble protesting. "I-I thank you, Madame," I stammered, "but I cannot. It's wonderful, only it's much too fine for me."

"A crown too fine for a queen?" she said, amused. "I've never heard of such a thing. Besides, it will go beautifully with that gown and shine like moonlight in your dark hair."

"The gown too?" I demanded. "You can't mean—"

"Not only do I mean for you to take it, but I insist," she said firmly. "You are Myrilla's queen, it is only right for you to dress as one. Sometimes greatness is best communicated through a gown."

"But I'm not a great queen!" I burst out. "I'm not. Forgive me, Madame, but it's the truth. Adam will tell you; I've made more mistakes over the past ten months than anyone has a right to, much less a queen. I feel as though I'm constantly fumbling through the dark."

The queen clasped my hands. "My dear, that's how we've all felt at one time or another. We're supposed to be strong and just and wise, but also possess grace and beauty. Our husbands carry swords and bows while oftentimes we can only arm ourselves with smiles and well-chosen words." She touched my cheek with frail fingers. "Of course you have made mistakes. All of us have. It's the great queens who admit their faults, not the ones who hide from them."

"I'm not sure Princess Aveline would agree," I muttered.

The queen closed the lacquered box and handed it back to the maid. "You mustn't be too hard on Aveline. She comes from a cruel court. Her sufferings are different than yours; nevertheless, she has suffered. That doesn't excuse her unkindness, but it may help you realize that in a different time or place she might have grown into a more tender person." She folded the blue silk wrapping and stood beside me. "Now tell me, Alcestis. What do you see in the glass?"

I gazed at my reflection. "I see a frightened girl."

"And I see a queen. More often than not, the two are the same." She met my eyes in the glass. "Now, thank me and you may meet the others in the courtyard."

I bent down and kissed her cheek. "Thank you, Madame." I glanced at myself in the glass again. I did feel very beautiful, and I found myself wondering how Adam would react when he saw me dressed so finely. "When shall I wear this?"

As if she had read my thoughts, the queen grinned at me. "When you are ready to fully claim my son's heart."

Our departure from Itomius was as solemn as our arrival was joyous. The people lined the avenue, still dressed in mourning and trying valiantly to summon enthusiasm. I felt awful waving goodbye; they had lost one of their beloved princes in the boar hunt, and now the second was abandoning them to his conquered kingdom.

The only good to come out Syrano's death was that I no longer feared the mountain pass. The fact that it halved the distance on our homeward journey made it that much more appealing. The day we reached it we led our horses at a slow pace through the roughly hewn gorge, with the mountains rising on either side of us. In some places it was so narrow we had to walk single file, edging past great rocks jutting out of the walls. I hardly noticed; I was desperate to be home, desperate to escape the blanket of tragedy that seemed to be draped over the whole visit. I wanted to wake up in my own bed and work in the garden and visit the temple. Even the constant worry over the crops and harvest would be a welcome change to the unbearable tension dogging me since the boar hunt.

When we reached the end of the pass, we stepped out of the shadow of the mountains and into the blazing sun. It shone so brightly that the horses shied in distress; I had to tighten my grip on the reins even though I wanted more than anything to drop them so I could shield my eyes. I turned from the sun to Adam, but he didn't seem to notice we'd emerged from the mountains. His eyes were glazed and his thoughts clearly far away, probably still in Itomius with his deceased brother. I wanted so badly to comfort him, to distract or engage him or whatever he required. The silence between us seemed to live and breathe throughout the journey. He hadn't spoken a word to me since we'd left his homeland, and I hadn't the faintest idea what to say to him.

So when he shaded his eyes against the sun and said, "Someone's coming," it gave me a start. I looked over at him and saw him gazing straight into the sun, down the slope and into the sprawling brush below. I could just make out the dark shape of a man, hunched over as he picked his way slowly through the neglected fields.

"He appears to be carrying something, Lord King," said one of the guards. "I'll find out his purpose."

The guard spurred his horse forward, but Adam held up his hand. "No. I'll go."

"Is that wise, sir?" began the guard uneasily. "We don't—"

Before the guard could finish his protest, Adam had descended half the slope alone. I could feel everyone in the party watching him in alarm as he rode toward the man, then turn their faces to me, waiting for my instruction. Instruction which never came, for I couldn't look away from Adam. It was as though we'd traveled back to the previous autumn, when he was nothing but a stranger to me. The foreign prince I'd been forced to marry. I watched him dismount and speak to the stranger, who I realized was hunched over from carrying a large sack on his back. The stranger placed the sack on the ground and opened it before Adam. I couldn't see what it contained, but when Adam looked inside he sank to his knees.

Suddenly frightened, I ignored the guards shouting for me to wait behind and drove my heels into my horse. I flew down the slope and dismounted at a trot, stumbling through tangles of briars and overrun honeysuckle to reach my husband, who was cradling his head in his hands. Thorns tore at my skirt and when I stood before the stranger I was shaking with rage and fear. I had just watched a princess bury her prince; I would not suffer the same fate.

"Who are you?" I nearly screamed. "What have you done?"

The stranger, a bearded man dressed in farming clothes, bowed deeply. "My name is Owan, Lady Queen," he said, his voice trembling as he turned his hat over and over in his hands. "Forgive me, I didn't mean to cause any alarm. I'm the head steward of the royal fields. Lord Turius told me I should inform the king as soon as his party returned."

My heart hammered in my throat as I pictured each possible disaster. "What's happened?" I demanded. "Tell me what you told the king. Immediately."

Before the steward could speak, I felt Adam stir beside me. He pushed the flaps of the sack aside, revealing its contents. At first I didn't recognize it, then Adam dipped his hand into the sack and scooped out a handful of what appeared to be large, coarse sand. He let it cascade between his fingers and into the sack once more. As it fell a warm, familiar smell filled the air and I realized it wasn't sand at all. It was grain.

My mouth opened, empty of words, as I stared at the sack. I had prayed so hard for this, pleaded with the gods again and again, begging for the fields to produce. Blood was poured onto the fields for this, all to appease the gods and try to win their favor. And here lay the proof that they had heard my cries. Unable to stand a moment longer, I dropped to my knees beside Adam. Above me, the steward relaxed his grip on his hat.

"It's the harvest, Lady Queen."

I nodded, my eyes watering from either the unforgiving light or the relief coursing through my body. I looked over at Adam and saw his face streaked with tears. They glowed like precious metal in the setting sun, and I realized for the first time how desperately he'd hoped for the wheat to grow too. Very gently, I put my hand to his cheek. He met my eyes and with a sound between a laugh and a sob he pulled me into his arms and wept golden tears into my hair.

XXV

The first days of Myrilla's harvest were the happiest I had ever known. Owan, the man of whom I had assumed the worst, turned out to be the forerunner of countless glad tidings. Once Adam and I had remounted and resumed our journey home, we spotted new joys around every corner. Not only had the wheat turned in our absence, but the other crops were thriving as well. Acres of corn stood tall, all green and gold. The apples were starting to ripen, ready for picking in a few weeks, and the fragrance of roses was so heady it nearly knocked me off balance as we approached the castle gates where Turius and the rest of the court were waiting to greet us. Crowds lining the road threw sprigs of rosemary at our feet and children rushed forward to crown us with plaited rings of wheat.

We were scarcely through the doors when Adam began talking of plans for my coronation, which he set to take place at the end of the week as the high point of the festival. That very evening he signed the papers to abolish the laws my uncle had written to keep me off the throne, tossing the old edicts into the fire. He wanted to speak to everyone involved, from the cooks charged with preparing the feast to Lilianne, who would act as priestess of Kore during the ceremony. When I offered to help he shooed me away, assuring me he wanted to organize the event on his own. It was his gift to me, he said. My sole task was to enjoy the harvest.

And there was so much to enjoy! I rode out every day, admiring all the gardens and groves and vineyards. The changes astounded me; fields that had once been barren and empty of hope now spilled over with crops. Yellow and orange squash, as long as my forearm, their meaty flesh nearly bursting out of their skins; large green melons with faint blue stripes, sweet and sour all at the same time; berries of every color, so juicy they stained my lips red and purple. Farmers presented baskets of food to us in the throne room, blushing with pleasure as we praised their work. Whenever I had a rare moment of freedom I'd slip into my garden to catch up on my tasks. Though, more often than not, I'd stretch out on my back and watch the sunlight playing in the rustling leaves of the trees overhead.

The most beautiful fields, of course, were the wheat fields. I wish you could know the pleasure and deep gratitude I felt, standing on the edge of Kore's field, watching the wind caress the wheat into golden waves. It seemed impossible that this was the very spot where I had performed the Blooding in the dead of winter. Cold and silent, it had held nothing but dirt and seed and fading prayers. Now it was bright, pulsing, and filled with life. I touched the head of a stalk of wheat, bent over backwards as though damaged by wind. The image carved into the temple wall flashed in my mind, the one depicting the God of Souls' hand reaching down into the wheat field. The wheat, I understood at last, wasn't bent because it was cowering. It had nothing to do with fear. It was simply ready for the harvest.

The day before the coronation I spoke with Lilianne after my temple prayers to review the finer points of the ceremony. It seemed simple enough, but our conversation kept me longer than I anticipated, and I had to rush back to the castle to meet Adam for our daily reception of supplicants.

I dashed cheerfully into the throne room and leapt onto the dais. I had expected to find Adam waiting on his throne, or else making his way through the corridors. Instead, standing near the servants' door, I spotted the last person I ever expected to see. My uncle.

"Queen Alcestis, I was hoping you'd arrive soon," he said, fixing his cruel smirk in place. If you have ever left someone in your past, hoping to erase the pain they caused, and then stumbled across them at a later time, you will know exactly how powerless I felt in that moment. A chill seeped through my fingers and toes and the muscles in my legs seized up, refusing to take another step. I had not laid eyes on this man since my wedding day nearly a year ago; even when the fire threatened the kingdom he and my aunt had refused to leave their house of exile in search of safety. Now here he was, approaching the dais and standing before me like a nightmare come to life.

"You're dressed quite finely," he said, when I stayed silent. "It appears your husband has no issue directing royal funds into a new wardrobe for you. I'm sure his soldiers won't thank him for that when their armor starts to rust."

A flush spread across my cheeks. "If you have a purpose here, uncle, I am willing to hear it," I said, my voice coming out louder than I intended. I wanted to be perceived as graceful and indifferent, coolly dismissing him, but my deep-seated fear rose to the surface and betrayed me. "If not, you may return to your house with Aunt Hestia."

"You misinterpret my motives as always, niece," he said. "I've only come to find out how you enjoyed your first foreign visit."

"Itomius is a beautiful country; it was an honor to spend time there."

He stroked his collar; even in the heat of summer he insisted on wearing his fur robe. I suppose it gave him some kind of comfort. A memento from his days as king. "It's a pity about the prince's death," he said smoothly. "Such a terrible accident."

"Indeed," I said, my stomach twisting at the memory of the boar hunt. "It is a great tragedy for Itomius, as well as my husband." Since our return, Adam had thrown himself into the coronation and festival, working himself to the point of exhaustion each night. I knew he was desperate for a project to help him through his grief, so I said nothing to deter his enthusiasm. But my worry for him kept growing.

My uncle, sensing the strain in my voice, smiled. To anyone else he would have looked like a doting relative full of compassion. I knew better. "It's a great responsibility you've taken on, niece, and I hope the weight of Myrilla doesn't prove too heavy for your fragile shoulders. I hear you're to be crowned tomorrow."

I lifted my chin a little at that. "You heard correctly."

"I'm sure it will be a beautiful ceremony. My own certainly was a spectacle not to be missed. We feasted for days; wine flowed from every fountain. People brought pitchers and jars and cups to the castle to fill them up. We had powder poured into the river to tint the water gold, like the wheat fields." He gazed wistfully toward the window, lost in his memories. "It was an endless parade of beauty, my coronation."

"I wouldn't remember," I said, determined to not let him get the best of me. "I wasn't invited to attend, if you recall."

My uncle ignored me, his eyes still fastened on the window. "I swore to the people of Myrilla I would be the greatest king they had ever known. I promised to make our name formidable, and to show the world just how strong we were. I came very close, many times. It was right in my grasp, and that filthy prince took it from me."

He clenched and unclenched his fist as he said this, though I don't believe he knew he was doing it. I watched him as he spoke, studying his eyes, alight with passion for the future he'd never brought about for the kingdom he'd stolen with his vile laws. I looked down at my feet and noticed for the first time he was standing beneath me, that now I was the one on the dais. He could no longer force me to do his bidding any more than he could force me to live in the tower again. The very thought was absurd, even laughable. I was so far out of his reach he could never touch me. In that single moment he utterly transformed. He was no longer a tyrant, a violent king to be feared. Just a pitiful and contemptible creature who would spend his final years in bitterness.

"Go home," I said, unwilling to argue further. "Go home to your wife and enjoy your memories, uncle. They are all that's left of your time as king."

He glared at me. "Take care, insolence is most unbecoming in a queen."

"It is not I who should take care, but you," I told him, my voice hard and steady. "You forget yourself. Look out the window. Look at the fields. Did you bring about the harvest?"

"No, and neither did you," he replied sharply. "The gods may have taken pleasure in you for the moment, but it will not last. It never does. Smile while you can, niece. Your triumph will not endure. Sooner or later you will have to pay in blood, just as I did."

"And whose blood did you use as payment? Not yours, surely. You were happy to spill it as long as it never fell from your own wounds. My father's, my mother's, anyone's but yours. Go home," I repeated, suddenly exhausted. "If you ever set foot in this castle again you'll be removed from Myrilla for as long as you live."

He didn't so much as flinch at my decree. He simply bowed and turned to leave the throne room. Before he reached the door, however, he stopped and looked over his shoulder. "I wish you well, niece. You certainly have your health. Though, you should know, you're not looking as well as I'd hoped. Or as the rest of the kingdom hopes, I should say."

I swallowed, sensing his trap. "What do you mean?" I asked, unable to resist.

"It's been many months since you married and your belly is as flat and uninteresting as ever. It appears the foreign prince came off poorly in our bargain. What good is a fertile kingdom if he's forced to share it with a barren wife?"

With one last bow, he pushed through the heavy doors and was gone.

I didn't tell Adam of my meeting with my uncle. It would have only upset him and I found no benefit to burdening him with the details. In a moment of spontaneity I suggested we take our dinner in the garden, so Adam had the servants pack our food into a large wicker hamper. He carried it himself from the castle and set it on a thick patch of grass once we'd closed the garden door behind us. The sun was low in the sky, casting the summer flowers in a rosy glow and edging the tree branches with molten gold. We ate quietly, listening to the bees humming at the end of their workday.

My uncle's words played over and over in my mind, particularly the bit about my failure in producing an heir for the kingdom. If he had noticed, surely others had as well. It may sound very naïve and foolish to you, but it never occurred to me that the people of Myrilla would expect me to have a child so quickly. Such a thought was almost amusing, considering how greatly Adam had despised me at the start of our marriage. And whatever affection I held for him now, it had yet to ignite any desire between us. It was a love too gentle, too fragile, to withstand such passion.

When we finished our dinner Adam picked up his lyre and tightened the strings. But before he started to play, he looked at me. "You've been quiet all evening, highly unusual for you. Out with it, Alyce. What are you plotting?"

I managed a smile. "You needn't fear; I'm not plotting anything." I looked over my shoulder. Just above the garden wall I could make out the tip of the north tower, where I had lived for so many years. The site of my most painful memories. Memories I still hadn't shared with Adam.

I pushed myself to my feet before I could lose my nerve. "Come with me. I want to show you something. Leave your lyre with the dinner things. We won't be gone long; we'll come back to collect them later."

He obeyed, placing the lyre in its lacquered box and following me to the garden door. "A mysterious errand? How thrilling. I am at your disposal, Alyce."

I led him into the castle and through the corridors until we reached the entrance to the north tower. I stood for a moment and studied it; not since Adam's army invaded had I so much as looked at this door. Servants scuttled past, ferrying empty trays from the court's dinner toward the kitchens. One rounded the corner too fast and nearly spilled the flagon of wine she was carrying on me. I barely noticed her hurried apologies; I had reached out and clasped the latch, and it took all of my strength to lift it and pull open the door.

The scent overwhelmed me at once, transporting me to the past. That damp, musty odor of stone left too long in the dark. I put my hand on the cool wall to steady myself, then started up the curved staircase without a word. Adam climbed the steps after me, though my heart beat so loudly I couldn't hear his boots on the stone. Higher and higher we wound our way up, until I stood at the door to the main chamber. With the handle caked in dust, it was already ajar, as though the servants who had cleaned the room following my uncle's fall had simply emptied its contents and then promptly forgotten its existence. Looking back, I'm thankful the door was cracked. I don't believe I could have summoned the courage to open it myself.

I touched the door with trembling fingers and gently pushed it. The hinges creaked violently, rusted and whining with neglect. The circular room opened before me and I stepped inside. Late evening sunlight poured through the narrow windows, illuminating the thick sheet of dust covering every surface.

Adam joined me and swept his eyes over the bare furnishings.

"What is this place?" he said, whispering as though we were in the presence of a ghost.

I swallowed the thick, hot tears that had sprung to my eyes. "This is where I grew up," I told him. "From the night my mother and father died until the morning you brought your army through the mountains, I spent nearly every day in this tower."

I felt him watching me in astonishment. I had never divulged so many details of my childhood before. It took a moment before he cleared his throat to speak. "What happened to them?"

"Nobody ever found out for certain. They became ill one winter and died soon after. Within hours of each other, in fact. The coughing sickness was especially rampant that year, and the physicians found no trace of poison." I looked down at the threadbare carpet, fraying on the edges. "Any number of causes are possible. Though there are some who say…" I trailed off and swallowed. "Some say it was more sinister than a simple illness. It probably won't surprise you that my uncle hated my father. They were brothers, and nothing my father did was ever enough to please Uncle Falwyn. When my parents died my uncle should have taken his place as regent until I was old enough to reign. Instead, he passed his laws to disown all royal female heirs and ordered that I be shut in this chamber. Then he and my aunt took it upon themselves to blot out any memory of me from the people—until he could shunt me off to the first foreign prince willing to take me as a bride."

I approached the small table below the window, lost in my past. "This is where I ate my meals," I said, running my fingers over the dusty wood grain. "Only one chair, you see? A few of my braver maids would stay with me while I dined. We'd hold whispered conversations in tiny snatches, careful never to say too much in case the guards outside the door overheard. When I was a young child this served as my writing desk, too. I had just begun to learn my letters when my parents died, and a maid named Iryna smuggled in paper and ink to make sure I continued my studies."

He watched me circle the edge of the room. "A screen stood right here," I said, motioning with my arms. "There wasn't a proper washroom, just a tub behind the screen. The maids would fill it with water so I could bathe. If the guards were in a good mood the maids would bribe them to heat up the water instead of leaving it cold. They'd drop sprigs of rosemary into the bath and perfumed steam would rise up, filling the chamber with the scent of Kore."

I stopped beside the bed and touched the mattress. Moths had chewed holes into the bedclothes, and a puff of dust rose from beneath my fingers. "This was my bed. It was never warm enough in the winter. No matter how many blankets and rugs my maids managed to sneak past the guards, I always lay shivering. In the summer it grew so hot I'd sprawl on top of the bedclothes in nothing but my shift, praying for a breeze to waft through the windows and cool the sweat on my brow. There wasn't a single morning when I awoke and didn't hope that it was all a dream, that I wasn't cursed to live in this wretched chamber any longer."

I walked to the other side of the bed and bent over. There, blended with the dust on the floor, was the small round glass I had used to study my reflection on the morning of my escape attempt. I held it gingerly and, using my sleeve, wiped the dust from the smooth surface. My own face greeted me, though I could scarcely believe it was the same one I had seen the last time I looked in this glass. All the dread and determination of that early morning came rushing back to me. The fear of what would happen to me if I were caught; the certainty that I would die anyway if I didn't try.

I carried the glass toward the high window, where the last orange light of sunset turned it into a pool of shimmering liquid. I stared at it, watching the light fill my hand until I couldn't see myself in the glass anymore. "I can't remember their faces, but I know they loved me. I wonder…" I said, my voice quavering, "I wonder what they would think of me now."

With faint footsteps Adam joined me. The threshers' cheerful songs carried to us from the distant fields, signaling the end of another day's harvest. He turned to me and touched my face, gently brushing my cheek the way a man does before kissing his lover. A thrill ran up my spine as I thought for a wild moment that he had planned to do just that, but he pressed his lips to my forehead instead.

"They would be endlessly proud," he said quietly, "just as I am. As I always will be. Alcestis, Queen of Myrilla."

XXVI

My coronation took place the following morning. Just like Adam's nearly a year previously, it was held in the throne room before the court while the rest of Myrilla stood outside the castle gates, waiting for the celebration to begin. With Lilianne acting on Kore's behalf, I knelt and lowered my head to receive the white-gold laurel wreath Adam's mother had given me, for there were no other crowns in the Myrillan treasury. I wore the white gown as well, and I remember thinking—with the bizarre clarity that often accompanies solemn events—that I hoped the stone floor had been sufficiently cleaned before the ceremony. The last thing I wanted was dusty imprints on my knees. I vowed to seek the gods' guidance in all my decisions and to protect Myrilla from harm, no matter the cost. The next thing I knew, Adam was holding out his hand to help me to my feet and the ceremony was over. I was Queen of Myrilla.

The feast wouldn't begin until later in the evening, but Adam had planned an elaborate tournament in my honor. The great expanse of green lawn outside the castle walls had been converted into a playing field for all kinds of sport and games. Swordplay, boxing, games on horseback, and a half-dozen other events I can't recall, culminating in a great archery contest. Tiered wooden benches were erected on scaffolding around the field for people to view the games, with a royal box in the very center. It was to this field that Adam and I walked, our way lined with people singing and showering flowers down upon us.

Half the stands were already filled with waiting Myrillans as Adam and I climbed the wooden steps to the royal box. They burst into deafening cheers upon seeing us, and a warm swell of pride rose in my chest. I sat in the ornate chair to Adam's right; the arms were carved to resemble a tangle of grapevines with a bunch of grapes for the sitter's hands to rest on. But instead of sinking into the chair beside me, Adam gestured to a basket filled with small wreaths woven from rosemary and wheat.

"Those are the prizes, Alyce," he said. "After each event you'll crown the victor, and then the next one will begin. I'm sorry I won't be here to see it, I know you'll do well."

"Where are you going?" I asked, alarmed.

"Did you really think I'd sponsor an archery contest and not participate?" he said with a sly wink. "Perhaps I'll enjoy the honor of being crowned champion by your fair hands." He bowed low and left the box, followed by a handful of other courtiers who planned to compete as well.

Shaking my head in mirth, I settled in my seat and waited for the games to start. It was very exciting; I had never watched so many different sporting events. Turius won the spear-throwing contest and another nobleman won the sword, but many of the champions were ordinary citizens. One farmer proved to be a vicious boxer, knocking his final opponent to the ground, unconscious, with a single hit. A vineyard worker won the wrestling tournament, and a young woman from the village took the wreath for the longest jump in the kingdom. I handed out the prizes with as much dignity as I could muster, making sure to smile graciously and share a kind word with all the participants.

Finally, it was time for the archery contest. The very air shifted in anticipation; everyone seemed to have come out to watch Adam shoot. One by one the caller introduced the athletes, and all waved politely to the crowd. Some had stamped confident smirks onto their faces, while others looked slightly ill at the prospect of competing against their king. Even I got caught up in the excitement, and sat on the edge of my chair as the caller made his last announcement.

"The final athlete in today's contest will be..." He drew out the pause to an unbearable length. "King Admetus!"

From the roar that greeted Adam's entrance, you would have thought one of the gods had walked through that gate instead of a man. Anticipation filled my belly as I watched Adam step onto the field. He was dressed in his finest armor—I recognized it from our wedding day—and he wore a simple laurel wreath on his head. The sun glinted from the hammered steel covering his chest and shoulders; he looked so strong and handsome I couldn't stop the blush creeping across my cheeks. He craned his neck, searching the faces in the royal box. When his eyes met mine his lips broadened into a huge smile and I found myself beaming back, as though we were a common boy and girl enjoying a summertime courtship, and not the king and queen of Myrilla. I wished I had thought to give him a scarf or little token to carry as a sign of my favor, the way a great lady in an old story would have done. Suddenly shy, I turned my face away, but when I glanced back he was still watching me.

The archers took their places across from the targets, spaced out in perfect military precision. There were a dozen or so in all, with Adam positioned in the very center.

"Your husband looks well prepared," murmured Lady Priscella, Turius's wife, from my left shoulder. "I've heard Turius talk of the king's ability with a bow. He sounds like a man of rare skill."

I nodded, not taking my eyes from Adam. "Indeed, he is."

"Then I take it you'll not want to wager against him?" she teased.

"Not in the least," I told her. "And more fool to anyone who does."

The caller raised his hand, signaling for silence. The crowd obliged and the archers finished testing their strings and reached for their first arrows. All the other competitors blurred into the background as I watched Adam. I could see the intense concentration on his face as he gazed at the target with fondness and mastery, the same way he gazed at his lyre before he began to play it. I knew that look well; nothing could break his concentration now.

"Each competitor will shoot five arrows," said the caller. "After the fifth arrow, the judges will tally the score according to where they hit the target and a winner will be announced. Archers, notch your first arrow and take aim."

In almost perfect unison, the competitors fitted their arrows to their bowstrings and drew. They all appeared experienced and self-assured—no green archers with wobbly elbows or slacken wrists to be seen. Adam, of course, drew his string in one seamless, fluid motion, his aim never wavering from the center of the target. He seemed oblivious to the eyes fastened upon him, or even the other archers. He could have very well been practicing in our private archery butts at the castle.

"Loose!"

I jumped in my seat, so intently was I watching that I'd forgotten the caller. The air filled with twangs and a series of soft thuds as the arrows found their targets. At once the crowd burst into applause and the caller raised his hand for silence once more as the competitors reached for their second arrows. All of them, except—

"What's the king doing?"

I leaned forward in my seat, along with everyone else in the stands, as Adam strode across the green toward his target. He gripped the shaft of his arrow and pulled it out with a deft tug. It left a small hole behind, in the precise center of the bullseye. He handed the arrow to one of the judges and, after a quick word which no one else could hear, Adam returned to his spot and reached for his second arrow. The box broke out in curious whispers, but no one could quite explain his intent.

The caller raised his hand for silence once more. "Archers, your second arrow, please. Now, loose!"

Once again, the targets were peppered with arrows, apart from Adam's, which only held one. And once again, when the others had lowered their bows he marched straight to his target and pulled the arrow from the bullseye. This time, however, the applause did not die down, it only intensified. It wasn't difficult to see why: there was still only one hole in Adam's target. His second arrow had punctured the exact same spot as the first.

The next two rounds continued this way. After each shot Adam retrieved his arrow from the target and handed it to the judge before returning to his place in line. The other competitors knew they were all playing for second, for no one else had managed to hit the bullseye even twice, much less four times in the same hole.

Finally, it was time for the last round. The caller raised his hand for silence and, amazingly, the crowd obeyed. No one could tear their eyes away from the astonishing spectacle of the king's skill. "Archers," he called, "notch your final arrows, and draw."

The green was so quiet I could hear the stretch of catgut and the creak of wooden bows bending in unison. A cool breeze picked up and the sun, hidden by clouds all morning, spilled bright light directly in the archers' eyes. I stood up and rested my hands on the box's rail, only dimly aware of the shuffle from the rest of the court rising to its feet as well. A few of the other archers squinted or balked at the strong sunshine, but Adam didn't flinch.

"Loose!"

My heart leapt in my chest and every head turned toward the king's target. After a split second of silence, the crowd burst into the loudest cheers yet. Adam didn't even have to pull out the last arrow; every eye could see it had fit the hole as cleanly and easily as the four that preceded it.

The caller was overwhelmed, to say the least. "I think there is no argument that King Admetus is the winner," he said, though I don't believe anyone was listening. "You'll find your prize waiting in the royal box, Lord King."

Adam was already on his way, though instead of making for the steps he leapt onto the scaffolding and began climbing. Giddy with laughter, I leaned over the rail and watched him scale the side of the box in his full armor. He finally reached the top and swung his legs over the rail and stood before me, breathless from the climb with sweat gleaming on his temples. The laurel wreath on his head was knocked askew and he looked at me a long moment. I say it was long, though it probably only lasted a few seconds. But it was full, full of hope and patience and joy and something like hunger, though not quite. It was more like the look in a man's eyes when he's thirsty from battle or a long day in the fields and stumbles across a cool, clear stream. I opened my mouth to congratulate him, to tell him how beautifully he had shot, when he moved very close to me and gently took my face in his hands. Then, without a word spoken between us or even the slightest hesitation, he kissed me.

I wish I could tell you the words I said after I shared my first proper kiss with my husband, but I recall nothing of the moments that followed. I only remember how hard my heart was beating, and how all the blood in my body seemed to rush from my feet to my face and back again. I remember that I didn't stagger from surprise; instead I felt strong and steady, like a tree spreading its roots deep into the earth and feeling safe in the knowledge that nothing, no storms or tempest winds, could ever shake the bond. The very same bond I felt with Adam in that moment. Adam, King Admetus, my husband.

When Adam drew his face away his eyes stayed locked on mine, brimming with warmth. I was only vaguely aware of everyone cheering, even the most stolid courtiers in the royal box, so happy were they to see their king and queen engaging in affection. But their proud cries were of little importance. For the first time since Adam's army had invaded Myrilla I didn't care what anyone thought or said of me. I had just kissed the man I loved.

He put his mouth close to my ear, and his warm breath tickled the downy hairs at my temple as he murmured, "My darling Alyce, I couldn't wait a moment longer."

A spark of laughter escaped my mouth and I threw my arms around Adam's neck. He may have lifted me up and spun me around, but I couldn't tell you for sure. As far as I knew I was already flying.

When the games were over we processed to the great hall and feasted for the rest of the afternoon and evening. The athletes regaled their tales and everyone ate until they felt like bursting. The feast lasted so long that it was well past midnight when Adam and I finally made our way back to our chamber, ensconced in the happy glow of celebration. Adam's arm held my waist firmly as he pushed open the door and ushered me inside. A small fire burned cheerfully behind the hearth; already the warm nights of late summer had turned cool. But I felt no chill that night. Indeed, a blizzard could have come roaring through the windows and I'd not have noticed.

"So, Lady Queen," said Adam, shutting the door behind us. "What do you command of your champion?"

I moved close to the fire and sank to the floor, too tired to climb into a chair. "I've never had a champion to command," I replied. "Tell me, Master Archer, what is a customary request?"

He sat in a chair and removed one of his boots. "Well, I believe duels are customary, but since no one would dare insult the honor of such a fine queen as yourself, we may have to be more creative than that. If you're hungry I can send for sweets from the kitchens, or something to drink if you're thirsty." He dropped his boots on the floor and paused. "Of course," he said, gazing at me thoughtfully. "I'd burn with envy against any cup that had the privilege of touching your lips before I had a chance to do so again."

I blushed and looked away; without a sound, he left his chair and knelt before me on the hearth rug. He put his hand to my cheek and slowly turned my face toward his. My chest had felt warm from wine all evening, but as soon I looked at him and remembered our kiss I felt sharp and alert, as though someone had poured icy water down my back. His eyes, too, held none of the lazy softness of a man who's been celebrating since well before sundown.

"Stay right here," he said, in a voice barely above a whisper. "I have something for you."

I couldn't have moved if I'd wanted to. I kept still, just as he said, bound by curiosity. I was nearly trembling with anticipation when he returned with a flat wooden box. He placed it carefully in my hands, kneeling before me. In the firelight I could see the image of a rose carved into the top of the box, bordered by sprawling vines. The wood was polished to satin, a brown so rich it almost looked red.

"It's incredible," I breathed, slowly turning the box so I could see the picture from all angles. "Your skill with a carving knife is unmatched, Lord King."

He gave a knowing smile. "Open it."

I looked up at him, but his face gave nothing away. My fingers found the latch and I lifted the lid almost reverently.

"Oh, Adam." My hand flew to my throat and for a moment I could not breathe. Inside the box, resting on the thinnest silk cushion, was a crown. It was the most beautiful object I had ever seen. Delicate and light, it seemed to float above the silk. It was a perfect circle of roses, wrought from wisps of gold so fine they looked like spun sugar. On a wild impulse I reached out my hand to touch it, then drew it back, afraid the crown would shatter in my fingers.

"I know you're fond of the crown my mother gave you," he said, gesturing to the gleaming laurel wreath in my hair, "but if you'll allow me the honor of seeing this one on you, just for a moment, you can wear whichever you favor best."

I nodded, my mouth suddenly dry. I lifted the laurel wreath from my hair and laid it carefully in the wooden box, now empty. Adam held the new crown, his calloused hands dwarfing it with their strength. The golden roses seemed to quiver at his touch. I leaned forward and kept very still as he placed it on my head. When I raised my eyes he was watching me with that same look of thirst he'd had after the archery contest.

"Thank you," I whispered. "It's beautiful."

He shook his head. "Not as beautiful as you."

Normally such a statement wouldn't be worthy of a second thought. But something deep inside me knew that this was no courtly talk, no polite Itomian prattle. I felt a great weight pulling me down, fastening me to the stone floor, forcing me to pay attention. Something grand was happening here. Something magnificent and grave and beautiful.

"You must realize it, Alyce," he said, taking my hand. "You must know how fair you are, in every sense of the word. You're gentle when others are rough. You're patient when others are demanding. You give when everyone else around you only takes." He bent over my hand and traced the fragile skin of my inner wrist. "I should know. You've given me more than I could ever deserve."

I frowned at the top of his head. "Adam, that isn't true. You're the most generous man I've ever known. No other king has done for his people what you have—"

"That's not what I mean." He gripped my hands and looked up, his eyes glowing. "The gods brought me to you, knowing that your strength and kindness and wisdom would wear away my hard, selfish edges and shape me into a better man. Can't you see that? They knew you would change my life forever. And not just mine, but all of your people's. Thanks to you, the gods made Myrilla fruitful again. Their favor has made you radiant. They could invite you to their holy mountain and you'd fit in perfectly. Goddess of spring, indeed." He brushed his fingers through my hair and white flower petals from the feast floated to the carpet.

I knew I should shake my head, tell him to stop with this foolish blasphemy, and ask the gods' forgiveness, but I didn't. My thoughts were filled with Adam. The respect and decency he showed me in our early time together, when he was under no obligation to do so. The kind words he used whenever he spoke to me, the care and attention he gave me even though I hardly ever deserved it. The way he made me laugh and always put my interests first. My heart hammered in my chest I found my eyes wet with tears. I blinked and they spilled down my cheeks, cool and soft.

Adam's warm thumb wiped the tears away. "The gods have my allegiance. You have my heart, Alyce," he whispered. "And with it, my deepest love."

I nodded, my cheeks still wet. "And you have mine."

With the smallest of smiles, Adam leaned forward and kissed me. I pulled him close, ready to be enveloped by his warmth. His lips still pressed to mine, he lifted me up from the hearth rug and into his arms.

Earlier in the day I had been crowned queen. That night I became the wife of a king.

XXVII

I woke the next morning with Adam's arm slung around my bare waist. The room was dark, with only a hint of grey light peering through the windows. In spite of the early hour I didn't feel the least bit tired. Just the opposite. My mind was a blur of excitement and plans. Careful not to disturb Adam, I turned over beneath the cool sheets to watch his sleeping face. My heart skipped merrily as I wondered if a tiny prince or princess was already growing in my belly. I considered slipping out to the temple early to make an offering to Kore so she might intervene on my behalf to the gods, in hopes of a blessed pregnancy. Then I remembered we were expected at the temple at midday. Only one rite remained in the harvest festival: the thanksgiving to the God of Souls. Then life would return to normal. Brimming with happiness, I ran my fingers through Adam's golden curls, burrowed into his warm chest, and slept once more.

The second time I opened my eyes, I was alone in the bed. I stretched in the tangle of sheets, staring up at the ceiling while the smell of breakfast wafted from the tray on my table. Eventually I sat up to eat before it turned cold, and on the tray I found a note from Adam. He wrote that he had left to visit his herdsman and would meet me at the temple before the ceremony of thanksgiving. (There were also promises of devotion and love talk, but I find that is best reserved for the husbands and wives directly involved. I'm sure you understand.)

After breakfast I bathed and dressed for the ceremony; it was a beautiful day with a clear blue sky streaked with only a few feathery clouds. I chose a gown in lilac and stitched in a vine of flowering yellow jasmine so that it wrapped the waist and crisscrossed the bodice. The crown Adam had given me was the final touch. I took it from the carved box and placed it carefully on my head, pinning it to my hair so it wouldn't slip. When it was secure enough to satisfy me, I beckoned to my maids and we left for the temple.

Our walk was cheerful and light; I didn't say much, I simply enjoyed listening to the maids whisper among themselves. Normally I would have joined in or offered my opinion on their topic of conversation, but I was engrossed with the scenery. The trees were heavy with leaves so deeply green they seemed to pull the branches toward the earth. As we ascended the hill I spotted the apple and pear orchards in the distance, where the fruit was nearly ready for picking. Already I could see the harvesters at work on the plum and cherry trees, and the late summer vegetable fields were almost depleted of their offerings. The scent of roses and lilies perfumed the air; I fancied I could put out my tongue and taste the sweetness of their fragrance as though it were syrup or wine. I found it difficult to believe it would soon be autumn, with the new planting season not far behind.

We drew closer to the temple and I couldn't stop myself smiling when I saw Adam waiting at the doors. He left the group of courtiers he was speaking with and skipped down the stairs. His eyes bright, he held my shoulders and lightly kissed my cheek.

"If it's possible, Alyce, you look even more beautiful than yesterday," he murmured, then tucked my hand into the crook of his arm. "Tell me I have the privilege of escorting you inside."

I nodded, squeezing his arm. "Of course, Lord King."

"Then come with me. Most of the court has arrived and Lilianne seems anxious to begin. Tell me again, what part must we take in the ceremony?"

I tilted my head closer to his as we ascended the steps. "All we have to do is throw our grain offering into the fire to show our thanks for the harvest. Lilianne will speak and make another offering to Kore, and we'll be finished."

"Sounds simple enough," he said, and then fell silent as we passed over the threshold.

At the back of the temple, below the carved panels, Lilianne paced back and forth before the alter, just as I'd found her dozens of times. The only difference between this and any other visit was the presence of Adam. He stood beside me, strong and straight as a pillar, and I silently thanked the gods for blessing me with such a fine man as my husband. We stopped a short distance from the altar, watching Lilianne, and waiting.

She reached into her pouch of grain and withdrew a handful. Not one speck fell to the stone floor as she weighed it in her hand. "Our king and queen, chosen by you, oh gods, acknowledge the fortune you have bestowed upon them in this rich harvest. For that they offer their thanks. Not because they feel worthy of such blessings, but because you are worthy of honor in times of both famine and harvest."

Adam and I stepped forward and held out our hands for the grain. Its sweet, nutty scent filled my nose and I felt it shifting and rolling against my skin. We carried the grain in our carefully cupped hands and cast it into the fire. It vanished at once, devoured by the flames. I looked up at the carving of the God of Souls' hand reaching into the wheat and smiled. Never had I thought I would see a fruitful harvest in Myrilla, and we had just enjoyed the most bounteous in our history.

Lilianne drew another handful of grain from the sack. "To Kore, the ever-faithful wife of the God of Souls, we devote this offering. You are more than the goddess of spring and wheat; you remind us all that we must die daily to ourselves and take the hand of death when it is offered to us. Only then will we truly follow in your footsteps." She turned so that her back faced us, and cast the second handful of grain over the fire.

Only one offering remained. To be precise, it was less of an offering and more of a casting of lots. On the Day of Collection, two mornings hence, a dedication would be made to the God of Souls, recognizing his power over all things living and dead. The chosen creature would grow sick and die, just as the remains of the wheat withered and died to nourish the earth in preparation for the next planting. It was similar to the Blooding, in that the item required wasn't known until close to the ceremony. Hares or doves were typical. I'd nearly forgotten about the Day of Dedication; I knew the workings of Kore's calendar much better than her husband's.

For the third time, Lilianne gathered grain in her hand. This time she scattered it on the marble floor instead of the fire. She stepped back and studied it carefully, a frown creasing her face. For several seconds she said nothing, but simply looked at the grain. I wondered vaguely how she knew what to seek out, for I saw no significance in the splotches and specks.

When she straightened up at last, Lilianne looked Adam in the eye and uttered the words that changed my life forever: "The God of Souls calls one of Myrilla's own. King Admetus is to die for the land."

As a child, when I learned of my parents' death, I felt a cold, sick sensation spread through my belly. It grew so intense that I vomited, right in the middle of the corridor. I remember thinking with absurd clarity that nothing would ever be the same, and that the gods had forgotten me. How else could such a dreadful thing happen? More than anything I wanted to travel back to the previous day, when everything was perfect and I was happy. In fact, I realized too late just how happy I had been, and that such joy would never again be within my reach. It is a misery unlike any other, to lose something before you fully learn how precious it is.

That is precisely how I felt, standing in the temple as Lilianne spoke those words. For a moment the temple was so quiet I could hear the birds calling to each other outside. I stared at the grain on the floor, then looked at Lilianne. Even though I knew it was foolishness, I opened my mouth to ask her if she was sure, if she had read it correctly. But the words cracked and broke in my throat. The marble shifted beneath my feet and Adam's hand closed around my elbow, steadying me. He didn't even look at me; he kept his eyes on Lilianne, his face drained of all color.

"I see," he said, with great effort. "Very well."

His assent, calm as it was, triggered an explosion of protests. From the corner of my eye I was saw one courtier after another pushing toward the front of the crowd, an angry jumble of arms and shouting lips. Turius's voice, predictably, rose well above the rest.

"There must be a mistake," he called out. "You've made an error, Priestess. You cannot possibly mean that King Admetus is the one who must die for the land."

The others agreed readily to this, though Lilianne remained unmoved. "The gods make no such mistakes."

"But the King isn't even native to this country. He is its savior, its liberator, but not one of its sons. You said yourself the blood must belong to of one of Myrilla's own."

"When this man swore an oath to rule Myrilla as its king, he became one of its people. One of Kore's people. The gods' blood flows in his veins now, the same way a branch grafted onto a full tree received the tree's sap."

Turius's voice rose in his rage. "Your inconsistencies trouble me greatly, Priestess. You speak of survival and life, yet you hold the death sentence of my king in your hand. If he were a tyrant, I would understand. Loose the gods' vengeance upon him and let the punishment lay as it falls. Let vindication and justice rain from the mountains upon any king who does his kingdom evil. But what kind of god demands the shedding of an honest king's blood? The gods of Itomius would do no such thing, I warrant."

Lilianne nearly smiled. "Your ignorance of the gods reveals itself more clearly with every word you speak. Compare the pantheon all you like, you'll change no minds. When the gods make a demand it must be answered. The die is cast; The God of Souls' hand has moved."

Turius swallowed. He gave Lilianne a hard look, then rested his hand lightly on his sword. "Very well. If the gods are so intent on their wishes they won't mind if I make public one last observation." His eyes flashed to me. "That crown suits you, Queen Alcestis. Tell me, will you wear it so happily when you're sitting on the empty throne of the king who gave it to you?"

I heard the metallic rush of a sword leaving its sheath and thought with horror that Turius was about to slay me, right there in the temple. But it was my husband who had called up his weapon. He pointed the sword directly at Turius, his hand steady as stone.

"The gods may tolerate your observations," said Adam, "but I will not. You are my brother-in-arms, but the queen is my wife. Hers is the higher binding. Be warned: the next treasonous words you utter against her will be your last."

Turius glared fiercely at Adam, and for a terrible moment I thought he might actually bait Adam into killing him, simply to be difficult. But just as I inwardly cursed him and his passion for fools he bowed low to me, so low I could see the back of his neck. I motioned for him to join the others; he obeyed, disgust stamped on his face. For a moment I was almost grateful for the distraction he had provided with his petty accusations. The anger of men is so much more easily borne than the anger of the gods.

As if she could read my thoughts, Lilianne turned her dark eyes to me. "We are the ones who must answer to the gods," she said. "They only answer us if they choose. Now, go. There is much to prepare."

Mutely, I obeyed, gripping Adam's hand with almost feral strength as we led the recession from the temple. The court's horrified stares followed us, and my feet fell heavily against the stone floor, as though made of stone themselves. We crossed the threshold into the sunlight only to be greeted by silence. The cheers that had followed us since our return from Itomius had completely dried up. Instead, the people seemed to recoil when they saw us. They didn't want to be contaminated by our ill favor with the gods.

Outside the temple Turius and Adam's other favorites remained in their whispering cluster, outrage pouring from their mouths like thick smoke. I felt their eyes boring into me, and I knew without question that the only thing keeping them from spewing further threats against me was Adam's promise to silence them permanently if they did so. I let Adam lead me down the hill, through the castle gates once more, and into my garden. The fragrance of sweet plums drifted toward me as soon as I unlocked the door and the flowerbeds erupted in a riot of late summer color. I closed the door behind me and stood back, watching Adam pace the length of the path. I hadn't the faintest idea what to say to him. I wanted to offer him comfort but how could I do that when I had none myself?

"Adam," I started, hesitating slightly, "tell me what you need. I'll do anything I can; I simply don't...I don't know what to do."

He gave a short, rueful laugh. "Neither do I, Alyce."

I joined him on the smooth path, wringing my hands. "Perhaps—perhaps Lilianne was wrong. Perhaps there's another way."

"She was quite clear in the temple. It's what the gods require, remember?"

"But she can't force you—"

He rounded on me. "She doesn't have to! Didn't you hear what she said? My own body is going to do this to me. There's no blade to fight off or fire to put out. I can't run from it. There's nothing to be done."

He said it with such terrible finality that I drew my last arrow.

"What if…" I began slowly, "what if the herdsman could help you? Tell him what's happened; he may have a solution we can't see on our own."

"I'm not telling the herdsman anything," he said bitterly. "Not after he didn't warn me about this. I see him every day, Alyce, and he said not a word. If he knew—and I've no doubt he did—he should have given me some indication. But he didn't. I had no idea he was so cruel."

I watched as he crossed to the bench where the lacquered case of his lyre was resting. He opened it and removed the lovely instrument, running his fingers along the carved wood. We had forgotten to return for it after our visit to the north tower; thankfully the weather had stayed dry. I was about to comment in that vein when Adam suddenly closed his fingers around the cords of the lyre and ripped them from the frame.

"Adam," I gasped, horrified. "Don't! You'll ruin it!"

He didn't answer me, just continued to tear the cords until they lay in shreds around his feet. Then he took the frame with the etching of laurel in his hands and bent it until the wood snapped. He broke it again and again, further destroying the lyre with each crack. Beautifully carved pieces fell onto the grass, silenced forever. When he finished all that remained were a few shards of pale wood; he looked at them as though he couldn't believe what he had just done.

I stared at him; I couldn't speak. He let the last pieces fall with the others, then fixed his eyes on me. He seemed so far away that I wondered for a moment if it he was out of his mind. I stepped backwards, frightened, as he strode toward me, but with a choked cry he dropped to the grass and embraced my knees. His cheek was wet with tears as he pressed it into my belly, and his shoulders shook from his sobs. Slowly, I sat on the path beside him and gathered him into my arms, struck into silence by the brutality of the gods.

XXVIII

I didn't dare leave Adam's side for the rest of the evening. We stayed in the garden all afternoon, and then took a private dinner in our chamber. I fought sleep as long as I could; I knew that the dawn would only bring us one day closer to Adam's death, and the thought of facing that was too much for me to bear.

When I woke, I felt as though I'd barely slept. I quickly realized I was right, it was still dark. Outside the window the stars shone brightly, assuring me that the earliest hints of sunrise had not yet arrived. I sat up slowly and looked down at Adam, unspeakably comforted by his steady breathing. I touched his burnished hair, which curled slightly at his temples, and ran my fingertips along his smooth cheek. The thought of the God of Souls devouring his health and ultimately taking his life made me sick with fear. Trembling, I slid carefully from the bed and dressed in the simplest clothes I could find in the dark. I only knew of one remaining hope: Adam's herdsman. And if Adam refused to visit him, I would go instead.

The corridor was quiet and still. The guards leapt to attention when I opened the door. I instructed them not to tell the king that I had departed at such an early hour, but that I merely wanted a breath of fresh air on such a fine morning. They bowed deeply, hands ever on their swords.

I set off for the mountain unaccompanied. No maids or attendants followed behind me. I knew it was the pinnacle of foolishness for a queen to undertake such a journey without any protection, but I knew I must go alone. Not for the sake of pride or sacred dignity, or anything as noble as that. Part of my heart was curious about what I would find, what the mysterious herdsman would say, or if I would even find him. But I am ashamed to admit that a larger part of my heart was terrified it would all turn out a great disappointment and I'd be left to return to the castle empty-handed. If that were indeed the case, I'd rather do so without any witnesses to my folly.

The road to the mountain was long, and while it began easily enough it soon turned treacherous. Gone were the carefully tended fields; it seemed as though every briar and weed the workers ever cut or burned had found new life in the shadow of the mountain. Thorns pulled at my clothes and scratched my hands. At one point I saw what appeared to be a staircase carved into the sloping stone, but it was so overrun with thorn bushes that I decided I'd rather climb the rocks instead. The stones were wet with morning dew; more than once my hand slipped and I clung to the mountain with my very fingertips, searching for any crevice or crack to grip. Several times I cursed myself for not bringing a guide, or at least asking Adam what path he took for his journey each day. I stopped to catch my breath, wishing I had thought to eat something before I left. My tongue prickled with thirst and my limbs shook with fatigue. My hands were bruised and cut from the thorns. So much for my plan of a discreet visit. As soon as Adam saw my battered appearance he would surely demand explanation.

Finally, the ground leveled. The rocky slope came to an end and I saw spread before me a smooth field. In spite of the chilly morning air the grass was dry and fresh, sprinkled through with fragrant wildflowers and blooming heather. Resting goats and sheep dotted the plain, perfectly safe and at ease. One ewe lifted its head and gazed at me with doleful eyes, then looked away without interest.

I heard running water and immediately searched for the source. The animals were no doubt perplexed as they idly watched me scouring the field. The trickling grew louder and louder until I located the clearest, loveliest mountain stream I'd ever seen. I had to fight through yet another patch of thorns to reach it, but I paid no mind to the scrapes and scratches; I plunged my face into the cold water and drank until I thought my stomach would burst.

When I lifted my head, I felt strangely content. I sat for a moment on the bank, listening to the stream carving its way across the mossy rocks. The sun still had not risen, though the stars had faded away into the predawn. I wiped the sweet water from my lips and looked over my shoulder at the mountain peaks rising far overhead; their edges stood out black and sharply jagged against the ever-graying sky.

I pulled myself to my feet and carefully picked my way back through the briars. The sheep and goats didn't bother to glance at me this time; a few shook themselves and stood, tearing up mouthfuls of grass, apparently deciding I meant no harm. I saw nothing of the mysterious herdsman, or any human being at all, for that matter. I was a bit annoyed, actually. Adam spoke so highly of him, and this so-called herdsman had the gall to abandon his creatures in the early hours, when wild animals were most likely to come hunting?

"Good morning."

I jumped, startled by the sound of a human voice. I looked across the field and saw the shape of a man, sitting on a rock. He leapt down easily and walked toward me. In the darkness I couldn't make out his face, though I felt his piercing eyes studying me. I did not have a chance to reply to his greeting before he spoke again: "Who are you?"

If I were a grand queen, properly trained and seasoned with experience, I would have taken immediate insult. I'd have delivered a cutting remark about his servile station and demanded he pay me the respect due my position. Then I would have wheeled around and left the mountain, eager to make my husband feel foolish for seeking the company of such a ruffian. But I was not a grand queen, and perhaps that is why I felt inexplicably small and guilty when the herdsman asked me my name. I had brought my selfish, savage thoughts to his peaceful mountain field. I was the intruder here, not he.

"Who are you?" he asked again, more sternly.

I gathered myself and replied, "Alyce. That is, Queen Alcestis. Sir."

"Very good," he said. Under his sternness I detected a hint of amusement. "And what brings you to my mountain?"

Again, a proper queen would have protested that no lowly herdsman could ever own any portion of her kingdom, much less an entire mountain. But he sounded so grand and fierce that I didn't question him. It seemed perfectly right and natural for him to own this mountain. And all the others along with it, in fact. "I'm here on behalf of my husband, Adam," I faltered. "Admetus. The King of Myrilla."

"Yes, I know you both well."

I blinked. "You know me? How?"

"Your husband speaks of you often."

"He does?" A confused pleasure spread through my belly. I felt strangely honored. "What does he say? Tell me, please."

The herdsman shook his head. "You may hear it another time, Queen. For now, tell me of your business."

The words poured from my mouth, tripping over my tongue and teeth in their efforts to be heard. My story was disjointed and poorly ordered; I had no notion if the herdsman could even understand what I was saying about Adam, and the harvest, and the God of Souls' demand for my husband's blood. Tears ran down my cheeks, blinding me and impeding my voice even further. My legs shook so terribly I had to sit down in the grass. Clumps of dirty wool and goat hair clung to my stained and torn clothes but I didn't care. Beside my knees I spotted a tiny white flower, its soft petals gently closed and waiting for the sun to coax them apart. I glared at it, furious with its pure beauty; it seemed to mock me and my pain. I moved my hand to rip it from the earth and crush it in my fist, but the herdsman spoke.

"So what is it you ask of me, Queen?" He sounded neither moved nor disturbed by Adam's plight.

I looked up at him, though his face was still shadowed by the lightening sky. "My husband trusts you. He says you are the wisest of counselors, the truest of friends and the best of men. He says…" My disbelief made my voice falter. "He says you have the ear of the gods. That you are bonded to them, that you share their lifeblood as no man ever has. That you have seen the God of Souls' face, and lived."

Again, the herdsman's voice betrayed nothing. "And do you believe what he says?"

"If he believes it, that is enough," I said sharply, my fear turning me nasty. "I am not the one dying of a silent disease, sir. What I believe scarcely matters."

"Then why are you here?"

"To save my husband!" I shouted. "Is that not plain? I did not come up here for the view, I can assure you. Adam is a great and wise king. He deserves life more than anyone I know. He's brought peace in a time when no one thought it possible. He is kind and good

221

and brave. And he credits *you* with all his success. That's why I'm here. I came here because Adam adores you. He won't consider doing anything to displease you. He speaks of you as if you're a god in the flesh, as if you dropped out of the heavens to take up post on this mountain," I finished, half amused at the absurdity of such a thought. I brushed a fresh wave of tears from my eyes. "I must be going mad," I muttered.

At that, the herdsman laughed. A loud, proper, gut-filling laugh that rang like music through the meadow. The sheep and goats lifted their heads and began baa-ing and braying, almost like they wanted to join in. The herdsman crossed to me and held out his hand, lifting to me to my feet. Even with the distance closed between us I still could not make out the features of his face. The sky behind his head grew brighter, shot through with orange and pink streaks, announcing the impending arrival of the sun. Not that I could have met his eyes if I wanted to. My sight told me he was not a giant; nevertheless, I have never felt as small as I did standing before the herdsman.

"You are not mad," he said softly. "And I know of your husband's illness. These mountains have enough eyes and ears to hear every word both spoken and unspoken in your land. I am sorry he is dying. It is a price no one was ever meant to pay. I can assure you, the God of Souls does not rejoice in any of his people's bloodshed."

The great sorrow in his voice almost made me believe he was even sorrier than I. I nodded tightly and tried to swallow the painful lump in my throat. "Then there's nothing that can be done." I said it not as a question.

"There is always something to be done," he replied, with something like grave amusement. "Call up your courage, Queen, for you hold your husband's life in your hands. The gods have not forgotten you."

My eyes dried up at once. "I'll do whatever they command."

"The king will only be spared if you can find someone to die in his stead. A substitute, who will willingly give their life so that he can be keep his own. If you can find such a substitute before the ceremony, the king will live."

My heart raced. All hope was not lost after all. The list of courtiers blazed through my mind, each soldier and lord more valiant than the

222

last, who had all promised fealty to the King of Myrilla under pain of death. This was just the sort of test they had prescribed to endure; surely their fortitude would prove itself in a time as desperate as this. I pictured them fighting their way to Adam, each one eager to fulfill their promise to preserve their king. Turius would probably climb the castle walls so he could have the honors.

"I will find someone, sir," I said. "I give the gods my word."

"And you have theirs," he said, solemn again. He looked over his shoulder and I caught a fleeting glimpse of his profile. "On your way now, mighty queen. There is great work ahead of you, and the sun will bring even more with him."

I spun in the grass and raced down the mountain. The descent was much easier than the climb. The smooth slabs of rock no longer seemed treacherous in the morning light, and the rough paths flowed like water beneath my feet. I pushed the briars and thorns aside, forming a plan in my mind even as I ran. Before I bathed or changed into clean clothes I would find Turius and have him inform the other members of the council. Adam, however, must remain deaf to the herdsman's advice. He would never consent to letting anyone die in his place.

I rushed up to the castle gates, hair flying. The stunned guards admitted me at once. I crossed the courtyards and burst through the doors of the great hall where I saw Turius standing near the head table, deep in conversation with another courtier. The look he gave me was carefully blank; he obviously wasn't pleased to see me. He acknowledged me with a bow and returned to his companion. I hung back, waiting for the courtier to depart before I approached.

"Turius," I said, as kindly as I could. "I'd very much like to speak with you."

He refused to meet my face. "With respect, Lady Queen, I have much business to attend to this morning."

"But—"

"Unless your need is urgent I'd prefer to speak another time."

"I believe you'll find it is quite urgent." A sharp edge crept into my voice. "It concerns the king."

His eyes narrowed. "What do you mean?"

I reported everything the herdsman had said, down to the details of the agreement. Turius clung to every word, and when I finished he sighed in relief. "So there is an alternative," he said. "Thank the gods." He thought for a moment, then seemed to reach a decision. "If we need to find a substitute, I will do so for you."

I did a bad job of hiding my surprise. "You will?"

"Yes, with joy. You are Admetus's wife; he needs you with him right now. Keep him calm, give him peace, and I will take care of this."

Tears rushed to my eyes. If he were anyone else I would have embraced him, but I simply rested my hand on his arm. "Thank you, Turius. You will never know what this means to me."

I started toward the door, but he called to me. "I know you dislike me, Queen," he said. "And I freely admit you are not the one I would have chosen for Admetus. Nevertheless, he loves you, and you seem to make each other happy. He is as close to me as a brother, and the reasoning goes back to when we were children."

I watched him, listening intently. Adam had never fully explained to me his friendship with Turius. "Go on."

"My father was a lord in Itomius; since Admetus and I were close in age we often took our lessons together. History, poetry and medicine, as well as swordplay and horsemanship. One day we were practicing archery in the fields near the river. There was a paddock nearby holding a bull, and when I ran to the target to collect my arrows the bull broke through the fence. He charged at me, and since I had no weapon, I was defenseless. The bull tore across the grass, frightfully fast; I truly thought I was about to meet my end. But then it stopped and fell, mere footsteps from me, with an arrow in its eye. Admetus had killed it with a single shot. At no close range, either. The bull never touched me."

He gave me a hard look. "Admetus saved my life. That is why I will find a substitute. I swear it."

XXIX

For once I didn't question Turius's word. Instead I did exactly as he instructed, and comforted Adam. Already the mysterious sickness had begun to affect him; his muscles ached and the beginnings of a fever slowed his mind. I suggested he rest in the garden, but his legs couldn't maneuver the steps leading down to the grounds. He couldn't polish his bow, for his hand was too weak to properly rub the wax into the wood. At dinner he was in too much pain to swallow whole bites of food, so I fed him warm broth in the privacy of our chamber. All these sudden changes unfolded before my eyes while I bit back tears and dragged the corners of my mouth into an unwilling smile. Even my most tender touch seemed to hurt him, so when I climbed into bed beside him that night I kept far away.

I was surprised, as you may imagine, when I felt his fingers brush my shoulder.

"Alyce, come closer," he murmured, his eyes half-shut in fatigue. "I want to hold you."

Heat poured from him and onto the sheets like clouds of steam. I lightly pressed the back of my hand to his forehead. "Your fever's raging. I'll get a wet cloth—"

"No, don't leave." His fingers curled around my wrist. Pearly sweat beaded on his brow and dripped down his neck. "Alyce, I must ask you something."

"Anything, Adam."

"Do you think…?" His brow furrowed with worry, he had to close his eyes from the effort of simply speaking. "Do you think Syrano will be waiting for me?"

"Perhaps," I said thoughtfully, stroking his hair. "There are some who say our loved ones greet us on our way to the gods."

He nodded. "I hope so." His body relaxed; he drew deep breaths through his nose. I thought for a moment he had fallen asleep when he suddenly said, "Alyce?"

"What is it, my love?"

"Do you think the God of Souls will be pleased? With me, I mean?"

My tears, which I had held back all day, spilled onto the hot sheets. I was drowning in the cruelty of the gods, who gave me the best of men as my husband, only to snatch him away. Our time was too short together; I would have paid any price to win a second chance at the last twelve months. With my fingertips I barely touched his closed eyelids, his lips, his cheeks. I thought of our conversation months earlier, about Kore, when Adam had said how extraordinary it would be for the gods to take a mortal man and turn him into one of their own. In a matter of mere hours he would find out if it were true.

"I can think of no one who would please them better," I whispered, brushing my tearstained lips against his.

For only the third morning in our marriage I woke with Adam still beside me. So much had happened since the ceremony that the days of him bursting into the room, hale and ruddy, after his visit to the mountain seemed but a distant memory. A relic of a perfect past. I thought of my conversation with the herdsman, and prayed that the fates would honor his bargain and spare my husband. I hadn't set eyes on Turius since he told me about Adam saving his life; I presumed he was working diligently to repay the favor. Again and again I tried to think of who he might contact. Adam's family in Itomius was too far away, though I had no doubt his parents would have come if there was time. The court was brimming with men who had pledged their lives to my husband, but I began to wonder if any of them would submit to such an ordeal. To die in an instant during battle is one thing, to suffer a raging illness is quite another.

Adam looked worse than ever. I tried to rouse him, but he waved me away, mumbling incoherently about his need for more sleep. His body was aflame with fever; nothing would lower it. I opened the door to ask for a cold cloth and found a cluster of servants pawing the floor like nervous ponies. Trina stepped away from the other maids and bravely approached.

"Will you take breakfast, Lady Queen?"

I shook my head. "I'm afraid there's no time. We must make our way..." I swallowed, forcing myself to say the words. "We must make our way to the temple." I looked over my shoulder at Adam, a withered shell of his former self. His legs would never be able to support him. "The king did not sleep well last night; we will require a litter."

Far too soon I was dressed, with the crown of golden roses resting on my hair, and standing by helplessly while four servants carefully lifted Adam's body onto the soft cushion of a litter. I spoke to him quietly, knowing he could not hear me, and explained that he would be carried to the temple; he needn't worry about walking. I assured him I would be there the whole time. When I straightened up I drew the curtains of the litter closed. Not out of shame, but because I knew Adam wouldn't want anyone to see him so physically depleted. He had always been strong, the pinnacle of a fit man.

I scarcely remember the walk to the temple for the Day of Dedication ceremony. I recall the vague blur of faces lining the path, and Adam's warm arm beneath my hand. No one said a word. Even the young farm children were silent, their eyes wide above dirt-streaked cheeks. I could only imagine their confusion. The whole business felt amiss. Dirty, tainted, as though we had done something wrong and were being punished for it. The sun burned away the last stray pieces of early morning clouds, illuminating my disgrace like a mirror.

We crossed the threshold of the temple and the men carrying the litter lowered it gently to the veined marble floor. They opened the curtains and pulled out the mat, with Adam stretched out on top. The whole court let out a little gasp when they saw him, unable to believe such a transformation could take place so quickly.

Ignoring them, I knelt beside the litter and clutched Adam's hand, unable to bear his pain. His skin burned from the fever and though his eyes looked directly into mine I knew he could not see me. He

227

had changed from a great and noble king to a wild animal, stricken with illness. I could scarcely believe this ashen creature was the same man I had grown to love so deeply. A sob clawed its way up my throat and I fought it, desperate not to waste my breath on foolish tears.

Lilianne stood in front of the altar. She held a sharpened knife in her hand and looked at me without a trace of pity. "It is time."

I glanced around for Turius. He wasn't there. "Wait, please. Give us another moment."

"There are no moments in the God of Souls' time, Queen. There is only now." She nodded to the litter carriers. "Bring forward the offering."

They started to lift the mat but I held tighter to Adam. "Wait," I said desperately. "Wait, I beg you—"

I stopped when a sudden shout rang out from the temple doors. Everyone turned to see the dark shape of a man, silhouetted against the sunlight, entering the temple. It was Turius, and he led a small animal on a length of rope. When my eyes adjusted to the stark light I saw it was a young ram.

A path opened up at once before Turius and the ram. He led the animal slowly through the crowd, stopping before Lilianne. The whole temple was silent apart from the soft click of the animal's hooves on the stones and my husband's wheezing, labored breaths.

"I have brought a substitute," said Turius, more reverent than I had ever seen him. He bowed to Lilianne and proffered the rope. The little ram stood dumbly, its large eyes fixed on the altar. "I hope that the God of Souls finds it worthy, and that he will spare our king in his good mercy."

I held my breath, watching Lilianne. I silently begged her to take the rope, to thank Turius for such an unblemished offering and perform the sacrifice. But Lilianne did no such thing. Instead she narrowed her eyes in disgust, her lips pursed so that I thought she might spit in Turius's face.

"This is what you bring the God of Souls?" demanded Lilianne, her voice filling the temple like thunder. "This is what your king is worth?"

Turius took a half step back, stunned by Lilianne's wrath. Then, apparently thinking this to be some sort of test, he rallied. "It is a clean ram, free of disease or flaw. The gods could not find a more perfect sacrifice if they searched the world over."

"Silence. You blaspheme beyond your knowledge. Perhaps if you hold your tongue now the gods will spare you yet." Lilianne pointed her dark, skeletal finger at the ram. "Beasts of the field do not sow grain and reap the harvest. The God of Souls demands man's blood and he will receive it. To offer anything less is to cheapen the gods themselves."

This time Turius did not argue. The ram bleated and the pitiful sound echoed like a child's cry. Adam's sweaty hand slipped in mine as Lilianne surveyed the gathered crowd.

"If a substitute is what you wish to offer, then tell me: who will take the king's place?"

No one spoke. The entire temple was still, as quiet as death.

"Is there anyone?"

The thick silence pressed against all of us. Then, with movements that hardly seemed my own, I leaned down and kissed my husband. I squeezed my eyes shut, my tears dripping on his face. My body felt numb and distant as I rose to my feet and said, "I will."

A chorus of cries assaulted my ears. My maids clutched at me, begging me not to do such a thing. I brushed away their pleas and hands, afraid that if I listened I would let them alter my decision. I walked with quick, wooden steps toward Lilianne, not daring to look back. I heard a voice in the crowd praising my courage and I nearly laughed. Courage was the furthest thing from my mind. Never had I felt such fear. My heart thrashed in my chest and my legs shook so badly I could barely keep my feet. "I will take his place," I said to Lilianne.

She nodded, her face blank. "Very well. Your hand."

I held out my left hand, and in a flash that somehow stretched into eternity, she lifted the knife and made a shallow cut into my palm. I felt a sharp sting and watched a line of bright red blood appear against my flesh.

Then came the sickness. It struck me all at once; for some reason I had thought it would come slowly and quietly, as Adam's had come, but I was wrong. Instead it burst inside me and spread its rotting agony through my fingertips. I gasped for air, only vaguely aware that I could no longer stand. Not from fear, but pain. I forgot the blood on my hand and clutched at my head, my heart, my stomach, every place that hurt. No scream could have properly translated the ache tearing through my body.

Outside of my darkening world, I heard the muddled roar of the temple. Lilianne's arms surrounded me, pulling me to my feet and draping garlands of greenery and flowers around my waist and shoulders. She wiped sprigs of rosemary across my palms, staining them with blood, then took the same herbs and brushed their bloodied, fragrant leaves across my cheeks, marking me as one who now belonged to the gods. I trembled and wept weakly as her hand pulled my golden crown from my head, replacing it with a band of plaited wheat and roses, nearly identical to the one I'd worn for my wedding. She held a cup to my lips and tipped it so that bitter lemon wine filled my mouth. I did not have the strength to swallow; I felt Lilianne's fingers stroking my throat until the liquid ran down into my belly. I coughed, repulsed by the sour taste, but she made me drink it once more before she pulled the cup away. My head lolled from the wine and strong arms lifted me onto the altar and somewhere in the midst of all that I felt Lilianne fill my hands with grain. Her words broke through my clouded ears, instructing me to offer the grain to Kore and the God of Souls upon my arrival to their kingdom. It was important, she said. It was the reason for all of this.

I could not even nod my head in reply. Somehow I turned my eyes to the gathered crowd, where among the blur of faces I saw a man shouting hysterically. It was Adam, restored to his glorious health as quickly as I had succumbed to my illness. He lifted his golden head and with his once more powerful arms tried to push his way to the altar, but a tangle of guards held him back. My weakened mind could not understand his words, only the anguish on his face. I closed my eyes, and the last thing I heard was my beloved husband crying my name.

XXX

I come now to the part of my story that many of you will not believe. You will say it was a dream, or a vision induced by some mind-altering substance. Perhaps you will even say I am mad, and my witness is not to be trusted. You may be right to doubt me; I often doubt myself. But when I opened my eyes there was no question in my mind that the gods were at work, because the first thing I saw was not feast tables or palaces built on clouds, or any of those pictures we're told to imagine as children. No, what I saw, rising clearly before my eyes, was wheat.

Instead of lying stretched out on the altar, I was in a wheat field. I was not afraid; indeed, I felt as though I had always been there. Any other experience up until that point faded away, the same way a dream that feels so real and vivid during sleep dissolves into dust upon waking. I watched the heads of grain sway above me, framing the sky. I was completely alone. It didn't worry me, though. Nothing could have worried me in that moment.

After a while I rose to my feet and surveyed my new surroundings. Wheat fields spread out in every direction, rippling in the gentle breeze. I felt neither cool nor warm, and as I stood there a sweet, delicious scent wafted through the air, enveloping me in a goodness I had never before known. I wanted to stand there forever, but then a few flecks of grain dropped from my clenched fists. The grain for the offering to the God of Souls. Terror spread through my belly as I remembered where I was and why I had come. I whirled around, searching for any sign of movement, but all I could see was wheat.

Then I spotted something in the distance. A figure was moving toward me, erect and bright. Soon I realized it was a young woman; to call her beautiful is almost an insult. She was radiant, the way the sun is radiant. Her loveliness preceded her much like the heavy scent of rain precedes a storm. Too late I realized with a pang of dread that she was walking straight toward me. I wished more than anything to hide, but there was nowhere to conceal myself.

Ever forward she came, closing the distance between us. I knew I should lower my eyes in shame, but I couldn't stop looking at her. Here was Kore, I had no doubt. It couldn't be anyone else. Tiny white flowers covered her hair like a delicate veil, and instead of clothes she wore swaths of roses and lilies and apple blossoms. I couldn't help thinking of all the times I had sewn flowers into my gowns, hoping to convey a similar picture, and seeing her now I knew how pathetically short of the reality I had fallen. Her skin gleamed like ivory and gold in the early light, and with each step she took the wheat parted before her. I bowed my head and studied the ground, not wanting to look the God of Souls' bride in the face and suffer the consequences.

The fragrance of rosemary washed over me when she finally halted. I started to kneel, but I felt a delicate hand touch mine.

"Save your reverence," she said, in a musical voice that made me want to both sing and cry when I heard it. "There are many who are more deserving."

"I can think of none," I whispered.

I heard the smile in her voice; indeed, I could feel its warmth on my cheek. "Why have you come?"

Shaking, I stretched out my hands, careful not to let any grain fall. "I'm here to make an offering to the God of Souls," I said, trying to sound strong. "I came in my husband's place. The herdsman—" I stopped, not sure if she would understand. "That is, an advisor told me that as long as I found a worthy substitute, Adam could live."

"Do you believe you are the perfect penitent?"

I started to say yes, but then a very strange thing happened. The breeze grew stronger, swirling around us and turning cold. I watched in amazement as the wheat, previously unremarkable, shifted in the wind, creating waves of gold and bronze, with pockets of shadow here and there. It was stunning, and somehow looked familiar. I turned back to Kore and shook my head.

"There's no one else," I said. "I had no other choice."

"Very well. Follow me."

She led me through the wheat, not once looking back. She walked so quickly I stumbled to keep up. The queer wind continued to blow, though I took little notice of it when I found myself ascending the steps of a great temple, not unlike Myrilla's, with one important difference: it had no walls. My feet fell upon the smooth, pink-veined floor, and far above my head hung the carved stone ceiling.

Kore stopped in the middle of the temple. "The God of Souls will now examine your offering," she said, beautifully solemn, like fresh snow. "But he can accept nothing other than a pure and blameless payment. I ask you again: are you the perfect penitent?"

Once more I started to assure her that yes, I was, but the breeze picked up once more. Because there were no walls to impede my view, I could see the endless fields stretching out below the temple. The curious light played across the plains, and I nearly spilled the grain from my hands when I realized what it was depicting.

Segments of my life, shifting from one to another with precision and speed, played throughout the wheat. Except I didn't see any kind acts or gracious gestures—the images you'd want to see if someone provided you a picture of your life. Instead I saw myself uttering every nasty comment I had ever said, every cruel glare or unspoken judgement. I saw myself speaking viciously to Turius, waiting for him to make me angry so I would feel vindicated in my dislike for him. I saw myself glowering at Princess Aveline, thinking unkindly of her without the slightest bit of remorse. I saw myself doubting Adam, again and again, never giving him the opportunity to do anything but disappoint me. Always assuming the worst of him and refusing to offer him love until the end.

Shame and humiliation swept over me, drowning me in despair. To have my endless catalog of flaws paraded before me—in the very presence of Kore, no less—obliterated any remaining shreds of hope I still held.

Kore's voice broke through the endless barrage of pictures. "What is your answer?"

"I'm not," I admitted, tears dripping from my eyes. A foul smell filled my nostrils, and it was such a severe change from the fragrance of the field that I cringed in disgust. Then I realized it was coming from my own hands. I looked down and saw the grain I had held for so long had begun to rot. I wondered how such a thing was possible, then remembered the cuts Lilianne had carved into my skin. My own blood had turned the grain into putrid clumps of decay.

It took everything in me not to hurl the grain to the floor. I turned to Kore wildly. "What can I do?" I asked her. "If I have nothing to give the God of Souls, what will happen to Adam? The herdsman fulfilled his promise, I must fulfill mine—"

I fell silent when a rushing wind filled the temple, as loud as a lion's roar. A bright light followed, so fierce I hid my face behind my rot-filled hands. I heard firm footsteps and thought I might be joined by my parents or Syrano or any of the other shades who had passed before me. Instead, when I looked up, I saw the herdsman.

His face was the very picture of kindness. He had a peace about him, a certain strength that emitted from his body like a pulsing light. Everything I had noticed when I visited his mountain struck me once more, only now it was pure and unfiltered, unhampered by the hazy mountain air. For the smallest instant my cares melted away, and I knew deep in my heart that all was well. Then I smelled the decaying grain in my hands and my anger surged anew.

"You told me to bring a substitute," I nearly shouted. "And I followed your instructions: I brought myself. You said nothing about perfection, you never said the substitute had to be blameless." I lifted my handfuls of grain. "Do you see what's happened? No god would ever want this offering now."

His gaze was endlessly patient. "You are certain of this?"

"Of course I'm certain," I snapped. "It's wretched." I could hardly see the filth through my cloudy tears. I couldn't believe the terrible turn this errand had taken. "I know I'm not perfect," I said, wiping my eyes on my sleeve. "I know I'm not Kore, who danced in the wheat fields and won the God of Souls' love with her virtue. I'm nothing compared to her; it's folly to pretend otherwise. I know I'm not kind or merciful or generous. I'm thoughtless and cold, and selfish with my desires." My voice caught in my throat. "What misery the gods must feel when they look upon me."

Instead of balking at my rampage, the herdsman smiled. "What misery, indeed? Turn and look, Alyce. See yourself through the gods' eyes."

I obeyed and found myself studying Kore, who had remained by my side. Her radiant beauty rushed at me, not diluted the least by my reluctance. The curtains of flowers, the sweet perfume, her laughter-filled eyes, all of it joined together to create the lovely, unattainable perfection of the God of Souls' bride. The longer I stared, though, the more I realized I recognized her. My courage grew and I finally looked her full in the face, only to find my own looking back at me. She wasn't Kore at all. She was me.

I gaped at the young woman—my perfected image. "H-how is this possible?"

The herdsman didn't answer. I gave a start when I noticed he had moved closer and was standing directly before me. He had stretched out his hands over mind, covering the rotten grain. Bright red blood coated his palms, which held wounds much like the ones Lilianne had cut into my skin during the dedication ceremony. I forgot everything but the herdsman, watching in amazement as the grain healed, growing plump and healthy once more. It had nothing to do with my worthiness, I finally understood, and everything to do with the gods. Kore—the real Kore, the one who tread the fields generations before me—hadn't won the gods' love, she had simply accepted it.

The roaring sound filled the temple once more, and as I squeezed my eyes shut against the wind I thought I heard a voice whisper, "We will meet again." But I may have just imagined it, for when I opened my eyes I found myself back in Myrilla, stretched out on the altar in the temple, with Adam kissing my face and sheaves of golden wheat pouring from my arms.

XXXI

As I write this last bit of my story, I'm sitting in the garden. It's the earliest days of spring, with crocuses blooming in clumps of purple and white and gold. The apple trees are heavy with blossoms, and pale green leaves are pushing out of the earth. I look at them and marvel at their courage; how much strength it must take to die back each autumn only to force their way out of the darkness once more in the spring.

Adam stands a short distance away, tuning his lyre. He still visits the herdsman each day, though sometimes he meets him in the fields instead of the mountains. Myrilla enjoys the peace that began with Adam's reign, and he continues to grow in wisdom as a king. He sets his lyre in its box and scoops our eldest daughter, Elna, into his arms. At six years old, she's the spitting image of her father. She has Adam's golden hair and bright, mirth-filled eyes. She has his penchant for stubbornness as well, much to the chagrin of her little sister. Maydene, at age four, already prefers the gardens to anywhere else on the castle grounds. It's touching to watch her talk to the flowers, encouraging them to grow and singing the little songs she's heard from me. She is the picture of charm and grace, and will be tall like her father.

In the basket beside my cushion lies our newborn son, sleeping soundly. His hair is dark, nearly black, and his eyes are still inky blue. We haven't named him yet, though we promised each other we'd agree on one today. A task unaccomplished so far.

"I still don't see why you object to Merwyn," says Adam, setting Elna on her feet. "It's a good name. It sounds like a fighter who's also a scholar."

I brush the baby's hair back from his smooth forehead. His tiny pink lips pucker as he dreams and his doughy fist squeezes the air.

"No," I sigh. "I don't think that's right."

"Then how about Byrle? Isn't that a favorite name in your family?"

"It is, but that isn't right either." I watch Maydene stroke the petals of a fading winter rose with her delicate finger. She's utterly engrossed in the plants; a sudden gale wouldn't disrupt her focus.

Adam drops onto the grass next to me. "Then what, Alyce? Any name you like. I simply want to know what to call our boy."

The baby stirs and I rock the basket, lulling him back to sleep. "I thought we'd call him Syrano." I look up at Adam. "What do you think?"

Adam peers into the basket, watching the baby's eyelids flutter. He has long, dark lashes that brush his cheeks when his eyes are shut. Smiling at me, Adam nods. "I think it's perfect, Alyce."

He kisses me, and we sit shoulder to shoulder, watching our little daughters play in the flowerbeds.

I don't know how my children will feel when they hear the unflattering rumors of their father, or if the myth-makers will have the final say in what kind of wife I was. After all, the first thing you learn about the truth is that it's rarely as simple as you think. But be assured: one day, before I pass from this life and join the God of Souls, I will tell them this story, as I have told it to you, patient Reader. The story of a girl in a prison tower who became a queen, of how a king's life was spared by a selfless herdsman, and how, thanks to the boundless love of the gods, the wheat grew once more in Kore's field.

www.ingramcontent.com/pod-product-compliance
Lightning Source LLC
Chambersburg PA
CBHW020406210626
46816CB00006BB/2143